Her heart poundi
Sarah start

Her eyes wer
reached Danie
and cry, to tha
kiss him and of
but most of all, s... wanted to feel her
daughter's small, sturdy body in her arms, to
smell the baby-sweet scent of her, to memorize
every detail of her chubby face.

She held out her hands to the little girl, who
studied her solemnly.

"No," Katie said softly, then laid her head
against Daniel's chest.

"She's not usually shy with strangers." He
winced. He shouldn't be calling his daughter's
mother a stranger, even if it were true.

Sarah knew it was foolish to be hurt, but she felt
a pang anyway. "Oh, Daniel, she's beautiful,"
she whispered. "She looks just like you."

The gaze he turned on her was disbelieving. No
one in his lifetime had ever mentioned beauty in
the same breath with him.

Dear Reader,

I hope you're now used to our new look, because this month's books certainly deserve to be found in the stores. First up is Kathleen Korbel's *The Ice Cream Man*, with a hero who isn't anything like he seems. After all, what self-respecting suburban mother could allow herself to fall in love with a man who delivers ice cream for a living? Not to worry. There's more here than meets the eye—all of it delicious!

Marilyn Pappano makes a welcome return with *Somebody's Baby*, a story that will break your heart, then mend it again. At fourteen months, Katie Ryan holds her adoring parents' hearts in her tiny hand, and she knows just what to do with them. She loves each one of them so much that they have no choice at all but to love each other just as much as they love her.

Lee Magner follows up her exciting *Master of the Hunt* with *Mistress of Foxgrove*, a sensuous, soul-stirring tale set in the beautiful Virginia hunt country. And new author Marilyn Tracy spins a Southwestern web to ensnare your heart as well as those of her hero and heroine in *Magic in the Air*.

In coming months you can look for books by more of your favorite authors: Nora Roberts (who has a special treat in store), Heather Graham Pozzessere, Kathleen Creighton, Barbara Faith and many, many more—as well as a few surprises. I hope you'll be part of the excitement.

Leslie J. Wainger
Senior Editor

Somebody's Baby

MARILYN PAPPANO

Silhouette Intimate Moments

Published by Silhouette Books New York

America's Publisher of Contemporary Romance

SILHOUETTE BOOKS
300 East 42nd St., New York, N.Y. 10017

ISBN: 0-373-07310-0

First Silhouette Books printing November 1989

Printed in the U.S.A.

MARILYN PAPPANO

has been writing as long as she can remember, just for the fun of it, but recently she decided to take her life-long hobby seriously. She was encouraging a friend to write a romance novel and ended up writing one herself. It was accepted, and she plans to continue as an author for a long time. When she's not involved in writing, she enjoys camping, quilting, sewing and, most of all, reading. Not surprisingly, her favorite books are romance novels.

Her husband is in the Navy, and in the course of her marriage she has moved all over the U.S. Currently, she lives in South Carolina with her husband and son.

October 1

Thirty-one days

Daniel Ryan stared at the calendar above his desk. October. If he lifted the page, he would see November first circled in red. That was his deadline. It would be one year since the Nashville lawyer had delivered his daughter to him, tiny, three months old, helpless—and unwanted by her mother. He could have her for one year, the lawyer had stipulated; then he had to return her to her mother. Thirty-one days more—that was all he had left with Katie.

Swiveling in his chair, he watched his daughter sitting on the rug in front of the cold fireplace. She was surrounded by bright-colored toys, but it was her own feet that interested her most. The tiny white Nikes that he had so carefully laced on only an hour ago were gone, one on the stone hearth, the other half-under the sofa. The socks were off, too, left in an untidy heap on the floor, and she was bent over, studiously looking first at one foot, then the other. The position was too much for her chubby body, and she rolled over, giving a startled cry followed immediately by a bright laugh.

Daniel felt a tightness in his chest. She was his daughter, with the same silky dark brown hair and the same unusual shade of dark blue eyes, and she was his life. How could he possibly give her back in thirty-one days to the mother who hadn't wanted her in the first place?

He couldn't. It was that simple. Sarah Lawson could make all the demands she wanted, but she couldn't take his daughter from him. Katherine Ann Ryan belonged to him, and she was going to stay with him. The sooner Sarah accepted that, the better.

He studied Katie as, feet forgotten, she reached for the Raggedy Ann doll that Mrs. Adams had made for her. The rag doll, with its carrot-colored yarn hair, was bigger than the girl, and its soft muslin face showed the stains of Katie's sloppy kisses. It was worn, soft and well loved.

He looked for some resemblance to the mother who had without hesitation given away her daughter to a man she hardly knew, but he could find none. Sarah Lawson had dark blond hair and brown eyes, nothing like Katie's. She had been thin and not too talkative, and had been willing to spend the weekend with a man she had met in a bar. She had seemed warm and giving, but she'd turned out to be cold. Selfish. How could he possibly let Katie return to live with a woman like that?

"Katie Ann," he called.

She turned toward his voice, breaking into a bright warm smile when she saw him. "Daddy," she replied.

"Daddy," he repeated softly, proudly. Not "Da-da." No baby talk for his little girl. Her vocabulary was limited, but the words she spoke were clear and correct. *Daddy, eat, drink, go, baby, Katie.* The word *mother* and its many variations were all but unknown to her. At fourteen months, *mother* was a foreign concept to her, one that meant nothing. He intended to see that it stayed that way. "Let's go to town, Katie."

She struggled to her feet, using the heavy coffee table to pull herself up. She had been walking for four months now and found it pretty easy once she got on her feet. She started toward the door, wearing nothing but a diaper and a T-shirt.

"Wait a minute. You can't go out half-dressed. It's too cool for that." He wished she could, he thought with a grimace as he scooped her into his arms. She was the sweetest, happiest baby a parent could ask for, except when it came to putting on clothes. She would go through life with no more than a diaper if it was left to her.

He picked up her shoes and socks, then took her upstairs to her room, next to his own. After laying her in the crib, he gathered a complete outfit and laid it on the mattress beside her. Months of experience had taught him to have everything at hand; that way she couldn't start removing the hated clothes while his back was turned to get the next layer.

She struggled and wriggled and chattered angrily at her father, but he succeeded in dressing her, shoes and all, then swung her up and hugged her. "You're a pretty girl, Katie," he whispered, hiding his face in her soft curls.

"Katie," she echoed in her little baby voice. She pursed her lips in an exaggerated pucker and left a wet kiss on his chin. "Go."

Rides in the pickup truck were a rare treat. She didn't even mind the infant seat that kept her securely strapped at Daniel's side. They carried on a lively conversation all the way into town, with Katie repeating words that she knew and gurgling nonsensical responses to everything else.

Daniel parked near the town square, underneath a red-and-gold banner announcing the annual fall Harvest Festival, and freed Katie from her seat. She looked longingly at the park, where two small children played together while their mother read a magazine in the cool morning sun. She was approaching the age where she would need exposure to other children at least occasionally, Daniel thought with a grim sigh. He wasn't quite certain how, but he would manage it. He would give her everything she needed.

Zachary Adams's office was located on the square in an old stone building. Daniel greeted the secretary, Zachary's sister, Alicia, with a polite nod, then asked, "Is Zach busy?"

"I'll see if he can talk to you now." She smiled at Katie, touching a hand lightly to the girl's hair as she walked by. A moment later she returned, gesturing to him to enter the office.

Zachary Adams was the attorney in the town of Sweetwater. He was also the only one in town who knew the identity of Katie's mother, and the only one who Daniel considered a friend. He greeted his unexpected guests with a warm smile.

They were an odd sight. Daniel, at six foot four and well over two hundred pounds of solid muscle, was the biggest man in the county. Perched on one hip and supported by a massive arm, Katie looked tiny and delicate, like a miniature baby doll in the arms of a giant.

"Hey, Katie," Zachary greeted her as he stood up. He came around the desk and tugged gently at her curls, and she graced him with her sweetest smile. "What brings you two into town?"

"I need some advice."

Zachary gestured to the chairs in front of his desk. He took one, while Daniel settled in the other. "I take it this has something to do with Katie," he said solemnly, "and the fact that your year is almost up."

Daniel nodded solemnly. "I want to get permanent custody."

Zachary had expected as much ever since the pretty lady lawyer had shown up in Sweetwater with Katie in tow. He knew his friend well, knew how he prized his solitude up there on his mountain, but knew, too, his loneliness. To Daniel, the baby had been an unexpected gift from heaven, and Zachary had known he wouldn't be able to give her up. Taking Katie from him would be like taking his reason for living. That knowledge made him word his response carefully. "What I would like to do, Daniel, is wait until the beginning of November. See if Sarah Lawson shows up. Then we'll move."

Daniel's scowl was fierce. "If she does show up, it'll be too late. She'll take her away."

Zachary watched Katie struggle against her father's restraining arm. "It's all right to let her down. There's nothing here she can get into."

As soon as she was on the floor, Katie took a few faltering steps, fell on her diaper-padded bottom and immediately turned her attention to removing her shoes. When she succeeded in removing one, she held it above her head, triumphantly calling it to her father's attention. His responding smile was edged with resignation.

"It won't be too late," Zachary said, returning to their conversation. "Because if Sarah does show up, you're not going to give Katie to her. I'll have the papers ready to file, and we'll ask the judge to leave Katie in your custody until the final disposition is made. Since Katie knows you, and her mother is a complete stranger, I'm sure he'll do it." He watched as Katie removed the second shoe, then peeled off her socks. That task completed, she rolled onto her hands and knees and crawled off to explore the office. "How well do you know Sarah Lawson, Daniel?"

He shook his head. "I don't." He had gone to bed with the woman, but he knew little about her beyond the fact that, between them, they had produced Katie. Sometimes it shamed him that he had been so intimately involved with a stranger, but then he looked at Katie, and the shame was replaced with love. If Katie had resulted from that weekend together, there could be nothing shameful about it.

"If she comes back for the baby and you take her to court, you're going to have to prove that Katie is better off with you, that Sarah is unfit to have custody of her. Does that bother you?"

"She gave her own baby away. She doesn't deserve to get her back."

"She didn't 'give' her away," Zachary disagreed. "She gave temporary custody to the baby's father. That doesn't make her a bad mother."

It did in Daniel's eyes. Any woman who didn't love her child enough to care for her, to love her, wasn't worthy of the title of mother. "I picked her up in a bar, Zachary. What kind of woman would go to bed with a man she met in a bar?"

Zachary's smile was amused. "That works both ways, Daniel. What kind of man would go to bed with a woman he met in a bar?" The smile turned into a grin. "That doesn't make you a bad father, does it? And it doesn't mean that Sarah is a bad mother.'' He sighed softly. "What I'll do is get in touch with a private detective in Nashville and see what he can dig up on Sarah. The more we know about her, the better prepared we'll be in court.''

"He'd better find something," Daniel said grimly, "because I'm not letting her have Katie. I can't.'' Although it was spoken quietly, calmly, it was a promise. A vow that he would never break.

Sarah walked across the yellowing grass, weaving her way around the stones, then stopped and knelt on the ground. Immediately she felt the cold damp seeping into her jeans. Everything here was cold, even on the hottest day of summer. She didn't think she could bear the winter's chill in this place.

"I have to go now," she murmured, reaching out to pluck a weed from the base of the white stone. "It's time." Tears filled her eyes and made her voice catch in her throat. For the past three years she had cried so easily. The tears had been the only outlet available to vent her sorrow, her rage and anger and bitterness, and she had cried, every day and every night. Now it was done. As soon as she had her baby in her arms, she would never cry again.

Katherine Ann. Almost a year had passed since she'd seen her little girl, since she had held her one last time. Katherine had worn a disposable diaper and a tiny pink dress, had been chubby and perfectly formed, with ten fingers and ten toes and dimpled knees and a tiny perfect Cupid's-bow mouth.

Now she was more than a year old. She was bigger, taller, walking and talking and helping to feed herself, and she wouldn't know Sarah from the man in the moon. But Sarah would know her. Her daughter might be a year older and completely different from the tiny baby she'd last held, but with a mother's intuition, Sarah was positive that she would know her.

She touched a hand to the marble headstone. It was like ice. For months she had been like that—frozen, unfeeling, as dead inside as Tony was. But Katherine wasn't dead; she was waiting in a tiny little town called Sweetwater, waiting for her mother to come and get her. Katherine was the bond that had kept Sarah going. "I'll come back," she whispered to the stone. "I'll never forget you. I'll never stop loving you."

Slowly, stiff from the chill, she got to her feet and walked away. She didn't look back at that lonely place. She didn't need to. It was burned forever into her mind.

Sweetwater was a three-hour drive from Nashville. Sarah sat for a moment in the car that held everything she owned: her clothes, worn but serviceable; a box of books; another box of pictures of Tony and Katherine and Sarah herself; a box of linens; and a fourth box of dishes, cheap aluminum pans and cheaper plastic plates and bowls. Once she'd had china and designer clothing, a television and stereo, an expensive car and a nice home. Then Brent had left, and Sarah had sold everything to pay Tony's medical bills, and it still hadn't been enough. She would work the rest of her life and never pay all his bills.

Beth had advised against this move. Let the final month in her agreement with Daniel Ryan pass, the attorney had insisted, then pick up Katherine as arranged. But Sarah couldn't wait any longer. She wasn't going to ask Daniel to return her daughter to her a month early, but maybe he would let her visit. Maybe he would let her see Katherine and help with her care for the next month, so that by the time November first arrived, Katherine would be used to her mother and would be happy with her.

She drove at a safe speed, not because she was cautious by nature, but because, after a hundred and fifty thousand miles, the secondhand car that had replaced her BMW didn't have the power to speed. She used the time to think, to plan her strategy.

If she knew more about Daniel Ryan, it would make her task easier, but, she was ashamed to admit, she didn't. He had told her a little about himself—where he was from, what he did for a living, that he wasn't married and, most importantly, that he loved children. His actions over the short weekend had told her more—that he was a good man, an honest man, a gentle man. She had thought at the time he was a man she could care about, if she'd had any caring left to give. But she'd given every part of herself to Tony, to the heartrending twenty-four-hour-a-day job of watching her son die.

She had been to Sweetwater a week ago had found Daniel Ryan's house and, luck being with her, had found an abandoned farmhouse only a few miles away. The For Sale sign had lain broken and faded by the side of the road, but she had deciphered the phone number. The real estate agent had been glad to unload the house; the owners, who lived in town now, were happy to have even a temporary renter after years of trying to sell. The place was in deplorable condition, but all that mattered to Sarah was its location. She would be close to Daniel. Close to Katherine.

She passed the highway sign declaring that it was ten miles to Sweetwater and began slowing down. The road that led to her new home was a few miles beyond that sign. Last week she had driven past it twice before getting its location fixed in her mind.

She turned off the narrow highway onto an even narrower gravel road. As it twisted and climbed its way up the mountain, gravel gave way to dirt, packed hard by the occasional traffic, baked hard by the sun.

It was nine miles to the house. Through careful questioning of the agent, she had learned that it was two miles farther by road to Daniel's house but less than a mile if she cut across the fields and through the woods. As soon as she reached her temporary home, she intended to find out if the information was correct.

Recognizing the faded sign still lying on the side of the road, Sarah slowed and turned into the driveway, steering to avoid the potholes, and parked near the house. What had once been a well-tended yard was no longer distinguishable from the open field that surrounded the house on all sides. She picked her way along the faint path, overgrown now with weeds, to the front of the house.

It was a neat boxy square, four rooms downstairs, four rooms up. Its straight lines were softened by the wide porch that circled along the side, across the front and down the other side, and by the intricately turned spindles that supported the porch railing. The house had last been painted blue gray, the shutters steel gray, the railing and spindles white, but the paint had weathered badly. It was cracked and peeling and in many places gone altogether.

This house had once been someone's joy, Sarah thought with a glimmer of sadness as she carefully stepped over the broken floorboards on the porch. Now it was neglected, forgotten, allowed to decay gracelessly. She felt as if *she* had been decaying, too, gradually withering away ever since Tony's illness had been diagnosed. But no more. For Katie's sake, she was taking control again. She had found the will to live again, to love again.

The key grated in the lock, straining to twist the rusted tumblers; then the door swung open. Footprints, hers and the real estate agent's, looked ghostly in the heavy layer of dust that coated the floor and everything else. Spiderwebs hung from the ceiling, and crackly brown leaves and twigs had blown in through a broken pane in the front window. It would take a lot of hard work, but she was used to hard work. She could make it habitable.

She walked past the sofa sitting alone in the living room, through the dining room and into the kitchen, where the refrigerator and stove that she had asked the agent to find for her stood, ancient but apparently serviceable, along with a rickety table and two chairs. She opened the refrigerator door, and a naked light bulb came on in the back. The air was musty but cool. Next she tested the faucet at the sink, watching the rust-colored water drain and slowly clear. As the agent had promised, the electricity was on and the pump was in working order.

Twisting the handle to the off position, Sarah raised her eyes from the sink to the window above it. Daniel Ryan lived on top of the mountain, the agent had told her. Through the trees bright with their autumn colors, she could make out a shape high on the mountainside. That must be his house.

After taking time only to change into a pair of tennis shoes, Sarah set out across the wide meadow. It was warm and sweet smelling there. In the spring and summer it would be filled with wildflowers. A few hardy ones remained in bloom even now. When she reached the woods, the land began to climb steeply, all the way to the top of the mountain.

There was a clearing at the top. Sarah remained at its edge, quiet and motionless in the cover of the dense growth. Her breathing was rapid and irregular, both from the hike and with anticipation.

There it was. Daniel Ryan's home. Katherine's home.

The house was beautiful, its hand-hewn logs blending into the rustic setting. The first Ryan had built the central portion, which was obviously the oldest, even to Sarah's untrained eye. Succeeding generations had added rooms as necessary, using the same native wood and stone, resulting in a rambling, welcoming structure.

A dusty dark blue pickup was parked at one side, between the house and the small cluster of outbuildings, but there was no sign of life. Sarah didn't know how long she stood there, watching, waiting, wishing for just a glimpse of her daughter, before aching muscles demanded that she move.

She would return to her house, she decided, and clean the bathroom, clean herself up and give her nerves a chance to settle. She wanted to be calm and in control when she saw Daniel Ryan again. She wanted to make a good impression on the man who legally had custody of her daughter for another thirty-one days.

She wanted to make a good impression on her daughter.

Daniel settled Katie into bed for a late-afternoon nap, then went outside to the porch. There were two rockers there, one on each side of the door. Both were large, handmade of pine, with a rich honey finish to protect the wood from the weather. He sat down in one and propped his booted feet on the rail in front.

It was already five o'clock, and he had accomplished next to nothing. The trip to see Zachary, followed by lunch and shopping, had taken up the better part of the day, and when they had returned home, Katie had demanded his attention. It wasn't easy being a single parent, especially with a baby—especially with a baby *girl*. He needed a woman around the place to do the womanly things—cook, clean, watch the baby—giving him a few free hours to work. The garden that kept their cabinets full and the small furniture business that paid their bills took a lot of time. So did Katie.

When this business with Sarah Lawson was settled once and for all, maybe he would hire a housekeeper. Or maybe he'd find himself a wife. Marcy, one of the waitresses at the diner, had made it clear that she was interested, and she didn't mind the fact that he had the baby, either. Of course, Marcy was interested in every man under the age of forty who walked through the door.

Who else was single in Sweetwater? He had never considered it before, because he had never considered getting married before. He had been totally self-sufficient since he was sixteen. He gardened and hunted and fished, cooked and cleaned, made his own repairs around the house, mended his own clothes, could even bake his own bread. He'd never wanted a woman except to satisfy his occasional physical needs, and that had never seemed reason enough to marry.

Sarah Lawson had more than adequately satisfied those physical needs.

He scowled at the thought of her. He'd never been able to completely forget her, not with Katie occupying every waking hour for the past eleven months, but he hadn't thought as much about her in those eleven months combined as he had today. It was natural, he supposed, with the deadline coming up. She would be on his mind for the next thirty-one days.

Would she come? He hoped not. In eleven months she hadn't contacted them or tried to see Katie, not even on her first birthday. It was logical to assume that she'd forgotten the daughter she'd given away. Although he hated to think that Katie's mother could be so cold, so cruel, that was what he wanted to believe—needed to believe. It would certainly benefit his case when he went to court.

The quiet of the afternoon was interrupted by the chug of a poorly tuned engine. Daniel's feet hit the floor with a thump as he leaned forward in the rocker. Trees obscured the driveway until it reached the clearing, but he caught a glimpse of yellow through the leaves.

Who would be visiting all the way out here? He hadn't had company since Zachary had brought his mother up, the day after Katie had arrived, to teach Daniel how to care for the tiny infant. He had no friends, no family close enough to drop in, and knew no one who drove a lemon-yellow car.

The car came to a sputtering stop some distance behind his pickup. Slowly rising to his feet, Daniel watched the driver get out. She removed her sunglasses, clenching them tightly in one hand, and started toward him. He muttered a low, violent, angry curse.

It was Sarah Lawson.

She stopped several feet away. Standing five steps above her, Daniel towered like a menacing giant and wore a fierce expression to match. Nearly eleven inches taller than Sarah, he had dark brown hair and darker blue eyes that radiated hostility. The lines of his face were harsh, rough angles that gave not a hint of the gentleness that she recalled.

For a moment her courage faltered. She had come to compromise, to bargain and, if necessary, to plead with him, but she hadn't remembered his being so hard looking. He probably didn't know the meaning of compromise, and her pleas would never touch him. Good Lord, what had she done in sending Katherine to live with this man?

"What do you want?"

His voice was a deep unfriendly rumble that sent a shiver down her spine. Calling on all her courage, she responded quietly. "Hello, Daniel."

The instant he heard her voice, he realized that he'd forgotten how it sounded—low, velvety, soothing, with a hint of a Tennessee drawl. Although she was a pretty woman, it was her voice that had attracted him most in the bar that night. Its slow smooth flow had reminded him of long summer nights, of heat and sweetness and need. Her voice had seduced him, as surely as *he* had seduced *her*.

His eyes narrowed at the memory, making him look fiercer, harsher. "You're a month early," he said flatly.

"I know. Can I see her?"

He shook his head.

She had expected a refusal, but it hurt just the same. Who was he to tell her that she couldn't see her own daughter? she silently lamented, and her conscience answered the question; he was Katherine's father. He was the man who had taken her in when Sarah couldn't keep her, who had raised her practically since birth. "Why not?"

He moved to the center of the top step, his legs wide, his arms folded over his broad chest. "She's not your daughter anymore. She's *mine*. You gave up your rights to her eleven months ago."

Stubbornly she shook her head. "No, Daniel, I didn't. Our agreement was for one year—nothing else."

"The year's not up yet."

"I just want to see her." Wanted to see her solemn blue eyes, to watch her smile crinkle up her entire face, to touch her baby-powder soft skin. She wanted to wrap her arms around Katherine's sturdy little body and know that losing Tony hadn't been the end of her world. She wanted to tell her daughter that she loved her, wanted to see proof that Katherine could love her, too.

"Come back next month," Daniel said callously, knowing that he wouldn't let her see Katie then, either. She would see his daughter only if and when the court said she could.

Sarah wanted to argue, to storm past him and into the house. But arguments would make him angry, and trying to storm past him would be like trying to shift an immovable object. He was big and solid and had no intention of letting her get close to Katherine. "Is she all right?" she asked softly.

"She's fine."

"She's walking? Talking?"

He nodded.

"Can she say much?"

Her eager questions stirred an unfamiliar sensation in his belly that he thought must be guilt. Zachary had warned him that they would have to accuse Sarah of being an unfit mother if they went to court, and Daniel had easily accepted that. But the woman standing before him now wasn't the cold, selfish, heartless creature he wanted to see. She was simply a woman anxious to hear about her child.

She gave away her baby, he reminded himself. Without the slightest regret, she handed her baby over to her lawyer to give to a complete stranger. She hadn't known that he would want Katie, that he would care for her or love her, and she hadn't cared. All she had cared about was getting rid of the child until a more convenient time.

"Yes, she talks," he said, his voice even and hard and cold. "She says 'daddy, Katie, baby, eat, drink and go.'" Deliberately he added, "She doesn't say 'mama' because she doesn't have the vaguest idea what it means. Do you?"

Sarah's face burned with a hot flush. She could tell him more than he ever wanted to know about what being a mother meant—about the sacrifices, the sorrows, the grief. It was the hardest job a woman could take on—a job too hard for many men. "When can I see her?" she asked in a voice that trembled only a little.

Daniel shrugged. "Not in the next four weeks. Go back to Nashville. You're not wanted here."

She took a step closer, resting one hand flat against the wood rail. "I'll go back when I have my daughter. Until then I'm staying here. I've rented the Peters place down the road."

He hadn't expected that, she saw with satisfaction. He hadn't expected her to come back for her daughter, and he certainly hadn't expected her to move in until she got her.

She started toward her car, then glanced back at him. "I'll be back."

"I'll have you arrested for trespassing."

She seemed to consider that for a moment before shaking her head. "I don't think so." She didn't believe that he would have the mother of his child arrested. It would lead to gossip and rumors that would most certainly center around Katherine. No matter what he thought of Sarah herself, he wouldn't expose their daughter to that.

She got in her car, starting the engine on the second try, and drove down the steep, winding road to her own house. The living room and kitchen were still filthy, but the bathroom gleamed. Tomorrow she would tackle the other rooms, but she had no plans to touch the empty room down the hall and the four bedrooms upstairs. After all, she would be here only one month, until she had Katherine back.

Katherine. She had chosen that name because it was beautiful, strong but feminine. All these months when she had cried for Tony and for her daughter, she had called her Katherine. But *he* called her Katie. Her baby wouldn't recognize the mother who had sent her away so long ago, and now she wouldn't recognize the name that mother had given her. For that, Sarah could thank Daniel Ryan.

She fixed a sandwich for dinner, took it outside and sat on the front porch to eat. She sat there until the sun had gone down, until yellow lights appeared in the woods to mark Daniel's house, until the night chill made her shiver uncontrollably and drove her inside.

In the bathroom she changed into a faded cotton nightgown that ended inches above her knees and glanced at herself in the full-length mirror mounted on the bathroom door. Three years ago her nightgowns had been silk and satin and lace. Her skin had been smooth and unlined, her hands soft and adorned with rings—diamonds and an emerald. Her hair, now short and untamed, had hung past her shoulders in glorious waves that had required twice-weekly visits to the stylist.

Then Tony had gotten sick, and Brent had disappeared from their lives. He had been ordered in their divorce agreement to help with their living expenses and Tony's medical care, but he had chosen instead to leave the state. He'd known that the Nashville district attorney's office didn't have the time or manpower to track him down and force him to pay, and Sarah certainly hadn't been able to. He had started a new, comfortable life for himself someplace else, forgetting his ex-wife. Forgetting his dying son.

Sarah sighed deeply. She wouldn't be able to give Katherine a life rich in material goods, as Tony had once briefly had, but she could provide the necessities, and she could love her. God, she had so much love to give her!

Shivering in the night chill, she returned to the living room. That afternoon she had given the sofa a good beating with the broom, stirring up clouds of dust. The sofa was still filthy and sagged dangerously in the middle, but, covered with every sheet and blanket she owned, it would be an adequate bed, if she could only stay warm enough.

There was no electric light in the room, but moonlight streamed through the uncurtained windows. Sarah tried to pretend that was the reason she couldn't sleep, that or the cold, but she knew it wasn't so. It was the loneliness, the disappointment at being so close to Katherine yet not being able to see her. Less than a mile away her daughter had eaten her dinner, had played and had a bath, and was now curled up in her crib, sound asleep beneath a warm blanket, but Daniel had deliberately kept Sarah from sharing those small daily pleasures with her.

She had known that he would be difficult, had known that he wouldn't want to part with the daughter who had counted solely on him for most of her life. She had been prepared to deal with that, to make offers. She could settle in Sweetwater, or wherever she could find a job nearby. She didn't want to cut him out of Katherine's life; he would still be her father, still be able to see her every day.

But he couldn't keep her.

Sometimes she was so jealous of him that she hated him. Katherine was *her* baby—*she* was the one who had spent nine months pregnant, who had endured the long, painful delivery, who was still paying the hospital and doctor bills, a few dollars a month.

But he was the one who had willingly taken in a daughter that he hadn't known existed, the one who had fed and clothed and raised her, the one who had rearranged his life to make room for a baby. The one who obviously loved her.

She owed Daniel a great deal. Without his help, she would have been forced to give Katherine up permanently. Keeping the baby would have been a full-time job, would have meant precious time away from Tony who had had so little time left. She hated that Daniel had been the one to soothe Katherine's tears, had been the one to watch her first steps and hear her first words, had been the one to receive her love, but she didn't regret what she had done. It had come down to a question of need. Katherine had a mother *and* a father, both of whom loved and wanted her. But Sarah was all Tony had. There had been no one else to be there for him, no one else to spend the long miserable days and longer agonizing nights with him. There had been no one else to love him. No one else to watch him die.

No, she didn't regret letting Katherine live with Daniel, but it had been the second hardest thing she'd ever done. She remembered the day Beth had taken the baby, barely three months old, soft and sweet and precious. Even though Sarah had known that she had no choice, she had felt as if her heart—or what was left of it—was being ripped away. Before it was done, she had suffered over the choice and over her decision. But the situation with Tony had left her no other choice, and the decision had been the only one.

She felt the familiar wetness fill her eyes and squeezed them shut. When would the tears run out? When would she be able to get through one day without crying? When would she be strong enough to put the past to rest, to let go of the sorrow, to face the future without fear but with hope instead?

The answer was clear and simple and sleeping less than a mile away. Katherine. When Katherine was back in her arms, back in her life, then she could go on. Then she would have a future. Then she would have a life.

October 2

Thirty more days

Daniel couldn't get that damn calendar out of his mind. He had always been aware of the time limits on the arrangement Sarah Lawson's attorney had offered, but it had been different then. Twelve months with a baby he'd never seen before had seemed like a lifetime. He'd had forever to get to know this new little child with Ryan hair and Ryan eyes, forever to learn to care for her and about her.

But he had fallen in love with her in about ten seconds. He had begun thinking seriously about lifetimes, about forever. Even then, he suspected now, he had decided not to give her back, not ever. After all, she was his *daughter*, a child of his blood, probably the only child he would ever have. Then, over the next eleven months, the emphasis had changed. She was *his* daughter—not Sarah Lawson's, not theirs, but his and his alone. She didn't need a mother—didn't need a damn thing from the mother who had given her away so easily. To Sarah, Katie had been a nuisance, a problem to dispose of until a better time. To Daniel, she was his love and his life.

He checked on her, playing—quietly for once—in her playpen. She hated the playpen, hated being cooped up, but the workshop was too dangerous to let her roam freely. There were too many sharp edges, and she was too curious.

Only yesterday he had searched her face for some resemblance to her mother and had arrogantly proclaimed that there was none. Since seeing Sarah yesterday afternoon, though, he could find the similarities. Her mouth, which was cute and pouty now, would be sensuous like her mother's when she was grown. The nose, too small and delicate to come from the Ryan side, was practically identical to Sarah's. The bone structure, too, was delicate and fine, unlike the harsh, angular planes of his own face.

He had deliberately overlooked the resemblance, he admitted, had refused to give Sarah any link to his daughter. As long as he recognized only Ryan features in Katie's face, he could forget about the Lawson blood. He could forget about Sarah's claim on Katie.

But now that he had seen Sarah again he couldn't forget. She was gently, softly pretty—slender, with small breasts and slim hips, with hair the color of honey, rich and sweet and thick, and eyes the same clear soft brown as a doe's eyes. In another twenty years, men would be looking at Katie the same way he had looked at Sarah. It wasn't a comfortable feeling.

And it wasn't comfortable knowing that with the slightest provocation he could desire Sarah again. Knowing the kind of woman she was, he could still want her again—which said a hell of a lot, he thought with a scowl, about the kind of man *he* was.

In the playpen near the door, Katie tired of her wooden ducks and cows and horses and imperiously swept them aside. "Daddy."

He absentmindedly answered her.

"Go," she suggested hopefully.

"Where do you want to go?"

"Sach."

He turned away from the chair leg he'd been sanding to look at her. "Go where?"

Pleased that she had his attention now, she extended her arms. "Go Sach."

He swung her up out of the playpen, making her giggle breathlessly. "Say Zach." He stressed the *z*, and she intently imitated him, sounding like a fat little bee. "That's good," he praised. "Now say Zach."

"Sach," she repeated with a grin.

Every new word was a celebration. Before long they would be having real conversations, with complete sentences. And Sarah would miss out on all of it. With a grimace, he pushed her out of his mind. She wouldn't spoil this special moment with his daughter. "Zach will be glad that you learned his name," he said, putting her back in the enclosure, "but we can't go see him right now. I've got to work."

Katie refused to release his arm. "Go, Daddy," she repeated. "Go Sach."

"We can't, Katie." He gently freed himself and returned to the workbench. As he reached for the sandpaper once again, the wooden animals he'd made months ago came flying out of the playpen as she unleashed a full-force temper tantrum. That must be another thing she'd inherited from her mother, he thought, steadfastly ignoring her cries. He had never been that angry in his life—not when his father had died, not when his mother had remarried and left him to run the farm alone, not even when he'd realized that Sarah was giving him Katie, like an unwanted souvenir from their weekend together.

Katie realized that the kicking and screaming were getting her nowhere, and she collapsed onto the quilt that covered the bottom of the pen, totally silent. She was rewarded by a quick furtive glance from her father, which she responded to with a big smile.

"You're a brat, Katie Ann Ryan."

She didn't understand the insult, but she knew the loving voice. "Eat."

"No, baby, it's not lunchtime yet."

"Katie!" she insisted.

He gave a shake of his head. For eight months she had been satisfied with being called 'baby,' until she had learned her name. 'Baby' was a fine name to call other things, in her opinion, but not *her*. Was Sarah also stubborn and opinionated? he wondered idly, then pushed all thought of her away once more. "It's not lunchtime, Katie. Settle down."

She obeyed him for all of five seconds before issuing her next command. "Drink."

"No," he replied sharply, once again turning his back on her. Days like this made a housekeeper sound even better than usual. If someone could keep Katie out of his hair for six hours a day, he could more than double his output here. Of course, quality was far more important than quantity. People didn't pay the prices that his handmade furniture commanded because it was readily available. They paid for the wood, the workmanship, the fine attention to detail that had earned him a reputation as a master craftsman in a part of the country where craftsmen abounded. Still, it would be nice to work a little more steadily, without constant interruptions from a bored, restless little girl.

Once again he sneaked a look at her. She was lying on her back on the quilt, her fingers wrapped around one chubby bare foot, murmuring quietly to herself. He started to smile until he understood the word she was repeating over and over and over. *No.* The one word he had hoped sincerely that, with her temper and obstinacy, she wouldn't learn.

Maybe seeing Zachary wasn't such a bad idea after all, he decided with a scowl. Katie wasn't the only one who was restless. The trip into town would keep her amused, and Daniel could tell Zachary that Sarah Lawson was here. Muttering to himself, he laid the chair leg aside once again and went to the playpen, offering his hands to Katie. "You win, sweetheart. Let's go see Zach."

Still lying on her back, she solemnly gazed up at him, then replied, very slowly and distinctly, "No."

"Come on, Katie."

"*No.*"

He bent to pick her up, but she wriggled away, shrieking, "No!"

She liked her new word, liked the way it made him react. Daniel could see it in the gleam in her dark blue eyes. He forcefully picked her up, holding her squirming little body tightly. He turned off the lights and shut the door, then started across the yard with the steady chant of "No, no, no!" shrill in his ears.

Yes, he was definitely going to see about a housekeeper.

Sarah sat in her car, staring at the building in front of her. Made of native stone, it was two stories high and bore the date of construction above the door. Nineteen eighteen—the year World War I had ended, her schoolteacher's mind supplied, but they hadn't called it that then. How could they have known then that another great war would follow?

She was procrastinating. The longer she sat here wondering about meaningless things, the longer she could delay the meeting with Zachary Adams.

Beth had advised her not to come here. After all, Adams was Daniel's attorney. It wasn't proper for her to approach him. Wait until next week, Beth had said, and she would come to Sweetwater and talk to Daniel Ryan and Zachary Adams herself. It would be better that way, Sarah admitted. Daniel couldn't possibly dislike Beth as much as he disliked *her*, and Beth knew legalese and would be able to carry on a conversation with Adams. But she had already waited eleven months and one day. She couldn't wait another week.

The sign painted on the door glass wasn't fancy: Zachary Adams, Attorney. There were no hours listed, but in a town like Sweetwater, if someone needed to see Adams and didn't catch him in his office, he would know where the lawyer lived, would probably have his home phone number, would know his habits. It was one of the benefits of living in such a small community.

She pushed the door open and was greeted by a young woman at the desk. "Can I help you?" the secretary asked.

"I'd like to see Mr. Adams."

"He's not in right now. He and Mayor Nelson went fishing out at the sheriff's place. He should show up in about fifteen minutes, depending on whether or not they're catching anything. Would you like to wait?"

Fishing. It brought her a grim smile. She'd gotten her courage up to talk to Daniel Ryan's lawyer, and he was out fishing.

"Yes, please," she replied, turning toward the row of chairs against one wall. There were errands she could run while she was in town, but if she left the office without seeing Adams, she wouldn't find the nerve to come back. She wasn't good at confrontations, at making threats—she didn't even *want* to make threats—but that was why she was here. All she wanted was to see her baby. Was that such a terrible thing to ask?

She sat on the edge of a worn leather chair, her hands folded tightly on her lap, and looked around. The office was comfortable, the furnishings old and inviting. It was a sharp contrast to Beth's ultra modern office in a Nashville high rise, and she had to admit she liked it better. But how, she wondered, could a town as quiet and small as Sweetwater support an attorney? And if Zachary Adams was a good lawyer, why didn't he go to the city, where he could probably earn ten times what he made here and still take mornings off to go fishing?

The secretary was reading a magazine, but she looked up occasionally, curiously. Finally she put the magazine away and turned her attention to Sarah. "Would you like a Coke or something?"

Sarah politely shook her head.

"My name is Alicia. Zach's my big brother."

At least that explained how Adams, whose business couldn't possibly be booming, could afford a secretary. Sarah had been told that there were advantages to having family. She had just never seen them for herself.

Although she knew she was being rude, she didn't offer her own name. It was on the document that Beth had drawn up for Daniel to sign, and there was bound to be a copy of it in Adams's files. She didn't want to see curiosity or, worse, derision in the friendly blue eyes. A man could lose interest in his marriage and family and leave his kids behind without support or money or love and still be considered a good man. But a woman who could give up her own child, no matter what the reason, was unnatural, was shunned and scorned. She had received more than her share of scorn from people in Nashville who knew about Tony. These strangers who knew nothing about the past three years of her life would be no different.

That was part of the reason behind her decision to say nothing about Tony. She knew the question would eventually be asked, if not by Daniel, then by his attorney or someone else. Why did you give away your baby? She would answer it—but on her own terms. She wouldn't rely on the details of her son's short sad life to make her own life easier.

"Are you new in town?" Alicia asked even though the answer was obvious. She had lived here all her life, knew everyone who lived within twenty miles of Sweetwater.

"Yes," Sarah replied.

"Really? Where are you—"

The question was interrupted by the arrival of a man—Zachary Adams, Sarah guessed, judging by the casual clothes he wore and the fishing rod in one hand. He smiled rather vaguely at her before turning to his sister. "Dinner at Mom's at six-thirty," he said with a charming grin.

"Oh, no," Alicia groaned. "I hate fish!"

"Too bad, sweetheart, because we caught a mess of them."

"Couldn't you put some of them back?"

"Afraid not." He balanced the fishing pole in the corner, then turned toward Sarah. "I'm Zachary Adams. Are you waiting to see me?"

Nodding, she rose to her feet, and he invited her into his office, gesturing to the chairs in front of his desk. He sat on the desk itself, his feet dangling. "What can I do for you?"

He was younger than she'd expected—her own age or a few years older—blond haired, blue eyed, tanned and incredibly handsome. How had Beth managed not to mention that to her last year? she wondered, then grimly answered the question. Because she hadn't been in any condition at the time to care about Daniel Ryan's good-looking attorney. She hadn't been in any condition to care about anything but Tony and Katherine.

He was waiting for her to speak, and she did so as soon as she was seated. "My name is Sarah Lawson."

She saw that the name meant something to him. He slid slowly from the desktop, his smile fading, and went behind it to sit. There he was all business. "Miss Lawson . . . you're early."

She smiled humorlessly. "That was Daniel's response, too."

"You've seen him and Katie?" he asked hastily.

"Just him. He wouldn't let me see Katherine. That's why I'm here."

Her use of Katie's full name was enough to tell him that she hadn't yet seen her daughter. No one could look at that sweet little devil and call her Katherine. It was too refined, too demure. "Miss Lawson," he began, trying to be tactful, "Daniel has custody of Katie for another month. Until then . . . he doesn't have to let you see her."

"I know that. I'm not asking to take her back early. I promised him a year, and he'll have it. I just want to see her . . . for a few hours . . . please."

The sheen in her eyes made Zachary uncomfortable. He toyed with a pen, twisting it in circles on his desk pad, watching it spin. "Miss Lawson . . ." He sighed helplessly and put the pen away, forcing himself to look at her. "What do you want from me?"

"I want to see my baby."

"That's entirely up to Daniel."

She clenched her hands tightly together. "My lawyer says . . . she says that I can sue and terminate the agreement."

Slowly Zachary shook his head. "But she doesn't recommend it, does she?" He remembered Beth Gibson well, knew that she was a beautiful woman and, more importantly, a damn fine lawyer. "If you and Daniel went to court today, I can all but guarantee that you would lose." He said it as gently as he could, but it was true. An unmarried mother who had willingly given her child wouldn't gain much sympathy in this part of the state, where old-fashioned values were still in style. Add the fact that Daniel Ryan was a respected member of the community who had taken in the child without hesitation, who obviously loved Katie and could support her, and Sarah Lawson faced a very difficult battle.

Her eyes when she looked at him were soft and dark with pain. "But don't you see? As long as he keeps my baby from me, I've lost anyway." She raised a slim hand to dry her cheeks. "Talk to him...please. Ask him...tell him..." Her voice faded.

Again Zachary shook his head. "No matter how much you want to see Katie, Miss Lawson, it's still Daniel's choice. I can't influence him on that."

"You can advise him."

He leaned back in his chair, crossing one ankle over the opposite knee, and idly traced his finger along the sole of his tennis shoe. "If Daniel asked for my advice on this matter," he said slowly, "I don't know what I'd tell him. I don't know if I could, in good conscience, recommend that he let you see Katie yet."

Sarah stiffened in her chair. "But she's my daughter."

"Yes, she is, and Daniel has custody of her for one more month." He started to end the conversation there, but added one more thing. "If you feel it's necessary to try to terminate the agreement, keep one thing in mind. I'll represent Daniel, and Ms. Gibson will represent you, and the court will appoint someone to represent Katie, because it's her best interests that are in question here. In the beginning, the judge will grant temporary custody to either you or Daniel, and Katie will stay with that parent until the suit is settled. If it's you, fine—you'll have your daughter. But if it's Daniel, Katie is going to live with him until the case is settled, which could take *months*. Miss Lawson. And it's a good bet that the judge would choose to leave her in the home that she knows with the parent that she knows. You could delay her return by two to four months, maybe even longer. Is it worth the risk?''

No, of course not. Sarah sat motionless, staring at his desk. Beth had warned her, had told her to stay away from Zachary Adams, from Daniel Ryan and the whole damn town of Sweetwater for thirty more days, and as usual she had been right.

''Do you have a phone number in Nashville where I can reach you?'' Zachary asked quietly.

''No. I'm staying here, and I don't have a phone.''

''In Sweetwater?'' The lawyer was clearly surprised. Little went on in town, Sarah suspected, that he wasn't aware of. ''Where?''

''At the old Peters place.'' The answer came from the doorway behind them. Sarah didn't need to turn to know that the deep hard voice belonged to Daniel. ''Right down the road from me.''

He came into the office, closing the door behind him. He had seen the yellow car parked out front and, suspecting that Sarah had come to see his lawyer, had asked Alicia to take Katie to the diner two blocks down the street and wait for him there. Sarah wouldn't catch him by accident with his daughter.

She slowly turned her head until she could see him. Once again she was taken aback by his size and by his hardness. Was this really the man she'd spent the weekend with, sharing his meals and his company and his bed? He had seemed so different then—gentle, sweet . . . special. Now he was simply intimidating—big, hard, fierce and rough. But Katie was proof that she *had* stayed with him.

''I think you two should talk,'' Zachary said. ''Calmly. Rationally.''

Daniel shifted his gaze from the lawyer to Sarah. In faded jeans and a faded red shirt, she looked young, thin and tired. There were dark circles in the delicate skin under her eyes, as if her sleep last night had been troubled. And well it should be, he thought, his scowl deepening. Whatever had prompted her to give up Katie might be settled, but her troubles were just starting. ''I have nothing to say to her.''

"Then you can listen to me," Sarah said quietly. "Will you sit down?"

Ungraciously he sprawled in the chair opposite hers, sullen, determined to be uncooperative. His legs were stretched out, long and heavily muscled beneath nearly new jeans, and his booted feet rested only inches from Sarah's feet, smaller, narrower, in badly worn sandals.

"I made an agreement with you a year ago—"

"Eleven months ago," he interrupted.

She nodded her acknowledgement. "I know you'll keep your word, and I'll keep mine. I don't want to take Katherine—"

"Katie."

The muscle in her neck started tightening. "I don't want to take Katie from you," she said, the tension apparent in her voice, "but I *do* want to see her. Those papers we signed said nothing about visits, and that's all I want. I'd like to be able to visit with her during the next month, until she comes to live with me again."

Daniel ignored the prick of his conscience. Was she really foolish enough to trust him to keep his word and return Katie to her? Surely she must realize how difficult giving Katie back would be—how impossible—now, next month or ever.

"No." His answer was flat, empty, signaling that the subject was closed. He fixed his coldest stare on her, daring her to argue, and she accepted the challenge.

"Why not?"

"Because she's *my* daughter."

The way he said it made her shiver. She was familiar with that kind of possessiveness. Tony had been *hers*, had belonged to her and nobody else, and she would have fought the devil himself to keep him. Was that the way Daniel Ryan felt about Katherine? Had he so easily forgotten that he hadn't produced the child on his own, that Sarah had had a greater part in it than he had? "No, Daniel," she said quietly. "She's *our* daughter. I couldn't have had her without you, and you couldn't have had her without me."

One part of him could admit that she was right, but the other side blindly denied it. Katie had no mother. All she had was *him*. She was his daughter, his child, his future, his hope. Without her, he would have nothing but the cold, lonely emptiness that he'd lived with for so many years. He couldn't face that again, couldn't face life without Katie. "You gave her away," he accused. "What kind of mother does that to her own baby?"

The look that came into her eyes was the saddest he had ever seen. It stabbed past the hard shell of his defenses and into his heart. "One who has no other choices." She had done what she'd had to do, but she knew that Daniel would never understand. He was strong, he was capable, he was a man. It would have been different for him. On top of that, even though he'd asked, she knew that he didn't want to understand. He wanted to believe that she was a terrible woman, a horrible mother who had no right to see her own child. That allowed him to justify turning her down.

He uttered a brief, vulgar word. "There are always choices. You were just too selfish to make the right one." He paused, then finished with a warning. "Stay away from my house. Stay away from my daughter."

The discussion was over. Sarah knew that she could stay and talk until her throat was hoarse, but she couldn't change his mind. She looked at Zachary Adams, who was staring intently at his desktop, uncomfortable with the entire situation. As she stood up, she extended her hand to him. "Thank you for seeing me, Mr. Adams. Beth will be in touch."

He stood up, too, and shook her hand, murmuring a grim goodbye.

At the door, Sarah stopped and faced Daniel once again. "It must be nice, Daniel, to be so perfect. To never make a mistake, to never be faced with choices that are all bad. It's just a shame that, in creating such perfection, a few things got lost. Things like humanity and compassion and understanding. But you don't miss them at all, do you?"

There was a tightness in his gut, as if he'd taken an un-expectedly painful blow. He stared at the place where she had stood long after she was gone.

This is ridiculous, he told himself. She was a stranger, a woman he'd spent one weekend with. She meant nothing to him. Why, then, should her insult carry such power? Of course, no man liked to be told that he lacked the qualities that made him human, but, coming from Sarah, the words should be meaningless. They sure as hell shouldn't hurt . . . but they did.

Zachary was the first to break the strained silence. "Maybe . . ." He cleared his throat and hesitantly looked at his friend. "Maybe you should let her see Katie." When Daniel started to protest, he rushed on. "Just a couple of hours a week, with you there. Is that asking so much?"

"It's *too* much. Just yesterday you were advising me not to give Katie to her if she showed up next month. Now you're saying I should let her spend time with her?"

"Yesterday we were talking about a woman I'd never seen before, and—"

Daniel interrupted angrily. "If you think she's that pretty, Zach, believe me, you can have her—easily. She went to bed with me; she'll jump at the chance to do it with you."

Zachary made an impatient gesture. "Shut up, Daniel," he commanded in a disgusted voice. "We're talking about a woman who would beg you if she thought that would make you let her see her baby again. Maybe you would get a kick out of that, out of seeing her on her knees."

Daniel's gaze dropped to the floor. He didn't want to make Sarah beg. He just wanted her out of his life, out of Katie's life. He wanted to continue living with Katie, caring for her, loving her, as he'd done the past eleven months.

He didn't want to lose her.

And that was what would happen. He was sure of it. Sarah would take one look at Katie and fall in love with her. And Katie—she adored everyone, but she would especially love someone as soft and pretty and sweet as Sarah. There would be ties between them that the little girl wouldn't understand, but she would feel them, and everyone else would know it.

If he ever allowed Sarah to get reacquainted with Katie, when they went to court, he would surely lose. The jury would take one look at him, the big fierce hermit who lived all alone at the top of a mountain, and at Sarah and the daughter who loved her, and they would give Katie back, and he would be alone—for the rest of his life.

Since he was unable to give the answer that Zachary wanted, Daniel changed the subject. "Did you find a private detective in Nashville?"

"I've got a call in. I should hear from him today or tomorrow."

"She said Beth would be in touch. Who is that?"

"Her lawyer, Beth Gibson. She's very good."

"Better than you?"

Honesty was stronger than ego. "A whole lot better," Zachary answered. "That's why she's got a thriving practice in Nashville, and I'm here in Sweetwater."

There was more to it than that, Daniel knew. Sweetwater was Zachary's home. The Adams family had settled here not long after Patrick Ryan had arrived some hundred and eighty years ago. Like Daniel, Zachary had roots here. Unlike Daniel, he also had family and friends and people who counted on him. He couldn't leave all that for the city.

Daniel vaguely remembered Beth Gibson from last year. She had been attractive in a sharp, flashy, sophisticated way, with long red hair and the only truly green eyes he'd ever seen that weren't courtesy of tinted contacts. He didn't remember anything else about her, except that she had brought him his daughter.

"You don't have any idea why Sarah sent Katie to you in the first place?"

Daniel shook his head. "But I could make a few guesses."

Zachary looked annoyed. "You know, Daniel, you may have to face the fact that Sarah might not be the cold, selfish, heartless bitch that you think she is. Why did you pick her out in the bar that night? What made you choose her over the other women there?"

The lawyer was asking him to remember the motivation behind something he'd done more than two years ago. Something private. Something he would rather forget.

Daniel had been lonely that night, lost, out of place in the bar, and Sarah had looked that way, too. She had been pretty; she'd had a nice smile, and that voice... Something about her had touched him from the beginning, in ways that were new and different for him. He had thought...

He scowled darkly. He'd thought a lot of things, and all of them had been wrong. She'd turned out to be nothing like the woman he'd thought she was.

Zachary was waiting for an answer. Why had he chosen Sarah? "Maybe because she was the one who was willing," Daniel said coldly.

"That was it—just sex? No attraction, no interest?" Zachary waited for answers but didn't get any. "Did it seem that she made a habit of that—letting strange men pick her up?"

"To tell you the truth, Zach," Daniel said, feigning boredom, "the weekend wasn't special enough for me to remember details like that. I can't even tell you if she was any good in bed."

Zachary was interested in the reason for the harsh statements. Was Daniel trying to convince him that the time with Sarah had been sordid and tawdry, and so she must also be sordid and tawdry? Or—and Zachary thought this more likely—was he trying to convince himself?

"So she was a whore who picked up men in bars and slept with them for kicks," Zachary said in a pleasant matter-of-fact tone.

A muscle clenched in Daniel's jaw at the lawyer's choice of words, though he didn't deny them. But he knew it wasn't true. He remembered other things about that weekend. Like the fact that the look in her eyes had been sad, lost. Like the fact that it had been a long time since anyone had held her close. Like the fact that she had slept the sleep of exhaustion both nights, as if a good rest was something that came as rarely as the close embraces.

He stood up, his nerves too highly charged to remain still any longer. "You do whatever it takes so I can keep Katie, all right?"

"Even if it means destroying Sarah?"

Daniel stared at him for a long time, his dark eyes bleak, then walked out of the office, the question unanswered.

Sarah didn't matter. He told himself that all the way home. Even if she was all soft and pretty, even if she was Katie's mother, she didn't matter. Katie was the important one. He didn't care what happened to Sarah as long as Katie was all right.

He glanced down at his daughter snoring softly beside him. She had enjoyed her short stay with Alicia. At the diner she had been the center of attention, and she loved attention. She had been playing the lovable cute baby for all it was worth when he'd picked her up, then had promptly fallen asleep as soon as she was settled in her car seat.

Dear God, he loved her. She was the only person in his life who he could say that about. Was this gut-wrenching fear the way divorced fathers felt when they lost custody of their children? When they were demoted from full-time fathers to weekend visitors, then finally replaced by stepfathers?

Well, that would never happen to *his* daughter. Just as Katie didn't know the meaning of the word *mother*, she wouldn't know what a stepfather was, either, not from personal experience. He would make sure of that.

When he approached the Peters place, he slowed down. The little yellow car was in the driveway, and there was a flash of red moving across the yard. Sarah, in her red shirt. He pulled the truck to the edge of the road and watched her for a moment. She was half carrying, half dragging an old wooden ladder. His eyes narrowed until he was scowling as fiercely as ever.

Surely she wasn't planning to use the ladder. Even from this distance he could see that it was in sad shape, having been left to weather and rot in the years the house had been empty. But when she leaned the ladder against the house, he admitted that she did indeed intend to use it.

He turned off the engine and climbed out of the truck, leaving the door open so Katie's sleep wouldn't be disturbed. There was no reason for him to interfere, he insisted even as he walked along the rutted driveway. She was a grown woman. If she chose to act like a damn fool, what business was it of his? He should get back into the truck and go home.

But he didn't. If she climbed that ladder, she would probably get hurt, and if she got hurt, God forbid, it would be left to him, as her only neighbor, to take care of her. By interfering, he was only saving himself from future problems.

Sarah adjusted the ladder against the house, setting it firmly on the ground. She had found it in the old shed out past the driveway, and she knew it wasn't very sturdy, but it was all she had. She couldn't very well go to town and buy a new one. She had tested the rungs, with the ladder lying flat on the ground, and they were weak, but she thought they would hold her weight long enough to get her to the roof. If they broke then...well, getting down would be a lot easier than getting up.

She stepped on the first rung, sliding her foot next to the side rail, hoping the wood would be stronger there. When she put her weight on it, it creaked but held firm. Cautiously she moved to the next rung, gripping the splintering rail tightly, hoping that the wood wouldn't give way beneath her.

She was more than five feet off the ground when the rung broke. The force of her weight hitting the next rung broke it, too, but the third one held her. She was breathing hard and her hands were burning from the slivers of wood she had picked up as she slid, but she was safe.

"What the hell are you doing?"

Sarah was so startled by the voice that she would have slipped again if Daniel hadn't caught her and lifted her, his big hands on her slender waist, to the ground.

He quickly withdrew his hands and settled them lightly on his hips. He had touched her only for seconds, but his palms were burning from the contact. She had been so light in his grasp, too light for a full-grown woman. He noticed again how slim she was and wondered about her pregnancy. Had she grown clumsy and heavy at the end? Had she had any difficulty giving birth to his daughter? Why had she gone through it alone, denying him the chance to help?

To draw his mind away from the questions, from her warm softness, he repeated his harsh question. "What are you doing?"

Her heart was starting to slow, her breathing returning to normal. She tilted her head back and met his blue gaze evenly. "I was going up to the roof."

"On that?" He gestured to the ladder with its aged and decaying wood, its cracks and splinters and broken rungs. "Are you stupid, or just putting on a good act?"

Desperate was more like it, she thought with a humorless smile. It had been cold last night and was bound to get colder. "There's something in the chimney," she said patiently, her voice made sharp by the effort it took to stay calm. "I don't want to build a fire until I clean it out, and since that's the only ladder here, I don't have much choice."

"This house has been empty for years. You need to have the fireplace inspected before you use it. Terry Simmons can do it for you, and he'll clean it while he's at it."

Sarah looked down at her hands to avoid his stare, keeping the palms turned inward, out of his sight. There were several large splinters in each hand, one deep enough to bring blood, each surrounded by angry red swelling. As soon as he was gone, she would dig out the wood slivers and bathe her hands. "I can't afford to have someone inspect it," she said honestly, "and I *have* to use it. It's the only heat in the house."

Daniel looked from the ladder to her. He should leave her here. Maybe the cold would drive her away. Maybe the realization of how inconvenient life could be up here would override this sudden urge to see his daughter, and she would return to Nashville where she belonged. And maybe she would make it to the roof and fall and break her neck, or maybe she would get sick from the cold, and damn it all, she was still Katie's mother. She had given him the most precious gift in his life.

"I'll get my ladder and check it," he said gruffly.

Sarah drew herself taller. She still had to tilt her head back to look into his face. "No, you won't. I'll take care of it myself."

"You can't."

She gave him a look that could only be described as haughty. "I'll manage." In the years since Tony's illness had been diagnosed, she had done everything for herself because there was no one to do it for her. She had learned to be alone, to be independent and strong, to make decisions and choices that no mother should ever have to make.

Before he could argue with her, she shifted her gaze to his truck. "Is Katherine with a baby-sitter?"

"Yes," he replied, and hoped that Katie wouldn't wake up crying and prove him a liar.

"You'd better go now," she said flatly, trying to hide her disappointment that another woman was caring for her daughter, holding her, feeding her, soothing her tears, while *she* wasn't allowed to see her. "I've got work to do."

"I'll be back in an hour or so." To ensure that she didn't try something stupid while he was gone, he pulled the ladder down and without effort heaved it across the yard toward the dilapidated shed it had come from. When it hit the ground it splintered into a dozen pieces, as he had known it would.

Sarah watched him walk to the truck, climb in and leave. She knew he would be back. After all, Daniel Ryan was a man of his word, wasn't he? He had said he would come back, so he would. He had said he would give Katie back at the end of the year, and he would do that, too. She had to believe in that, had to believe in *him*. It kept her going.

Daniel grumbled all the way back into town. It was a trip he normally made only once a month or so, but now he had made it three times in two days—all because of Sarah Lawson.

Katie's stubbornness had definitely come from her. Her refusal of his help hadn't been the standard "oh, you don't need to do that but I'll accept anyway" turndown. She didn't want help—or was it only *his* help that she didn't want? If it had been Zachary or old man Peters or any other man in the county, would she have turned *him* down, too?

He was satisfied with most areas of his life, but he was well aware of more than a few insecurities when it came to women. By no stretch of the imagination could he be considered attractive, and a lot of women were put off by his size. His solitary life-style had given him peace, but had left him lacking the social graces demanded by most women. They weren't easy to talk to, to confide in, to be intimate with, physically or emotionally. It was easy to believe that women—Sarah Lawson included, in spite of their weekend together—found him as unacceptable as he imagined he must be.

But it didn't matter. He didn't want a woman's interest, especially Sarah's. He had the only things he needed to be happy: his land, his business and Katie. There was room for a woman—just not much desire for one, and even less need.

Bonnie Adams, Zachary's mother, agreed to keep Katie for a few hours. It was the first time Daniel had ever left her with anyone else, except for the hour with Alicia today. Bonnie politely probed the reasons behind his unusual behavior, but he just as politely brushed her off.

"Supper's at six-thirty, Daniel, if you'd like to stay when you pick her up again," she invited when it became apparent that she wasn't going to learn anything from him.

He gave a noncommittal response, kissed Katie goodbye and left for the nineteen-mile drive home. When he passed Sarah's house—old man Peters's house, he amended; nothing around here belonged to Sarah—it was quiet. He continued up the mountain to his own house, loaded a long aluminum ladder into his truck and went back to Sarah's— to the Peters'—place.

There was no sign of her. She was probably inside, he guessed, watching the soap operas or doing something else totally useless. He stuck a flashlight into his back pocket, carried the ladder to the same spot where the wooden one had stood, wedged it firmly in place and climbed the rungs to the top.

The roof needed a lot of work, he noticed as he made his way carefully across it. The chimney needed work, too; many of the bricks were cracked, and the chinking was gone in great patches. The house needed a tenant who would love it and keep it in good repair, or it needed to stand empty until it fell in on itself. What it *didn't* need was someone like Sarah, who didn't know how to take care of it and couldn't do it on her own, anyway. She wasn't needed by anyone or anything here; why couldn't she accept that and leave?

Shining the flashlight into the chimney, he found the obstruction that Sarah had seen from below: several years' accumulation of birds' nests built on the ledge inside the chimney. He removed them and tossed them off the roof in the back, then shone the light on the brick sides. Considering how long the house had been empty, the chimney was remarkably clean. Old man Peters must have cleaned it when he and his wife moved out.

He put the flashlight into his pocket again and climbed carefully down the ladder. Living alone for so many years had taught him caution. If he was injured on his mountaintop, it could be weeks before anyone found him, so he didn't take risks.

Why then, he wondered grimly, did he go looking for Sarah as soon as he was back on the ground?

He found her in the living room. The room was empty except for the old broken-down sofa placed in front of the stone fireplace, but it was as clean as soap and water and hard work could make it.

She was sitting on the floor in front of the broken window, her head bent while she worked diligently with a pair of tweezers.

"You ought to get that window fixed," he said gruffly, gesturing to the broken pane.

Sarah nodded without looking up. "Mr. Peters is supposed to be out sometime this week."

"Tell him to fix those broken boards on the porch, too."

She nodded again.

Moving a few steps closer, he watched her for a minute, then asked, "What are you doing?"

She looked up then, her cheeks a faint red, her eyes unquestionably damp. "I have a splinter from the ladder," she replied softly, extending her right hand to him.

Little more than an hour ago, she had made it clear that she didn't want his help. Now she was silently asking for it. He should have felt some satisfaction, but he didn't. He didn't want to take her hand, didn't want to touch her again. But, just as he hadn't walked away earlier, he didn't do it now.

"It's not a bad splinter," she said as he sat down in front of her, "but I'm right-handed, and I can't seem to get hold of it, and I'm afraid I might have pushed it in deeper than it already was."

He took the tweezers, then her hand. It was warm. Soft. Dainty. The palm was marred by little red pricked areas where she had removed other splinters, but there were no calluses, no roughness. Whatever work she had done in Nashville, if she had worked at all, hadn't left any marks.

It wasn't a splinter in the meaty part of her hand near the base of her thumb, but a good-sized chunk of wood. Old wood and soft skin, he thought with a silent sigh. Removing it was going to be painful, and he would just as soon not do it himself. "Maybe you should see the doctor."

"No." She said it quietly, with a faint shrug, but she meant it. She had spent the better part of the past three years in doctors' offices and hospitals, and, God help her, she was *never* going near either one again.

"It will hurt," he warned.

She looked at it for a moment. "What will happen if I leave it alone?"

"It'll fester, swell. It may break open and expel the wood, but, most likely, it will get infected, and you'll still have to go to the doctor."

"Then you take it out."

The look in her eyes made him cold inside with sharp-edged panic. She shouldn't do that, shouldn't look at him with trust in her soft doe's eyes, shouldn't trust him not to hurt her any more than necessary. Didn't she understand by now that he despised her, that he didn't want anything to do with her, didn't even want to live in the same county with her?

But here he sat, in her house, willingly holding her hand, hesitant to start the task because he didn't want to cause her pain. With a dismayed sigh, he laid her hand on his leg, holding her wrist to steady it, and began probing in the open flesh with the tweezers. He heard her gasp, felt the muscles in her hand go taut, but he kept searching, ignoring the trickle of blood from the injury.

She concentrated on his hands, blocking out the pain in her own. They were twice the size of hers, big and strong and capable. They were calloused from years of hard work, and his fingers were nicked and scarred in a dozen places. And they were gentle. Even though he hated her, he touched her so gently.

"There." He eased the wood from her flash. Once it was out, the blood flowed more freely, and he held her hand, watching it.

As reluctant as he had been to touch her, now he didn't want to let her go. But he did, slowly, sliding his hand away from hers, his fingertips trailing over her skin. He set the tweezers on the floor, went into the kitchen to get a towel and returned to wrap it around her hand. "Do you have firewood?" he asked, his voice still low, still deep, but uncomfortable now.

"No," she murmured. "But I'll take care of it."

"I'll bring some—"

"No," she repeated. She had to tilt her head way back to see him standing over her. Awkwardly she got to her feet and faced him stubbornly. "I know you feel obligated to do these things because you're a man and I'm a woman and Katherine's mother. But I didn't come here to impose on you. I've been taking care of myself for a long time, and I can do it now. I appreciate your offer, but it's not necessary."

Stubborn and proud, he thought, gazing down at her. It was an admirable combination, but one that could keep her pretty damn cold through the night. If she couldn't afford to have Terry Simmons check the fireplace, then she couldn't afford to buy firewood, either, and she certainly wasn't capable of cutting it herself.

Well, he had plenty of wood, and it would cost him nothing to share it with her, because she was right. He was a man, and in his corner of the world, men took care of women as much as they could. Besides, in years to come, when Katie looked at him with her sweet blue eyes and asked about him and her mother, he didn't want to have to tell her that he'd treated Sarah badly.

She lifted the towel and looked at her hand. The blood was clotting, thick and dark. She replaced the makeshift bandage, then met his eyes. "Do you have a picture of Katherine?"

He did, in the worn wallet out in the truck, and dozens more at the house. But he didn't offer to show her any of them. "Why do you call her Katherine?" he asked instead.

"Because that's her name."

"It's too big a name for a tiny little girl."

She smiled faintly. "Daniel was too big a name for a tiny little boy, but your mother never called you Danny, did she?"

Slowly he shook his head, then pointed out the flaw in her argument. "But I was never tiny."

No, she agreed silently. A tiny baby couldn't have grown into such a big man. What a sense of security he must give Katherine and the women in his life. "Have you ever been married?" she asked curiously before she could stop the question.

For a moment the tension that held his face in a perpetual scowl had eased, but now it was back, and his eyes were as dark as a stormy winter sky. "No. I have no need for a wife. I don't need anyone."

Sarah folded her arms over her chest, hugging herself for warmth against the sudden chill that had come from inside her. "Then you're a lucky man, Daniel Ryan," she said with a soft sigh. "A very lucky man."

October 4

Twenty-eight days, counting today

Daniel tried to ignore the clock ticking in his head, counting down every minute of every hour left with Katie. He tried, too, to ignore the guilt inside him, but it was just as relentless as the passing of time.

It was his own fault for going back down the mountain Tuesday afternoon with a load of firewood. Sarah had tried to refuse it, but he had ignored her protests and continued unloading it, stacking it neatly near the shed. The problem—and the guilt—had started when she'd walked back to the truck with him. Perched in Katie's empty car seat had been a ragged-eared teddy bear, her favorite toy—the only toy she had brought with her from Nashville and her mother. Sarah had reached through the open window and picked it up with trembling hands, then had hugged the bear, hiding her face in its baby-powder-scented fur, and sobbed.

He had never been comfortable with women, and, like many strong men, a crying woman made him feel helpless and foolish. He had stood there, his hands at his sides, staring dumbly at her, an unwilling witness to her grief. She had regained control quickly, had thrust the bear into his arms and dried her cheeks, then apologized and thanked him for the wood and the help, and practically run into the house.

He had told himself to forget the incident, but he couldn't. The image of her tear-streaked face and swollen eyes, of her slim body shuddering with sorrow, refused to leave his mind. She was desperately unhappy, and he was responsible. He was the only one who could give her what she wanted: time with her baby.

Letting her see Katie was the decent thing to do, the compassionate thing, and he had always been a decent, compassionate man, hadn't he? What would it hurt? It would mean the world to her, but he told himself that to Katie, Sarah would be no different than Bonnie or Alicia Adams, just a sweet-smelling woman with soft hands and a soft voice, just another woman who loved children. As long as he stayed with them, never left them alone together, wouldn't it be all right?

He didn't like playing the bastard, he admitted, didn't like the guilt that was eating him up inside. As much as he wanted to hold out, he wanted to give in more. He wanted to be fair—to Sarah and especially to Katie—and there was only only one way he could do that.

He finished his coffee and rinsed the cup in the sink. Katie would be waking from her nap soon. If she was in a good mood, he would dress her and take her for a visit. She would like that, even though she wouldn't understand the significance of it. Even though she wouldn't know how much it cost her father, or how much it meant to her mother.

Sarah sat on the sofa, her knees drawn up to her chest, her chin resting on them. The three rooms of the house that she was using were so clean that they sparkled, and now she had nothing to do. There was no television or radio to distract her, no books to read, no work to be done. Nothing to do but relax.

Unfortunately, in the months she'd spent spent nursing Tony, she had forgotten how to relax. She had forgotten how it felt to have an hour or two for doing absolutely nothing, and now she had twenty-four of them every day. How was she going to stand this for the next twenty-eight days?

It was a beautiful fall day, the kind that drew travelers from all over to this part of Tennessee to admire the weather and the glorious colors of the changing leaves. She considered going out to the porch, where she could do the same thing she was doing now, only surrounded by beauty. But maybe she had forgotten how to appreciate beauty, too, she thought wistfully, because the only beauty she had any interest in seeing was that of her little girl's face.

She had driven into town that morning and placed a call to Beth. Her friend hadn't been surprised by the way things had gone at the meeting with Daniel and Zachary, but at least she hadn't said, "I told you so." She had confirmed everything Zachary had said and told Sarah once again to do nothing until she could get there herself. "I'll be there next Tuesday," she had promised, "and we'll talk about what action to take then."

The only problem was that Sarah didn't want to take any action against Daniel. He was simply trying to protect his daughter, *their* daughter, in the only way he knew how. Taking him to court wasn't the right way to handle things. What she needed was to convince him that Katherine didn't *need* to be protected from her. She would never take their daughter away from him, would never cut him out of her life, but how could she make him believe that? He thought she was selfish and cheap, a terrible person and a worse mother. Without knowing all the facts, why should he believe anything she told him?

All the facts. She sighed bleakly. Should she relive the pain and the sorrow for him, so that he might think better of her? Was his opinion so important? Yes, of course it was—he was Katie's father. But was it more important than her desire to be accepted as she was—without excuses, without explanations, without opening her heart and her soul for his inspection? She didn't know.

The sound of an engine in her driveway drew her out of her hopeless thoughts. Maybe Mr. Peters had come to fix that broken window. She had covered it with plastic, taped securely to the frame, but nothing would fix it like a new pane of glass. She rose from the sofa, the wood floor cool on her bare feet, and went to the door to look out.

It was Daniel's truck. Slowly she stepped onto the porch, stopping at the top of the steps. Just as slowly, he climbed out of the truck and came to a stop in front of it. He stared at her for a long time, never moving, never speaking. He had done that that night in Nashville, Sarah remembered, and a faint smile touched her lips. But that night his eyes had been warm and gentle, and there had been a definite degree of male interest in them. Today they were hard and steely, measuring, judging.

Her sigh was heavy and weary. She was tired of being judged, of being condemned by people who didn't know what she'd been through. Maybe if she told Daniel about Tony, about the constant care his illness had demanded, about the lack of money and a decent place to live, about the emotional strain of watching him die bit by bit—maybe it would make a difference. Maybe it would erase the derision from his eyes.

Or maybe he still wouldn't understand, she admitted grimly, remembering his words in Zachary's office. *There are always choices, Sarah. You were just too selfish to make the right one.* Maybe she would give him everything, and it still wouldn't be enough. Maybe he would still blame her, still condemn her, still hate her. Could she risk that?

Not yet, she decided. Not until he knew her. Not until he could see her as a loving mother, a caring person, and not some horrible creature who gave away her baby.

She moved down the steps, stopping on the bottom one. "Hello, Daniel," she said quietly.

Abruptly he moved, returning to his truck. Sarah watched, her face lined with bewilderment, until he returned. In his arms was Katherine.

Her heart pounding, Sarah started toward them, unmindful of the rough ground beneath her tender feet. Her eyes were damp with tears when she reached them, and her hands were clasped tightly together. She wanted to laugh and cry, to thank God and Daniel, to hug and kiss him and offer him anything in the world, but most of all she wanted to hold her daughter, wanted to feel that small sturdy body in her arms, wanted to smell the baby-sweet scent of her, wanted to memorize every detail of her chubby little face.

"Katherine." The name came out on a breath, a soft, insubstantial prayer. She held out her hands to the little girl, who studied her solemnly with eyes as dark and as blue as her father's.

"No," Katie said softly after a moment, then laid her head against Daniel's chest, her fingers curling around the open collar of his shirt.

Sarah knew it was foolish to feel hurt—the child didn't know her, couldn't remember her—but there was a pang deep inside anyway. Blinking away the tears, she raised her hand to stroke Katie's soft curls. "Oh, Daniel, she's beautiful," she whispered. "She looks just like you."

The gaze he turned on her was disbelieving. No one in his lifetime had ever mentioned beauty in the same breath with *him*. "She's not usually shy with strangers," he said gruffly, then winced. He shouldn't be calling his daughter's mother a stranger, even if it was true. "She just woke from her nap." He shifted her to his other arm, then tickled her chin. "Katie, this is Sarah. Let her carry you while I get some stuff out of the truck."

"No," Katie murmured, clinging tighter to him.

"Katie—"

Sarah laid her hand on Daniel's arm. "That's okay. She's forgotten me. Don't make her come if she doesn't want to. Why don't you come inside?"

He gave a shake of his head. "I brought some wood to patch the floor."

"But Mr. Peters—"

"Leon Peters is seventy years old and slower than molasses. By the time he gets out here, the whole porch will be gone." He climbed the steps, skirted the hole and set Katie down. She toddled to the rail and immediately plopped down on her padded bottom. "Watch her, will you?"

Sarah nodded, taking a seat nearby but not close enough to threaten the girl. While Daniel unloaded tools and boards, Sarah watched Katie, and Katie stubbornly ignored her, picking up a dried leaf, crumbling it between her fingers, then reaching for another. When she tired of that, she leaned back against the rail, wrapped her hands around one bare foot and studied Sarah.

"Where are her shoes?" Sarah asked, glancing at Daniel when he returned.

"She doesn't like to wear shoes—clothes, either, if she can help it. It's a game we play. I put them on, and she takes them off." He looked pointedly at her own bare feet. "Where are *your* shoes?"

"I don't like them, either."

Her smile made her look years younger. Daniel grew still, saw in hand, and watched until it faded. She was so lovely, so fragile looking. What had the last year been like for her? he wondered, searching her face for some clue. Why had she given away her baby for a whole year when she had so obviously wanted her?

With a scowl, he turned to his job. He was getting soft, letting a pretty face affect his thinking, his judgment. The reasons why Sarah had given him Katie didn't matter. Nothing could excuse what she'd done. *Nothing*.

While he removed the broken boards, then measured and sawed the new ones to fit, Katie and Sarah continued to study each other. Finally Katie scooted closely enough to touch Sarah's foot. After a moment, she laid her foot, sole to sole, against Sarah's. "Katie," she murmured.

"You're a pretty baby," Sarah responded.

The toddler emphatically shook her head. "No. *Katie*."

"She doesn't like to be called 'baby,'" Daniel said, fishing a hammer from the toolbox he'd brought. "Can you steady this?"

Sarah knelt across from him, holding the board still while he hammered in the first nail. There was a rustle behind her; then a fat little hand appeared on the board beside hers.

Sarah turned her head to see Katie on her knees next to her, smiling brightly. "Hi," Katie said in her sweet little voice.

This was her daughter, Sarah thought, feeling the ache deep inside. The last time she'd seen her, Katherine had been three months old, able to do little but smile and cry and occasionally laugh. Now she was walking and talking, dressing herself—or at least undressing herself. She was friendly and happy and probably more than a little stubborn. She was growing up, and Sarah had missed so much of it.

Lord, she wanted to hold her, wanted to wrap her arms around her and let Katherine's warmth fill all the empty places inside her. But she forced herself to keep her hands flat on the board. When her daughter was ready to be touched, she would let her know.

"What do you do with her while you work?" she asked, turning to look at Daniel.

He was bent over, his face only inches from hers. Knowing that he would see right into her eyes if he looked up, he kept his gaze on the board he was nailing down. "I keep her with me."

"Doesn't that make it kind of hard?"

"Why should it?" he asked, his tone defensive. "You don't even know what I do."

She smiled. "You make furniture, mostly pine but some oak. Tables, desks, chairs, rockers—things like that."

Then he did look, and all he saw were her eyes, soft, brown, gentle. "Did you have your lady lawyer check me out?" he asked snidely, reacting against the corresponding gentleness that she stirred within him.

"No. You told me yourself. In Nashville." He had been willing to talk—uncharacteristically, she had guessed, for he seemed a man of few words—and she remembered it all. "You're thirty-four, you've lived in Sweetwater all your life, you don't like the city even though you occasionally have to do business there, you have a workshop at your house, and your work sells in expensive shops all over the South. Your father is dead, and your mother remarried when you were sixteen and moved to Florida, where she lives with her husband and their three children. You like working with your hands, like living alone, you like these mountains, and . . . you love children.''

Tears dampened her eyes. When he'd told her that he wanted children, it had been a pleasant piece of information, no more important than anything else about him. But when she had finally admitted that she had to give Katherine up, she had been grateful to know that Daniel would want her, that he would love her.

He *had* told her those things, Daniel realized. It made him uncomfortable—and angry—that she had remembered them for two years. "Do you want to know what I remember about that weekend, about you?" He paused briefly before telling the lie. "Nothing, except that you were so willing to sleep with a man you'd never seen before."

Sarah knew he was lying. He had wanted to see her again, had asked to see her the following weekend. She had turned him down as quickly, as gently, as she could. There had been no room in her life for a man. Those two days and nights had been a precious gift from Beth, a respite from her constant care of Tony, a time to rest, to think for a short while about living instead of dying. Those two days and nights had been all she had to give.

Would Daniel ever understand the kind of need that had led her to spend that time with him? Did he have any idea what it was like to be alone and frightened and unhappy, to be so hungry for a night's peace, for another person's touch?

She sat back on her heels, running her fingers through her hair. "Maybe it meant nothing to you, but it was special to me, and for the things you gave me, I thank you." She stood up and walked to the end of the porch, sitting on the peeling floor there.

"What things?" Daniel asked, bewilderment taking the sharp edges off his anger.

"Katherine."

"Her name is Katie, damn it! She doesn't answer to Katherine."

As if to prove him right, Katie looked up when he spoke. She grinned first at her father, then at Sarah, and repeated her name.

Most mothers had the privilege of choosing their daughters' names, Sarah thought, but Daniel refused to give her even that much. She could accept that. Tony's illness had taught her a great deal about accepting things that couldn't be changed. In comparison, calling Katherine 'Katie' would be easy.

"What other things?"

Peace, affection, gentleness. He had made her feel wanted, needed, protected. For one weekend nothing had been able to touch her. For one weekend she had felt secure. But she gave a slow shake of her head. "Nothing you would understand, Daniel."

Muttering a curse beneath his breath, he hammered the remaining boards into place. While he worked, Katie left his side and wandered down the length of the porch toward Sarah. She didn't get too close, only watched her curiously. After a moment, she sat down, back against the rail a few feet away. A few minutes later she inched closer, then closer still until, by the time Daniel finished patching the floor, Katie was right next to Sarah.

He put his tools into the truck, then gave both females a harsh look. "Let's go, Katie."

"No."

He wasn't in any mood for this. "Come on," he demanded. "Let's go home."

Katie reached across and slid her hand inside Sarah's, then looked defiantly at her father. "No."

Her action turned him cold all the way through. Wasn't this exactly what he had feared—this bond between mother and daughter? He had been wrong to bring her here, wrong to give in to Sarah Lawson, even a little bit. It was a mistake he couldn't afford to make again.

Reading the foreboding in Daniel's eyes, Sarah scrambled to her feet and opened her arms to Katie. The little girl went to her readily. Sarah picked her up and carried her to Daniel, placing her in his arms. "You're a sweetheart, Katie," she said, her voice rough and unsteady. Leaning forward, she placed a light kiss on the girl's cheek. Then, standing on her toes and straining, she placed her second kiss on Daniel's chin. "Thank you for letting me see her."

Her touch made him go all stiff and hard. With a sigh she stepped back and folded her arms over chest. "You know, Daniel, if you ever decide to quit hating me, maybe we could be friends. For Katie's sake?"

"Friends?" He repeated the word as if he didn't know its meaning. "Why would I want to be friends with you?"

"Because I'm your daughter's mother." Because she needed a friend. And because, she suspected, so did he. But she knew he would never admit it, would never admit even the possibility of needing anything from her. "In spite of what you think, Daniel, I'm not a bad person. Give me a chance to prove that to you."

He didn't want her to prove anything. He only wanted her to stay away from Katie, to disappear from the face of the earth and leave him alone with his daughter.

Sarah sighed at the implacable expression on his hard features. Couldn't he see that she was trying to make things easier for all of them? Couldn't he relent even a little?

When she spoke again, she sounded tired, defeated. "Can I see her again?"

"No. You asked for a visit, and you got it. There won't be any more." He said it quickly, sharply. He couldn't let Katie spend more time with Sarah, couldn't let this bond between them develop into anything stronger. It was the only way he knew to protect his daughter...and himself.

"That's not fair, Daniel!" Remembering how uncomfortable Tuesday's tears had made him, she strained to keep these new tears under control, even though her eyes burned mercilessly. "You can't bring her here and let me look at her and talk to her, then take her away again!"

Her thick emotion-charged voice stirred his guilt, making it prick sharply at him. He reacted instinctively, defensively, hardening himself against it, against *her*. "Life isn't fair," he reminded her harshly. "It wasn't fair to Katie when you gave her away. It isn't fair of you to come back before my time is up.''

''I don't want to take her from you!'' She breathed deeply, trying to calm the shudders inside. ''I want to see her, that's all. I want to hold her. I want to play with her. I want...'' Her voice broke with the tears she could no longer contain. ''I want to be her mother.''

''Too bad you didn't want that eleven months ago.'' His sarcasm was cold, heavily laced with derision. ''But it wasn't convenient to be her mother then, was it?''

She stared at him for a long moment, her tear-dampened gaze meeting his damning eyes. If he knew about Tony, would he stop judging her, stop hating her? She decided the answer was no. He believed what he wanted to believe. He'd twisted his memories of their weekend together into something cheap and shabby, had deliberately forgotten the gentleness, the specialness, because the memory of a whore having sex with a stranger better suited his needs. That made it easier to condemn her for giving up Katie. It made it easier for him to hate her.

And it made her want more. She wanted him to remember that he had been attracted to her, that he had liked her, that in some small measure he had cared for her. She wanted him to have faith in her, and she wanted to know that when she told him about Tony, he would care. Tony deserved that much. *She* deserved that much.

''I have always been her mother, and I have always loved her. Please...''

Daniel slowly shook his head. He didn't know what she was asking—please let her see Katie? Please give her daughter back? Please quit hurting her?—but he was saying no to everything. He would give her nothing—no understanding, no sympathy, no time with Katie. ''Twenty-eight days. You can see her then.'' He insisted to himself he sounded deeper and rougher than usual because he'd seen his daughter choose Sarah, even briefly, over him. Not because of the sorrow in Sarah's soft brown eyes. Not because she seemed to need Katie almost as much as he did.

Certainly not because he felt her pain and shared her fear and wanted to soothe both.

With a muttered oath, he walked away, Katie secure in his arms. Sarah watched until they were gone before slowly sinking down to sit on the first step. Then, as she had done on a regular basis for three years, she bowed her head and cried.

October 6

There had been times when Sarah had believed that just one glimpse of her daughter would make the year's separation bearable, but she had been wrong. Thursday's brief visit with Katie had only made her want more. It had stirred an ache deep inside her, throbbing, relentless. It had kept her awake the past two nights—hurting, feeling, thinking, planning.

Her plans were simple in concept. Daniel didn't trust her; she would earn his trust. He condemned her; she would make him understand. He despised her; she would make him remember the affection he'd once felt for her.

Simple in theory, difficult in practice. How would she earn the trust and understanding of someone who *wanted* to hate her?

She plunged her hand into the bucket of soapy water by her side and wrung out the rag, then began scrubbing the top panes of the front window. She had to stay busy, had to keep herself occupied, or she would go mad, so she had turned to housework. In the past two days she had waxed the wood floors, gotten on her knees and scrubbed the kitchen linoleum, washed all the downstairs windows from the inside and was now tackling them from the outside. When that was done... She stifled a sigh and rinsed out the rag. When that was done, she would find something else to do.

When she heard the truck on the road she stubbornly refused to turn and look. Daniel had gone by an hour earlier—she'd seen him from the living room, had seen how he'd stared straight ahead without so much as a glance at her house—and now he was on his way home again. The knowledge that Katie was probably with him made Sarah's fingers clench into a fist around the soapy cloth.

In spite of her intention to ignore him, the unmistakable sound of the truck turning into her driveway brought her head around. Daniel parked behind her car, shut off the engine and climbed out. Her hopes rising, Sarah looked closely, but as far as she could tell, the infant seat was empty. He'd left Katie with a baby-sitter, she realized, disappointment tight around her heart. Rather then expose her to Sarah, he'd taken her to stay with someone else.

Soapy hands on her hips, she waited for him at the top of the steps. She looked belligerent, ready for a fight, Daniel thought, and he could probably give her a good one, but that wasn't why he'd come.

He stopped at the bottom of the steps. The height of the porch put her a few inches above eye level with him. She didn't wait for him so speak, but asked sharply, "What do you want?"

He offered a single envelope. "You don't have a box, so the mailman left this in *my* box."

Drying her hand on her jeans, she took the letter. She knew without looking that it was a bill. The hospital and the doctors were patient. Aware that she was a single parent with no insurance to help cover her and Tony's medical expenses, they had never pressed her for payment and had written off many of their bills. Because they had been good to her and Tony, had done all they could to help, she paid what she could. "Thanks." Her curt, sarcastic tone embarrassed her, but she made no effort to apologize.

Daniel knew he'd been dismissed with that brief word, but he didn't go. The return address of the Nashville hospital had roused his curiosity, and he had to know. "Is that for Katie?"

"That's none of your business." She clutched the envelope tightly, as if he might try to take it from her.

"It *is* my business. Do you still owe the hospital for her delivery?"

Raising her eyes to the sky, she gave a humorless laugh. Sometimes she felt as if she owed half the medical community in Nashville. Then she looked back at him, her expression serious, her eyes challenging. "I never asked you for money, so it's *not* your business."

"But you could have." He climbed one step, and they were eye to eye. "You should have."

"That was what my lawyer said." She folded the envelope and tucked it into her hip pocket, then crossed her arms over her chest. "But I chose not to."

Why not? he wondered. Why hadn't she sued him for payment of her medical bills? For child support? Why hadn't she tried to get as much money from him as possible? Wasn't that what women like Sarah did when they found themselves in her situation? "If you'll give me the account number and the balance, I'll pay it."

Sarah clamped down on her temper. She had to earn his trust, make him remember the affection he'd once felt for her, remember? Snapping at him because he wouldn't let her see Katie might make her feel better, but it certainly wasn't the way to go about making him like her. "I appreciate the offer," she replied, and the antagonism and sarcasm were gone from her voice. "But I'll pay my own bills."

"You can't afford to pay them." He'd seen her car, her clothes, had seen how bare the house was. She was barely scraping by, while he had more money than he needed. "Besides, they're not *your* bills. If you hadn't gotten pregnant, you wouldn't have had the bills, and if I hadn't . . ."

Under other circumstances she might have been amused by his reluctance to put his part in Katie's conception into words. Today her mood was too fragile for amusement. "If you hadn't had sex with me. That's as good a way of putting it as any, isn't it? If you hadn't had sex with me, I wouldn't have gotten pregnant. Where is she?''

The sudden subject change didn't unnerve him. "With a friend." When he'd left the house over an hour ago to get the mail, he hadn't planned to leave Katie with anyone—hadn't even planned to see anyone. But after the four-mile drive to the nearest junction, where a row of rural mailboxes stood, he'd found a letter to Sarah with his mail and had known he couldn't take it to her while Katie was with him, then still refuse to let Sarah see her. He wanted to protect his daughter and himself, but he wouldn't resort to cruelty to do it.

That had meant another drive into town, where he'd left her once more with Alicia Adams. It also meant another long drive back to pick her up.

"Are you really going to make me wait until the first to see her again?" In spite of herself, she sounded hopeful, as if she couldn't quite believe he could be so stubborn, so hard-hearted.

Her hopefulness fanned his guilt, making it twist and coil in his belly. Unused to the feeling and not liking it one bit, he responded with a single harsh word. "Yes."

"Daniel—"

"The first." He turned and started toward his truck.

Sarah followed, catching up with him as he reached it, grabbing his arm. "Wait a minute! Why are you doing this to me? I've never done anything to you—except give you a daughter who you obviously love a great deal. Why are you punishing me?"

He looked at her hand, so small and fine boned against his heavily muscled forearm. On the surface it appeared that he was strong and she was weak, but he knew there were different kinds of strengths. He could crush her physically, but she could so easily crush him, crush his spirit and his emotions. He was strong, but she had power. He had to protect himself against that power.

He stepped back, causing her hand to fall, then climbed into the truck. "I'm not punishing you," he said through the open window. "I'm holding you to our agreement."

"I don't want to take her away from you," she whispered in despair.

He gave no reply, just started the engine and backed out of the driveway.

I'm holding you to our agreement. Daniel winced as the words echoed in his head. He had looked Sarah in the eye and lied to her without the slightest hesitation. He had no intention of honoring their agreement...and no qualms about using the papers they'd signed to make her believe that he *would* honor it.

He really was a bastard.

October 9

It was Tuesday, the ninth of October. Twenty-three days until November first. Twenty-three days until Katie was back with her mother, where she belonged.

Sarah sat on a bench in the town square, idly watching the traffic that passed. A little over two hours ago Beth had arrived at the house with the news that she'd made an appointment with Zachary Adams for this afternoon. She had insisted that Sarah come along, even though she would be excluded from the meeting. Sarah had spent the past hour on this bench, ignoring the curious looks sent her way by the occasional passersby, watching the cars, wondering what was going on inside Zachary's office.

Beth had agreed that a lawsuit to terminate their agreement wasn't a wise plan of action. All she could do was try to convince Zachary to reason with Daniel—not, she'd added dryly, that she believed Daniel Ryan was a reasonable man.

Sarah smiled faintly to herself. From the first time she'd met him almost a year ago, Beth had been dismayed by Sarah's choice in lovers. Beth preferred handsome, elegant, sophisticated men; in a pinch, she could make do with cute, bright or charming. She'd seen nothing in Daniel to excuse Sarah's affair with him and had decided that it could only be blamed on her fragile mental state at the time.

She couldn't have explained it to Beth even if she'd wanted to, Sarah thought. How could her friend understand that it had been *right*? Being with him, talking to him, making love with him—it had all felt so right. So good. So special. She had no doubt that under different circumstances they could have built something permanent from that weekend.

But the circumstances hadn't been different. And they needed to be explained, Beth had insisted. That was the only way to get through Daniel Ryan's tough exterior to the goodness and gentleness that Sarah claimed were underneath. He loved his daughter dearly, so he would understand that Sarah had loved her son dearly. He would understand and would forgive and would let them be together. Let her tell Zachary about Tony, Beth had pleaded, so that Daniel would know the truth.

But Sarah had refused.

She shivered in the bright afternoon sun. How many times had she seen the shock and criticism and condemnation in people's eyes when they'd learned that she had sent her baby daughter away? Natural mothers didn't willingly give up their children. No matter what the sacrifice, a good mother kept her child.

It was a common, if unfair, reaction, one of Tony's social workers had told her. People wanted to believe in the maternal instinct, in the goodness of all mothers. When a mother lost custody of her children, they automatically assumed that she was a bad mother. When she voluntarily gave up that custody, they assumed she was a bad person. It was based on ignorance and self-righteous attitudes, but it hurt all the same. Sarah could attest to that. She still remembered the pain, when her very soul was already aching from the loss, of being told by a friend that she would have found a way to keep both Tony and Katie *if she had really wanted to*. Even those who had understood had still been appalled by her decision.

How would Daniel react to the truth? she wondered. She was afraid that he would still judge her, and she was afraid to see that damning look in his eyes. What if he, like the others, thought that she hadn't done enough—that she hadn't tried long enough, hadn't prayed often enough, hadn't worked hard enough? What if he believed that she had taken the easy way, that without regard for Tony or Katie, she had chosen the path that was best for herself?

Well, she hadn't taken the easy way, and she wouldn't take it this time, either. She wasn't going to tell this man who despised her such painfully intimate details of her life. She wasn't going to demean her son's memory by using him to influence Daniel's opinion. She wasn't going to give in, to plead for understanding and forgiveness, when she hadn't done anything wrong.

She smiled wryly. That was a good, strong stance to take now, but after a few more weeks—or even a few more days—without her daughter, she might be willing to do all those things and more just for the chance to see her again.

Daniel parked next to the fancy German car, giving it a derisive look as he climbed out of his dusty truck. He'd seen the car a couple of times before, when the flashy redheaded lawyer had come to tell him about Katie, and again when she'd brought his daughter to him. According to Zachary's message, she was back now to "talk." Well, *he* didn't want to talk. In fact, he'd driven nineteen miles into town just to tell her that. Sarah hadn't changed his mind, not with her arguments and requests and pleas, and her fancy lawyer wouldn't, either.

He went into the office, tapped on the door, then walked into Zachary's inner office. With barely a glance for the redhead, he faced the other man. "Alicia said you wanted to see me."

Zachary rose easily to his feet. "Thanks for coming. Is she staying with Katie."

"Yes." Finally he looked at the woman. His expression wasn't friendly.

"Daniel, you remember Beth Gibson, Sarah's lawyer?" Zachary asked.

He remembered her, all right. She was pretty, expensive and fancy, and she didn't like him one bit, he knew. From the first time they'd met, she'd made no effort to hide the fact that she found him totally unsuitable—as a man, as her client's lover, as Katie's father. It showed in her condescending smile, in her cool, aloof manner and in her cold emerald eyes. But he didn't give a damn what she thought of him, because he didn't give a damn about *her*, either.

"Mr. Ryan," Beth said, managing, as he had known she would, to make his name sound distasteful. She rose from her seat and offered her hand, smooth, long fingered, with perfectly groomed nails.

Daniel considered refusing the handshake, considered refusing any contact with her at all. He was annoyed with Sarah for bringing the woman here, felt irrationally angered by the threat the big-city lawyer was supposed to represent. But in spite of his feelings, he shook her hand quickly before turning back to Zachary. "I assume this is about letting Sarah see Katie."

Before Zachary could answer, Beth did. "You do realize, Mr. Ryan, that instead of giving you temporary custody of Katherine, Sarah could have turned her over to the state. You probably never would have known that she even existed."

"So I should show my gratitude by letting her play mother now that it's convenient for her." Daniel shook his head in disgust.

"Not 'letting her *play* mother,' Mr. Ryan. She *is* Katherine's mother."

He faced Beth again, his angry dark eyes meeting hers. "And *I* am Katie's father, and for the next twenty-three days, *I* have sole custody."

"Daniel, Beth..." Zachary came around his desk to stand between the two. "Beth, would you please wait outside while I talk to Daniel?"

She wanted to refuse, to argue with this man that Sarah had so foolishly chosen for a fling, but because he expected her to argue, she left willingly though spitefully.

When the door closed behind her, Zachary sat on the corner of his desk. "Look, I don't know what Sarah and Beth are planning, but they could create a lot of problems, Daniel."

"What kinds of problems?" he asked grudgingly.

"When you sue Sarah for custody, they're going to try to make you look like the worst father imaginable. Everything that you say and do now could be used against you then. Beth Gibson is an expert at twisting someone's words and beliefs and perceptions into something totally different to suit her client's needs."

Daniel walked to the window behind the desk, staring out at the square. "You're saying I should give in."

"Not give in. Be reasonable. Be fair. Then, when we go to court, we can say that you gave Sarah generous visitation rights completely of your own free will." Zachary was silent for a moment. "I know you wish that Sarah would simply disappear without a trace and leave you and Katie alone, but that's not going to happen, Daniel. You can't cut her out of her daughter's life."

Daniel considered the lawyer's advice while he studied a slim figure in the park across the street. Her back was to him, but there was no mistaking that cap of honey-blond hair. How smugly satisfied she must be, he thought with a trace of bitterness, knowing that she was going to get her way. She was going to win, and he was going to lose. "You didn't see them together."

"Sarah and Katie?"

Daniel nodded. "She was charmed by her." He realized that his statement wasn't clear—who was charmed by whom—but it worked either way. Sarah had seemed to think Katie was the most precious thing in the world, and Katie had liked *her*, too. When Katie had first come to live with him, he'd read magazine articles about the bonding between a baby and its parents, but he'd never understood it as clearly as he had that day last week. Katie liked everyone she met, but she'd never exhibited that kind of attraction to any of them, had never chosen anyone else over her father.

In a dull monotone, he recited the details of last week's visit—how Katie had refused to leave with her father, how she had wanted to stay with Sarah. With her mother.

Zachary didn't say anything for a long time. Because he understood Daniel's fears about losing the girl, the reassurances he could give wouldn't mean much. "Daniel . . . when you go to court to get permanent custody of Katie, I can't guarantee that you'll win. You know that, don't you?"

Daniel turned from the window and sat down. He knew, but it wasn't a possibility that he wanted to face. How could he live without Katie?

"In the event that Sarah does win, it couldn't hurt for her to owe you a few favors, you know? If you antagonize her and treat her unfairly now, she might decide to retaliate once she has Katie back."

Daniel's expression was stony. "If she wins and the judge orders visitation, she can't interfere."

"No, but she can certainly influence how Katie feels about you. She can certainly make things difficult for you." Zachary returned to his seat, leaning back comfortably. "What I'm saying is that you should cover all the possibilities. We'll go ahead with the custody suit—I'll have everything ready to file on the first, and the private detective in Nashville has promised me a report no later than the twenty-fifth-but in the meantime, make friends with Sarah. Let her see Katie. Show her that you can be a fair man."

In other words, Daniel thought cynically, lie to her. Let her think that he *was* being fair, that he was being a friend, while at the same time he was planning behind her back to take her to court. Deceive her, use her, then hit her with the truth. Was he that good an actor? Was he that hypocritical? Grimly, he turned away from the answer. "All right."

Zachary didn't ask for an explanation of exactly what he would do. Daniel never did anything by half measures. When he'd agreed to take care of Katie, even knowing that it was temporary, he'd put his whole self into it, heart and soul. Now that he'd agreed to befriend Sarah and give her access to her daughter, he would go all the way. "If you want the terms in writing, we'll need to discuss them with Beth first."

"No. This is between Sarah and me." Daniel stood up and glanced out the window. She was still sitting on the bench, looking small and so alone. "I'll be in touch," he said quietly as he started toward the door.

Beth looked up from the magazine she was reading as he passed through the waiting room. She knew from his somber expression that Sarah had won this battle, although she refrained from commenting.

Daniel crossed the street and followed the winding sidewalk to the bench where Sarah sat. Without waiting for an invitation, he sat down at the opposite end, his big hands clasped together.

Sarah looked up, surprised by his appearance, then she realized that she shouldn't be. Since Katie was the topic of discussion this afternoon, she should have expected Zachary to notify Daniel. This time she wasn't even the faintest bit hopeful that he might have their daughter with him.

He was staring at his hands, and she directed her gaze in that direction, too. They were big hands, the fingertips marked with the cuts and scars, the palms ridged with the calluses; she had noticed the day he removed her splinters. Hardworking hands, she thought. Capable hands. Like the man.

She didn't know how many minutes passed before he broke the uneasy silence. She expected to hear anger in his deep, rumbly voice. She was surprised by defeat.

"Why did you bring your lawyer here?" He admitted that it was the logical thing to do, that it was what he would have done in her position, but, irrationally, he felt betrayed. As he'd told Zachary, this was between him and Sarah—not him, Sarah, Zachary and the redhead.

Sarah gave a simple shrug. "I called her last Tuesday. Before you brought Katie to the house." After a brief pause, she reached out to touch his arm. "Daniel, I don't know what she told you in there, but I don't want to take you to court. I have too much respect for you for that."

He looked sharply at her. *She* respected *him*? That was more than he was capable of believing.

"Do you know how many men divorce their wives and refuse to pay even a few hundred dollars a month to help feed and clothe the children they helped bring into the world?" she asked, her voice sharp with the remembered pain that she had married one of those men. "Yet you took in a child you hadn't even known existed, who you'd had no say in planning...." Her voice grew soft. "A child whose mother you hardly knew. And you've raised her and cared for her and loved her. Yes, I do respect you, Daniel, very much."

He shifted uncomfortably on the bench. That wasn't the kind of speech the Sarah he'd condemned for so long was supposed to make...but he wanted to believe it. He wanted to believe that she thought well of him.

Drawing her hand back, Sarah gave a soft sigh and gazed around. Above the streets on two sides of the square fluttered banners announcing the date of this year's Harvest Festival: Saturday, October twentieth, right here in the square, from 9.00 a.m. until the music ended. She wondered idly what kind of festival a small town like Sweetwater put on, if it was similar to the country fairs she'd been to. Would there be rides and candied apples and game booths? Would Daniel bring Katie to ride the merry-go-round and eat cotton candy and play with the other small children in town?

Her smile was wistful. How she would like to share something like that with her daughter.

Now that her attention was elsewhere, Daniel felt safe in looking at her. Curiously, a great deal of his hostility was already gone. In deciding to make her a part of his life, he had unknowingly eased the resentment and anger he felt, not *for* her, but *because* of her. Because he'd known that he needed to hate her, but hadn't really been able to. Because he'd wanted to see her as his enemy but remembered her too clearly as his lover.

Now it was safe to see how pretty she was, how delicate. Now it was safe to remember their weekend in Nashville as it had really been—sweet, endearing, important. Now it was safe to admit that once he'd wanted much more than an affair with her, much more than two brief days and nights.

"As soon as your redheaded lawyer is gone..." He paused over the words. He didn't want to sound begrudging or resentful, didn't want her to think he'd been forced into this. "Come to the house. You can see Katie."

When he stood up, so did Sarah. Unmindful of the curious eyes on all sides of the square, she rose onto her toes and pressed a quick, joyous kiss to his lips. "Thank you, Daniel. Thank you so much. You won't regret this."

Flushed a deep bronze, he stepped back and saw old Henry Walters and Leon Peters sitting on the bench in front of the hardware store, looking in his direction. Within an hour it would be all over town that the city girl living in Leon's house had kissed Daniel Ryan right in the middle of the park. Small-town gossip being what it was, the townsfolk would make the logical leap from a kiss to a sweet baby girl who had appeared out of nowhere last November. Oh, well, he thought resolutely, he couldn't keep his personal life secret forever, and he couldn't keep the identity of Katie's mother secret much longer, either.

October 12

Friday was bright, sunny and cold, a sure sign that winter was on the way. Daniel hugged Katie close to his chest as he quickly covered the distance between his house and the workshop. Once inside, he continued to hold her while he turned on the heat; then he settled her in the playpen. With both hands, she tugged her knitted cap off, leaving her hair standing on end; then she grinned at him. "Go play, Daddy."

He studied her as he removed his jacket and hung it on an intricately carved coatrack next to the door. Next he removed her coat. "Play, huh? Did Sarah teach you that?" Two days with his daughter, and Sarah was already teaching her new things. He wasn't quite sure how he felt about that.

"Sair," Katie murmured. "Sair play."

She was so bright, picking up new words and ideas so easily. His daughter was growing up—*their* daughter, he corrected—and Sarah had missed so much of it: Katie's first steps, her first words, her wet kisses and energetic hugs and even her stormy tantrums. Most of all, she had missed being called Mama. How would she feel when she came in today and heard her daughter call her by name?

He knelt beside the playpen, picking up a wooden horse that had been thrown free and laying it back inside. "Not 'Sarah,' Katie. Say..." The word stuck in his throat. How could he encourage his daughter to call Sarah Lawson 'Mama?' At the same time, how could he not? "Say 'Mama,' Katie."

She picked up the horse and stuck its head into her mouth. Daniel gently removed it, but she immediately put it back.

"Can you say 'Mama'?"

"No."

He couldn't help but grin at the naughty gleam in her dark eyes. "You're being a snot."

"'Not," she echoed around the horse's head.

With a laugh, he turned to the worktable that filled half the room and took a seat on the high stool. The chair he was working on lay in pieces—legs, rungs, slats, arms, seat. Two chairs sat in the corner, waiting for their mates before they would be shipped to the man in Augusta who had commissioned them. Daniel had already shipped a table and a china cabinet that matched.

The pieces were sturdy, plain, functional. Their beauty lay in their simplicity—smooth, clean lines and graceful, flowing curves. Each piece had been carefully fashioned, sanded until the wood was satiny smooth and given a finish that would protect it for years.

Ever since he had sold his first rocker six years ago to a collector sent out by Zachary, he had put long hours into each piece. With no wife or children, they were to be his legacy, something that would continue as strong and beautiful as ever, long after he was dead.

But now he had Katie. The Ryan name would die with him, but the family would live on through her and her children and her children's children. And the work that had been a true labor of love was now a business—no less loved, but business all the same—because now he had a child to support.

He fitted the chair together, testing each joint, searching critically for some small flaw. He didn't find one, though. The Ryan name stood for quality, and he didn't accept anything less.

In the playpen, Katie chattered, lining up her toys, rearranging them, hugging first one, then another. Was she happier than usual, Daniel wondered when he glanced at her, because she knew that Sarah would come today as she had come yesterday and the day before?

It was getting harder to put Sarah out of his mind. The easy, graceful way she moved. The low, slow sensuous drawl of her voice. The soft, trusting look in her eyes. The sorrow, the pleading, the happiness, the dignity. Every time his mind was idle, she slipped in, enticing him, touching him, stirring his guilt, his needs, his loneliness. She made him remember, made him feel, made him . . . want.

Wanting wasn't so bad, was it? She was a beautiful woman. Wasn't it natural that he should want her? As long as he didn't *need* her . . .

He sat for a long time, his hands idle, his thoughts two years distant. He had gone into that Nashville club looking for a drink, nothing else, but the moment he'd seen Sarah, he'd known that she was special. He had been drawn to her in a way that no woman had ever drawn him. His heart, always racing miles ahead of his mind, had immediately considered the possibilities of a future, of permanence and commitments. If he could have those things with any woman, he had known instinctively that it would be her. He had believed that she felt it, too, that rare sense of belonging. How could the bond exist for him, but not for her?

But it hadn't. The weekend had ended, and he had asked to see her again, had been willing to make the long drive into the city again the following weekend. But she had quickly, bluntly, turned him down. Those two days had been all she was willing to give. That was his first clue that she wasn't the perfect woman he'd made her out to be. The proof had come a year later in the form of a sweet brown-haired, blue-eyed baby.

So she wasn't perfect. That didn't mean she was horrible. She loved Katie, didn't she? He wasn't too familiar with love, other than his own, but wasn't that what he'd seen in her eyes when she played with their daughter?

But if she loved Katie, why had she given her away? Why hadn't she wanted her?

Before he could push the questions away, there was a knock at the door. It was Sarah, dressed in jeans and a sweatshirt that swallowed her. Her hair was tousled by the light wind, and her cheeks were colored an attractive pink by the cold. Where's your coat? he wanted to ask. Why did you walk through the woods wearing clothing too thin to protect you from the wind's chill? But it wasn't his place to chastise her. It wasn't his place to take care of her. He turned back to his work without saying anything at all.

Sarah gave Katie a brilliant smile and swung her up when the girl raised her arms. "Hey, sweetheart," she said, brushing her cold lips over Katie's warm fat cheek. "Good morning, Daniel."

His only greeting was a nod.

Sarah found another stool on the opposite side of the table and perched on it, holding Katie in her lap while they watched Daniel work. "You do beautiful work," she commented.

He glanced up swiftly, then down again. "Thanks."

He didn't take compliments easily, she'd noticed. Because there had been too few of them in his life? It was a shame, because he was a bright, talented, sensitive man. He was the most special man she had ever met, but telling him so would only embarrass him.

Katie tugged at Sarah's shirt until she looked down. "Go play?" the little girl asked hopefully.

"And what do you want to play?" Sarah asked, bending to nuzzle the girl's round belly. They were limited in their choices since they couldn't leave the workshop. Daniel hadn't laid out any rules or restrictions, but Sarah could read the wariness that slipped into his eyes every so often. He didn't yet trust her enough to leave her alone with Katie, but she didn't mind. If the truth was told, she enjoyed his company almost as much as Katie's. In the past two days he had worked hard and said little, but he was *there*—strong, quiet, reassuring. She liked that about him.

If the truth was told, she silently repeated with a harmless edge of sarcasm, she liked a lot of things about him. She liked his commitment to Katie, to his work, to his land. She liked his gentleness, his sensitivity, his vulnerable self-consciousness when he was complimented. She liked his hands, so strong and capable, and his size that made her feel as if nothing could harm them while he was around. Most especially, she liked his unwavering devotion to Katie.

Katie was struggling to get down, and Sarah let her, then followed closely behind her. At the playpen, they gathered all the toys and carried them to an empty corner where they sat down to play.

Daniel listened to them as he worked. Sarah's voice was different when she talked to Katie—softer, more alive with emotion. He'd read once that babies reacted to their mothers' voices more than their fathers' because of the softer, higher tones, and he would bet now that it was true. *He* would rather listen to Sarah's voice than his own any time.

Katie talked, too, mostly nonsensical chatter, coupled with the few words that she knew. He noticed that there were new ones—*dog, kitty, bird, teddy.* How had she learned so much from Sarah in only two days? he wondered grimly. Maybe he hadn't spent as much time with her as she needed to help her learn. After all, since they didn't have a television, she didn't watch *Sesame Street* or other educational programs, and she was never exposed to other kids. All she had to depend on was him, and maybe he wasn't enough.

It was a disquieting thought, one that nagged at him through the morning. He was still considering it when Sarah returned Katie to the playpen for her nap.

"She's a handful," Sarah said when she was sitting across from him again. "I don't know how you manage."

"Maybe not very well," he muttered without thinking.

"Why do you say that?" She didn't wait for him to answer. "She's a very happy, bright, well-adjusted kid, and that's all your doing."

"She needs more attention than I can give."

"Because you have to work?" Sarah rested her elbow on the tabletop and cupped her chin in her hand. "Obviously you can't quit working to devote yourself one hundred percent to her." She smiled suddenly, broadly. "You're facing one of the biggest problems in every working mother's life: dealing with the guilt. You have to work and you have to take care of her." She shrugged philosophically. "You do the best you can. And you've done a good job, Daniel."

She only hoped that she would do as well next month when Katie came to live with her. She would have to leave the child with a baby-sitter or in a day-care center rather than try to work around her, as Daniel did, and she worried over how Katie would respond to the change.

"Do you think she'll like me?"

Her unexpected question stopped Daniel's work, and he slowly raised his head to look at her.

"I mean, living with me. She's so used to you and your house. I wonder sometimes if she'll be happy with me."

The guilt was a sudden pain in his gut, clawing and twisting. How could he look into her eyes, seeing the fear and the love so strong that they brought tears, and lie? How could he say, "Sure, she'll like living with you," when he had no intention of ever letting Katie go?

Sarah gave a sudden sigh. "Beth used to say that I worried too much, but...I've had good reasons for worrying." First Tony's illness, then the divorce, then her pregnancy. Even though Tony's doctors had assured her the disease wasn't hereditary, that the baby she was carrying was at no higher risk than any other baby, she had worried about it, had worried about the effects of the stress and the exhaustion on the baby, had worried about all the other dozens of things that could go wrong with a pregnancy. But nothing had gone wrong. Katie had been born perfect, healthy and beautiful.

He wanted to ask what those reasons were, but he was afraid. If her life hadn't been easy and carefree and self-centered, he didn't think he wanted to know, not yet.

He continued to work in silence. He was used to silence. Along with no television, he had no radio, either. He'd grown up with only the sounds of nature—the birds, the wind, the animals—and had always felt at home with the lack of noise. Now, though, it bothered him...or, more precisely, *her* silence bothered him. He asked the first question that came to mind to break it. "Where are you going when you leave here?"

"I'm staying." She saw the startled look in his eyes, though he tried to hide it, and smiled. "Not in that house, of course, but in town. In Sweetwater. That way you can see Katie as often as you want, and she'll be able to come up here and stay with you. Of course, everything depends on me finding a job in Sweetwater. It's such a small town, but there's got to be something."

He stood up on the pretext of stretching, then walked to the window to look out. It was still bright and cold outside. He was starting to feel that way inside. "What kind of job?"

"Anything. I can work hard."

He turned to look at her. She was slender, delicate. Insubstantial. Hard work would break her. She was the kind of woman who needed to be cared for, the kind of woman who needed to be supported. The kind of woman he needed.

Hearing his own thoughts, he gave a shake of his head. He didn't know *what* kind of woman he believed she was anymore. Every time he saw her, his opinion of her changed...to match his changing feelings for her?

Sarah read his thoughtful look as skepticism. "I *can* work. I used to teach school, but I could do anything that paid enough to support us."

He responded to the least important part of her claim. "What grade did you teach?"

"Second." She smiled briefly, remembering the pleasure she'd found in teaching, in working daily with a roomful of lively, eager children. "But I haven't taught..." She broke off with a sigh, then continued, "In three years." Since she'd given birth to a beautiful little boy who suffered from liver disease. It seemed so long ago that the doctor had told her that Tony would die without a transplant. With his next words, he'd taken even that faint hope from her, when he'd explained the negative factors: the chances against finding a compatible donor in time, the cost, the tremendous risk of the surgery itself. She would have found the money somehow, would have risked the surgery, but she'd never been given the chance. Tony had died before a donor had been found.

She was a second-grade schoolteacher. Daniel was dismayed. He had gone to bed with her, and spent an entire weekend with her, and hadn't known that. What other important things about her had he neglected to learn during that weekend?

All of them, he decided after a moment. In the two days he'd spent with her, he had learned nothing—just that she was lonely and that he was immensely attracted to her. He hadn't learned that she'd had a job, if she had friends or family—parents, brothers, sisters, maybe even a husband. He hadn't learned anything.

"What about your family?" he asked. "Do they live in Nashville?"

"I don't have much family, and what I do have is scattered all over Tennessee. There are some aunts and uncles and a few cousins, but I don't really know them. I haven't seen any of them since my mother died ten years ago."

"And your father?"

She shrugged. "The last I heard, which was years ago, he was living in Oregon. He and my mother divorced when I was little. I don't know him."

He came back to the table and sat down, but didn't pick up the chair leg he'd been working on. "Have you been married?"

Sarah studied her hands for a long time. She didn't want to discuss her marriage with him—didn't want to admit how badly it had turned out, how poorly she had chosen. She didn't want to bring even the memory of another man between them. But she wouldn't lie to him. She expected honesty from him; she had to give him nothing less. "Yes, I was married."

"Were you married when we met?" It was an ugly thought. She had seemed so sweet, so good, that he'd never considered the possibility that she could have been married, could have used him to be unfaithful to her husband.

She heard the suspicion in his voice. Maybe she'd given Katie to him because she'd been married, the little voice was suggesting to him, because her husband had objected to raising another man's child. She gave a shake of her head. "No. He divorced me about a year before I met you."

"Why?"

She wasn't offended by the question, simply because it was Daniel asking. Because he was Katie's father. Because he was a good man. "There were—" she searched for a word that would encompass all the reasons Brent had left her without explaining any of them "—responsibilities to being married that he didn't want to accept. He didn't want to grow up."

Life had been one long party to Brent. With him and Sarah both working, there had been money to spend on nice things and good times. He hadn't wanted to spoil that with a baby. When she had accidentally gotten pregnant, she had expected him to mature, to give up the easy fun and settle into the role of father, but he hadn't. Then Tony's illness had become apparent, and Brent had disappeared from their lives.

Biliary atresia. That was the correct term for the disease that had ended Tony's life. The average life expectancy for patients with the surgically noncorrectable form of the disease who were unable to obtain transplants was about eighteen months, but Tony had lived two-and-a-half years. Looking back on the last months of his short life, Sarah didn't know if that was a blessing or a curse.

Daniel watched her, his dark eyes somber. She had forgotten that he was there, he realized. She was lost somewhere in the past, in an immeasurably sad past, if her expression was anything to judge by. Had this sorrow been responsible for her decision to give Katie away for a year? He couldn't ask. He didn't want to learn any details of her life that might make him regret the action he was taking to keep Katie.

As if cued by his thoughts, Katie woke up. She rolled onto her knees and looked around, her eyes heavy with sleep, her expression drowsy and befuddled. Then she saw Daniel, and a smile lit her face. "Daddy," she murmured. After a yawn that crinkled her entire face, she shifted her eyes to Sarah, studying her for a long time with a solemn gaze so like her father's.

Sarah had left the stool and was on her way to the playpen when Katie spoke again. "Mama." It was soft, hesitant, but clear and sweet, the most precious word Sarah had ever heard.

She picked up Katie, hugging her close, then walked over to Daniel. "Thank you," she whispered, carefully balancing Katie while she leaned forward to kiss him.

She had intended only a quick kiss, one of gratitude, but the instant her lips touched his, she paused. It had been so long since they had kissed, *really* kissed, and she wanted to savor it—the firm line of his mouth, the fragrant woodsy scent of him, the strength in his body where it touched hers.

Hesitantly she probed, and his lips parted beneath hers. His hand came up to rest gently on her back, steadying her, and his other hand circled around Katie to reach Sarah's shoulder. He considered turning away from the table so he could pull her close and cradle her against him, but decided that he wanted it too badly to do it. He made do with her arm pressed against his chest, her hip against his leg.

He let her control the kiss, took what she gave, but didn't give back, didn't interfere. He accepted the delicate intrusion of her tongue, submitted to its slow searching strokes and finally yielded to desire—hers or his, he wasn't sure and didn't care—and became the aggressor.

Sarah leaned into him, letting him help support Katie, and gave him control, gave him everything. He tasted dark and strong, her dazed mind thought. Like need. She recognized the need because she had felt it herself—once for Brent, now for Daniel. First and second. First and last.

Daniel moved his arm from around Katie's back and brought his hand to Sarah's neck. His big fingers stopped there, grasping her firmly, pulling her closer... just a little closer. The hunger was bubbling up inside him, sending restless, edgy, heated sensations through him. He knew what it was like to love her, to feel her slim, fragile body beneath his, to fill her so completely, so thoroughly, as to create a new life. He knew how she moved, how she responded. He remembered her ragged breathing and her ragged cries, remembered how the tension wound itself through her until she exploded, leaving her limp and exhausted. And he wanted that now—all of it. *Now.*

Annoyed by the lack of attention and by her father's arm excluding her, however slightly, from their closeness, Katie gave a frustrated wail. "No, Daddy, play!" she cried, shoving his arm with all her strength.

Sarah responded to the interruption first, gently, sweetly ending the kiss. She leaned against him for a moment, until the trembling inside calmed, then took a step back.

Daniel's face burned with an uncomfortable flush. He released Sarah awkwardly and refused to meet her eyes. "I, uh... I'll see about... lunch."

She didn't offer to help him fix it. He slid off the stool away from her, got his jacket from the coat tree and stepped outside.

"I think your father's a little bit flustered," she said softly to Katie as they watched him through the window.

Katie laid her hand on Sarah's cheek. "Go?"

"Not yet. Let's give him a little time alone." Sarah turned away from the window and set the girl on the floor. They played happily for the next fifteen minutes, but Sarah's thoughts were on the kiss. Of course Daniel was flustered. He had tried, judged and convicted her before she'd even come to Sweetwater. Probably the last thing he'd expected was to still be attracted to her. But why wasn't *she* the slightest bit fazed by the kiss?

Oh, she had been disturbed, all right, but all her responses had been good ones. They could be grouped together under a variety of names—lust, desire or, if she was very lucky, love. She wasn't casual enough for lust or foolish enough to believe that what she felt for Daniel was love—not yet, at least. But did she desire him? She respected him, liked him, admired him and, yes, she admitted with a slow smile, she desired him.

"It's easier for me," she remarked, uncaring that Katie couldn't understand her. "You see, your daddy thinks he has to protect you from me. He thinks I'm not a very good person. So naturally he doesn't want to want me. But I *know* he's a good person. I know he's a good, honorable, decent man, so it's all right for me to want him. Besides, he's your father. What could be better than Katie's mother falling for Katie's father?"

Katie solemnly listened to the whole speech, then stood up and started toward the door. "Go. Eat."

"All right. I guess he's had enough time to settle down." She found the girl's jacket, hustled her into it and zipped it up, then held her hand as they walked to the house.

Daniel came outside to get them for lunch, then stopped on the porch to watch them. They walked slowly, at Katie's let's-look-at-everything-along-the-way pace. He grew cold waiting and wondered once again why Sarah wasn't wearing a coat. This time, searching for anything to cover up the uneasy gentling taking place inside him, he harshly asked. "Where is your coat?"

Sarah looked up while she helped Katie negotiate the steps. "I don't have one," she admitted blithely. It was the truth, but more than that, it was an easy way to silence him. As she'd expected, he was so surprised that he didn't know what to say. With a smile, she walked past him and opened the door for Katie. After a moment she glanced at him. "Are you coming in?"

He turned to face her. "What do you mean, you don't have a coat? It gets cold up here."

She shrugged and followed Katie inside. "It wore out last winter. Katie, let's wash your hands. Come into the bathroom."

Slowly Daniel closed the door behind him, shutting out the chill. Sarah's easy admission stunned him. He'd known that she didn't have much money, but this...! This was unacceptable. "How are you living?" he asked as soon as they were seated at the table.

"I saved money from my job for the past few months." Aware that she couldn't go to Sweetwater five months early, she had found a job shortly after Tony's death. It hadn't paid much, but she'd been able to save enough to support herself, if she lived very carefully, for six weeks or so. "It'll last until Katie and I find a place to live in town and I can start working again."

"How much do you have now?"

The easy, careless tone was gone from her voice when she looked up at him. "I believe we had this discussion before. It's none of your business, Daniel."

This time he didn't drop it, but pressed on. "Can you buy a jacket? Can you afford that?"

She dropped her eyes from his and concentrated on ladling vegetable soup into Katie's bowl. She could make the purchase if it was necessary, although it would mean skipping this month's payments to the obstetrician and the radiologist. She just didn't feel it *was* necessary. How could she spend money on things for herself when she owed so much money to others? Besides, when it was cold like today, she would be outside only for the twenty minutes it took to walk up the mountain in the morning and down again in the evening. Later, when she was making some money, when she had an income again, it would be soon enough to buy herself a coat.

"Sarah—"

"Not Sair," Katie interrupted, waving her baby-sized spoon for emphasis. "Mama."

"Hush," he ordered without looking at their daughter. "Sarah, if you need help..."

She should have lied to him. She should have told him that she'd left her coat at home because she hadn't realized how cool it was. Maybe he would have believed her, or maybe he wouldn't. But it probably would have avoided this conversation about her finances. She just wasn't used to anybody caring about her, she admitted to herself.

"I don't," she replied quietly, firmly. "A year ago, two years ago...I did. But now I don't." Now all she needed was Katie. Everything else would be all right then.

He wondered about those dates, when she'd asked him to take Katie and when they'd had their affair. What else had been going on in her life at those times? Whatever it was, had it led her to have an affair with a stranger? Had it caused her to give up their daughter?

For a moment Sarah thought he was going to ask her for an explanation, and she was going to have to easily, politely refuse. But the moment passed, and he didn't ask. He didn't want to know, she thought, and the idea both relieved and saddened her—relieved her because she was spared the refusal, saddened her because maybe he simply didn't care.

They talked little through the rest of the meal. Katie welcomed all the attention they could give, so she was the buffer between them. After lunch Daniel cleaned up Katie and changed her diaper while Sarah rinsed the dishes and put away the remaining food. When they got ready to go out again, Sarah fastened Katie's jacket, then stood up to find Daniel offering one of his own jackets.

"It's obviously way too big for you," he said awkwardly, "but it'll keep you warm."

Pride prompted her to refuse, but good sense made her accept it. "Thank you." She put the jacket on, snuggled into it, smelled his scent as it settled around her and smiled impishly. "You're a good man, Daniel Ryan."

October 14

Sarah woke with a yawn and a stretch on Sunday morning, then quickly dove beneath the covers again. Once again the fire had gone out, and the room was so cold that her yawn had formed a frosty cloud. She had always taken central heating for granted, had known that with the twist of a dial she could keep the house comfortably warm. It wasn't that simple with a fire. When the logs burned brightly, the room was warm, sometimes even hot, but as the logs burned down, the temperature dropped, too. That meant adding more logs from her rapidly dwindling supply.

She rubbed her cold nose with her warm hand, then slid lower under the covers. As she saw it, she had only two choices: either she asked Daniel to give her more wood, or she rationed what was left to make it last until the end of the month. Of course he would be more than willing to deliver another load of wood. He might not give graciously—he'd been stubborn, curt and insistent when he'd brought the first load—but he gave freely, willingly.

It was a shame he wasn't married and raising a big family, Sarah mused, because he was a natural caretaker. He had been born to take care of things, of animals, of people.

She'd seen it in his work, with the few cows and horses he still kept, with Katie, and even with herself. He didn't love her the way he loved everything else, but he was willing to take care of her.

But if he was married, there would be no place in his life for *her*. Another woman would claim his time, his attention, his kisses, and he would never even look at Sarah. She found herself suddenly, selfishly glad that he'd never found someone to share his life.

What did he do on Sundays? she wondered, slowly working her feet free of the blankets. If she got used to the cold gradually, her theory went, it wouldn't be such a shock to get up. Did he take Katie to church, or was it just another workday, as yesterday had been? Surely he took one day off to rest, to play with Katie, to do nothing except what he wanted to do. When she was up and dressed and warm again, she would make the walk up the hill and find out.

She let the covers slide up to her knees. The muscles in her legs clenched and tightened, then slowly relaxed.

She worried that he was getting tired of her. He hadn't said or done anything to make her think that—no, once he'd decided to let her see Katie, he'd given her unlimited access. In the past four days he hadn't complained when she arrived right after breakfast and stayed until dinner. In fact, he'd seemed, in a reluctant, grudging sort of way, to enjoy her company himself. He had occasionally talked to her, explaining his work, telling her a little about the Ryan family, recounting stories about Katie's time with him. And once he had kissed her. Well, kissed her back, she was forced to admit.

The covers were up to her waist now. Since everything above that was covered by her nightgown, she threw back the blankets, sat up and swung her feet to the floor. The wood was like ice, and she worked out the morning stiffness in her joints quickly as she hurried to the bathroom to change.

She had done laundry last night, washing her clothes in the kitchen sink rather than making the long drive into town to a Laundromat. Now her jeans and shirts hung semi-frozen over the bathtub. If it remained sunny today she would hang them outside, then bring them in by the fire tonight, she decided as she tugged on her last clean pair of faded jeans.

Getting ready to go was a simple matter of running a comb through her hair. She didn't wear makeup—hadn't even owned any since her supply had run out long ago—and all her jewelry had been sold. Even if she'd wanted to, there was nothing she could do to make herself look more attractive. This, she thought with a faint frown, was as good as it got.

Daniel's jacket *was* much too big for her. Where it probably reached his hips, the hem came closer to her knees. The sleeves extended several inches past her fingertips, and there was practically enough fabric for her to wrap it around herself twice. But Sarah liked it. She liked that when she breathed deeply she could smell his scent. She liked knowing that it was his.

After locking the house she slid the key into the coat pocket, then rolled back the sleeves as she walked across the field and into the woods. She scuffed her feet through piles of brown crackly leaves, kicked occasional pinecones and climbed over rocks and fallen trees that blocked her path.

She'd been born and raised in the city and had never spent any time in the mountains before this. She envied Daniel the pleasure of growing up surrounded by such beauty. It would be a wonderful place to raise their daughter so that she could learn to appreciate nature the way her father did. Sarah would bet that Daniel knew the name of every tree, plant and flower that grew on his mountain. Maybe he would teach her and Katie together. Maybe, even after November first came and she and Katie went to live in town, he would still let Sarah share their time together.

She gave a forlorn sigh. *Maybes*—they characterized her entire life. Maybe Brent was a wonderful man, the one she'd been dreaming of all her life. Maybe they would live happily ever after. Maybe he would change his mind about not wanting a baby once it was born. Maybe the doctors were wrong about Tony. Maybe he would be the exception, the one who would live. Maybe it wouldn't hurt to spend the weekend with this sweet, gentle stranger from Sweetwater. Maybe she could take care of a baby *and* a dying child. Maybe Daniel would let her see Katie early. Maybe he would share their lives with her. Maybe he would learn to care for her. Maybe he would even learn to love her.

Was there no end to her dreams? How many times did she have to be disappointed before she gave them up? Brent had been a selfish bastard, Tony had died, she'd had to send Katie away, and Daniel wasn't going to fall in love with her. It was that simple.

Then she thought about that kiss. It had affected him as much as her. She hadn't had vast experience in that area, but she *had* been kissed by a few other men, and none of them, not even Brent, even in the beginning, had been like this. And there had been their weekend in Nashville. Daniel had no more been in the habit of picking up strangers than she had. There had been something special between them from the start, something that couldn't be explained by hormones, loneliness or lax morals. Maybe they could find that bond again. Maybe they could strengthen it into something lasting.

She grinned, an easy, carefree grin. More *maybes*. *Maybe*, after thirty-one years of dreaming, it was too late to change.

Daniel glanced at the clock above his desk, then his eyes dropped to the calendar beneath it. Eighteen days before Sarah came not to visit but to claim her daughter. Eighteen days before Zachary filed the lawsuit that would take Katie away from her. Eighteen days to be friends.

He wasn't sure when he'd begun to think of her that way. There were people in town whom he knew well, people he exchanged small talk with, but that wasn't being friends— it was part of living in a small town. Zachary was the only friend he'd had in years...and now Sarah. For eighteen more days.

She was late this morning, but that was all right, because Katie had gone back to sleep as soon as she'd eaten breakfast. Was Sarah sleeping in, too, on that lumpy broken sofa she used as a bed? He could offer her a bed—there were several in the empty rooms upstairs—but instinct told him that her pride would take offense. It was a different matter from the firewood, when he'd insisted, or the coat. She could sleep on a lumpy sofa without endangering her health, but she had to have a warm room to sleep in and warm clothes to wear.

It was silly of him to worry over her. She was a grown woman, married and divorced—a mother, for heaven's sake. She should be taking care of people, not being taken care of herself. But she was so thin, so slight, so fragile looking. She roused every protective instinct he had, but only because she was Katie's mother. Only because having a child together created ties that couldn't be easily broken.

He glanced at Katie, sleeping on a quilt in front of the fireplace, then went to the window, laying his hand against the pane. Although the air was still cold, the sun was bright. By afternoon it should be warm enough to take Katie out, maybe to have their lunch outside. She'd loved their summer picnics in a field of wildflowers or the quiet, cool shade of the woods. They could go to the stone wall out back, where there would be room for Katie to play and plenty of sun to warm them. She would like it…and so would Sarah.

Would Sarah carry out her plans to live in Sweetwater after she'd lost Katie? he wondered somberly. Or would she be so angry, so hurt, that she would want to get as far away from Sweetwater—and him—as possible? One thing was sure; she would hate him. For breaking his word, for lying to her, for deceiving her with every day, every hour, they spent together. But Sarah's hatred was a small price to pay for getting Katie. He could bear that.

But what if she didn't lose? What if *she* got Katie and *he* was left with nothing? Zachary had warned him of the possibility, but it wasn't one he wanted to consider. Life without Katie would be unbearably lonely. Sarah had said that he could see their daughter whenever he wanted, but even daily visits wouldn't make up for the fact that she was living elsewhere. He would still be lonely and miserably empty.

As Sarah was? his conscience prodded. He'd found it convenient in the past year to create two sets of completely opposite emotions—one that truthfully portrayed his own feelings regarding Katie, another that he was certain described Sarah's feelings. But he had been wrong. Wouldn't losing Katie be just as unbearably lonely and miserably empty for Sarah as it would be for him? There was no way they could survive a custody battle without a great deal of harm on one side or the other or both.

But they had no choice. There were two parents and only one child. Someone had to lose. And it had to be Sarah.

He returned to his desk and sorted through the papers there. There were orders to fill, letters to answer, bills to pay. In the past four days, with Sarah there to keep Katie amused, he'd accomplished more work than he had in the previous two weeks. Whatever else the next two weeks were, they should be productive ones.

The knock at the door pulled him across the room. He let Sarah in, taking the jacket from her and hanging it next to his. Her cheeks were flushed, her smile warm. "Good morning," she greeted him softly, immediately noticing Katie asleep on the floor.

It had already been a good morning, he thought dryly. Why, then, did it suddenly seem better? "Have you had breakfast?" he asked, watching her move into the center of the room.

There he went again, Sarah thought, her smile deepening. Taking care. "I don't eat breakfast. It's too early in the day to face food. Were you working?" She gestured to the clutter on his usually neat desk.

"I was just going through the mail."

"Go ahead. I won't bother you." She sat down in a nearby rocker, kicked her shoes off, then drew her feet onto the seat. While Daniel hesitantly returned to his desk, she took the time to look around. She had been in this room numerous times since last Wednesday, but she was delighted anew every time.

The room was large, with exposed beams and rough log-and-mortar walls. On one end a wall of rock rose to the ceiling, framing the fireplace that was the house's primary source of heat. The furniture was of pine, handmade and massive. Gathered in front of the fireplace were a sofa and two rockers, the lines straight and clean, the plump cushions oatmeal colored. There were tables, bookshelves and cabinets, and on the far side of the room, a desk, chair and pine file cabinets. The wide planked floor was bare except for a rug at the door and another in front of the fireplace, where Katie lay.

There were few homey touches—a couple of photographs, none of them of Katie, scattered here and there, a half dozen bright-colored pillows, a wicker basket overflowing with toys—and the overall look was strongly masculine, but it was warm and comfortable. It was a welcoming room.

Daniel considered the orders that he'd received. Some, those received from the retail shops he contracted with, had to be filled. The others, individual orders from people who had seen his work somewhere, went into a separate pile. He would fill them if he had time, but with the court case looming... He glanced at Sarah, contentedly rocking back and forth, and pushed that thought from his mind.

Sliding his chair back, he asked, "Do you want some coffee?"

She focused her dreamy gaze on him. "No, thanks, I don't drink it. I'll get it for you, though."

He started to protest, but she was already on her feet, coming for his cup.

"I'm the one intruding here," she said when she returned with the refilled cup. "I might as well make myself useful."

"I told you that you could see Katie," he said gruffly, her remark about intruding pricking edgily at him.

"But you didn't expect me to be here all day, every day, did you?" she asked matter-of-factly as she pulled the rocker closer to his desk.

"Yes, I did." He had the satisfaction of surprising her into silence for once. "It's not a problem."

A week ago he would have thought spending more than ten minutes with her was a problem. She smiled serenely, pleased with the progress they were making. "Are those orders for your furniture?"

He glanced at the papers he held. "Yeah."

"Business must be good."

"Ever since country-style decorating became so popular, everyone who can afford it wants handmade solid wood furniture."

"Will you do all those?"

"I don't have time now. I'll fill as many as I can."

Sarah drew her shoeless feet onto the seat again. Daniel glanced at them and thought of Katie, asleep with one sock on. The other was in the kitchen, and her shoes were somewhere between her room and the dining room. Like mother... The cliché died away unfinished.

"Why don't you hire someone to help you?"

"Because then I couldn't truthfully say that the pieces are made by Daniel Ryan."

She smiled sheepishly. "I suppose people pay for the name, too, don't they? They don't want to buy a chair made by John Smith, Daniel Ryan's assistant. But you could get someone to help with the less important jobs. You could still do the designs and have control and oversee it all."

He shook his head. "About the only part I'd want help with is this, the paperwork."

"Well, when you get married, your wife can do that."

The innocent remark caused similar reactions in both of them. Daniel looked uncomfortably away and tried to relax the stiffness that had spread through him. Sarah was stiff, too, displeased with the idea of Daniel married... to somebody else.

Turning back to his work, he said flatly, "I'm not getting married."

She didn't know what pushed her—the lack of emotion in his voice, the hostility in his manner or her own stubbornness—but she asked the question anyway. "Why not?"

"I have a daughter. Why would I need a wife?"

Was that how he saw marriage? she wondered unhappily. As a means of getting a child? "What about love, Daniel? Happiness, satisfaction, understanding, friendship? What about other children—sons, more daughters? A wife can give you all that."

He swiveled the chair around to face her. His expression was dark, challenging. "Did your husband give you those things? Did he make you happy? Did he satisfy you? What happened to the love and the understanding and the friendship when he divorced you? What about the children, Sarah, the sons and the daughters? Where are they?"

Daniel watched the color disappear from her face, and she huddled tighter, shrinking away from him. Her eyes were wide with shock and brimming with tears. She looked as if he'd struck her without warning or provocation, and *he* felt that way too. What right did he have to throw her marriage in her face? He knew nothing about it, didn't know the reasons it had failed, or if she had loved her husband—or if she still loved him.

He knelt in front of her and reached out, his big hand unsteady, to touch her. "I—I shouldn't have said that." The words came out slow and rusty. It wasn't an apology, exactly, but it was the closest he could come to one.

She accepted his gesture in her own way—by kissing him. She leaned forward in the rocker and slid her arms around his neck, then touched her lips to his, slowly, deliberately. This was the chance she'd been waiting for since Friday, the chance to see if that first kiss had been a fluke or evidence of the attraction between them.

It was no fluke. She tasted the warmth, the hunger, the urgency, immediately. How long had this need been inside her? Two weeks? Two years? A lifetime? There were no answers to her questions, only more questions. And demands. And pleas.

Daniel raised his hands to her arms. She was so small, like a child. But this was no child's body. This was no child's kiss. This was Sarah, the mother of his child. The woman of his long-ago-but-not-forgotten dreams. Sarah.

He pulled her closer until she was on her knees in front of him, the chair rocking with her sudden movement. His hands were gentle when they lifted her against him, when they slid over the straight line of her spine to her neck and higher, into the soft thick strands of her hair. He touched her, held her, kissed her, thrusting his tongue into her mouth and tasting the sweet flavor that was her. She fed his hunger, fed the wild, primitive need that was burning through him, making his muscles quiver in protest of his rigid control.

Sarah felt his desire in the intensity of his kiss and, lower, in the powerful masculine swelling of his loins. Oh, yes, he wanted her. He might still despise her, might—in spite of his recent behavior—still hate her, but he wanted her. For a woman who'd had nothing for so long, wanting could be enough. If that was all he could offer her, it was all she would ask for.

This time it was Daniel who ended the kiss. He had to force his mouth from hers, had to command his hands to release her. His body protested the loss of her warmth, and one hand, defying his order, came back to gently cup her cheek.

Sarah waited for him to speak, but she saw that he didn't know what to say. Neither did she. She felt an absurd desire to pretend that nothing had happened, and an equally absurd desire to talk about it, to take it apart and analyze it. In the end she did nothing.

His hand slipped from her face and rested nervelessly at his side. If he were a different kind of man he might hide the intensity of his response behind a crass, empty joke. Or he might carry her to his bed and ruthlessly, carelessly, take what she'd offered. But he could be only what he was—a little embarrassed, a little disturbed, a little confused and a whole lot aroused.

She sat back on her heels, bumping the chair. "I, uh...I forgot what we were talking about."

He nodded once, but he hadn't forgotten. They had been talking about marriage. About Sarah's marriage. About whether her husband had satisfied her. If he'd made her happy. Somehow, after that kiss, the answers were more important than ever, but he couldn't ask again. Not now.

A flush of uneasiness crept into her face as she moved clumsily into the rocker. "Would you like me to go away until Katie wakes up?"

Saying yes would be the easy way out. But did he want this to be easy? "No. It's all right." He returned to his chair and settled in as comfortably as he could under the circumstances. He was starting to sort the order requests by date when Sarah suddenly spoke again.

"I like being kissed by you, Daniel."

His face flushed, his hands grew still, and for a moment, so did his heart. Then he slowly continued his work. He liked it, too. He liked it a lot.

As Daniel had predicted, it was warm enough by one o'clock for them to have their lunch outside. He carried their food and a quilt and led the way, and Sarah and Katie brought up the rear. When they'd reached the site he'd selected, Katie wandered off to look at a lone scarlet wildflower while her parents spread the quilt on the yellowing grass.

"This is pretty," Sarah remarked, sitting down. The backyard sloped steeply, and a stone retaining wall had been built to slow the inevitable erosion. The area where they were was small and clear and surrounded by brightly colored trees. "It must look kind of bare around here once all the leaves are gone."

Daniel lay on the opposite side of the spread, leaning on one strong arm, and watched Katie. "The pines are still here, so we don't lose all the color."

Sarah followed his gaze. Wearing pale pink corduroy overalls and a white sweater, Katie looked adorable as she crouched beside the flower. She touched its petals gently, but made no move to pick it. Daniel had taught her well, Sarah thought with a surge of warmth for the man who had raised her daughter.

She looked at him again, her eyes measuring. He was dressed as usual in jeans and boots, and a red shirt stretched across his massive chest. Once the shirt must have been the color of Katie's flower, but now it was faded to a soft rosy hue and fit with the easy comfort of well-worn fabric. The jeans were faded, too, and snugly followed his flat belly and the long, powerful lines of his thighs.

He was the biggest man she'd ever seen, and she knew some people, especially those who didn't know him, found that intimidating. She'd seen some of the curious looks he'd drawn in Nashville. It was a shame he wasn't what the world called handsome. In a society that placed more value on looks than on character, being handsome would have made his life easier. Still, she found an undeniably attractive quality in the hard, rough angles of his face.

Uncomfortable with her staring at him, Daniel looked sharply at her. Sarah smiled and turned back to Katie. "That's a flower," she said as the girl sank to her knees to study it more comfortably.

Grinning, Katie repeated the word, somehow fitting all the sounds into one syllable. When she lost interest in it, she went on to a leaf, then a rock.

"Do you ever see your mother, Daniel?" Sarah lay down on her side, facing him, letting the sun's warmth seep into her.

He took a moment to lazily wonder about her interest before he replied. "Not very often. Once every few years she and her husband come by for a few hours when he's got business in this area. The last time was . . . three, four years ago."

"They live in Florida." Sarah knew that was correct, but waited for confirmation. Daniel gave it with a nod. "And they have children."

"Two sons and a daughter."

"You have half brothers and a half sister." She was pleased with the idea. She had always thought she would have liked having brothers and sisters, if her father hadn't taken off for distant horizons when she was so young, or if her mother had ever trusted another man after that.

He gave a shake of his head. "I haven't seen the kids in five or six years." He'd never thought of them as family. In fact, since his mother had left so many years ago, he hadn't really thought of her as family, either. She was the woman who had given birth to him, the woman who had raised him after his father's death, the woman who had left him here alone at the age of sixteen to fend for himself. But she wasn't his family. Katie was. Only Katie.

"So you're not close to any of them."

He looked at Katie and understood the disappointment that colored Sarah's voice. His mother was Katie's only grandparent, her children Katie's aunt and uncles. "No."

"Does she even know about Katie?"

"I told her." He looked away, his eyes dark and hard, his mouth a narrow line. Her only response had been a card, asking for a photograph, and the promise that they would visit "sometime." Nearly a year later, "sometime" had not yet arrived.

The ache around Sarah's heart was for Katie, whose grandmother hadn't bothered to come and see her, but also for Daniel, whose mother hadn't shown enough interest in his only child to visit her. "My mother would have loved her," she said, her voice thick with emotion. "She would have liked you, too." She smiled faintly when he glanced at her. "My mother was old-fashioned. She valued things like honesty, respect and trust. Dependability, fidelity, honor."

Daniel flinched at the list. Had he exhibited any of those qualities in his dealings with Sarah? He certainly hadn't been honest with her; he was betraying her trust and destroying his own honor, and he would lose her respect. If dependability and fidelity entered into the picture, he would probably let her down there, too.

Lost in the memories of her mother, Sarah didn't notice his response. "She thought a woman's first responsibility was to her family—and a man's, too. If she had lived to see Brent..." It would have broken her heart. She had always regretted her own poor choice of husband. If she'd known that her daughter's choice had been equally poor, she would have been immeasurably sad.

"Is Brent your husband?" Daniel was surprised by the flare of jealousy, sharp and ugly. He had never been jealous, hadn't even believed he was capable of it. But then, he had never had anyone to be jealous of—and he still didn't, he warned himself. A couple of kisses didn't give him that right.

"*Ex*-husband, please."

"Is Lawson his name?"

"Yes." She'd had the option of using her maiden name again, but for Tony's sake, she hadn't wanted to. Maybe it had been silly, but she had wanted to have the same last name as her son.

"Do you still love him?"

The question hung between them, connecting them, locking their gazes. Sarah's eyes were clear and thoughtful. Daniel's were harder to read—solemn, cautious, remote. He was disturbed that he'd asked such a question. He was even more disturbed by how badly he needed to hear the answer.

"No."

It was the answer he'd wanted to hear—plain, simple, no room for doubt. But he wasn't sure he could accept it. "How long were you married?"

"Four years."

"And you didn't want the divorce."

"Why do you say that?"

"You said that *he* divorced *you*. Not that the two of you had decided to get a divorce, or that you'd left him. *He* left *you*. You didn't want it, did you?"

As a mother, she had been appalled at Brent's reaction to their baby—his lack of love, his lack of concern. She hadn't wanted anything to do with a man who could turn his back on his own son. As a wife . . . No, she hadn't wanted the divorce. She had still loved him, had still hoped that things would change and be all right again. It had taken her a long time to accept that Brent would never change and that things might never be all right again. "No." She said it with a sigh. "I didn't want the divorce."

"So how can you be sure you don't still love him?"

Her smile was weary and sad. "I'm sure, Daniel. Believe me, I'm sure." She sighed again. "No more hard questions today, okay?"

He nodded his agreement. They had eighteen more days for questions. That was time enough to learn about her. Today... today they would enjoy their daughter.

Sarah stood on the porch, her face turned westward, judging the descent of the sun. She would get home with minutes to spare, she decided, before the sun set and turned the woods dark and mysterious.

"I can give you a ride home." Daniel made the offer routinely, although he knew there was little to fear in the woods. Unless she fell and hurt herself, she would make it home all right. Still, she was a woman.... She was Sarah.

But, as she'd done on the previous four days, she gave a shake of her head. "No, thanks. This has been a very nice day, Daniel. Thank you for sharing it with me."

Quickly she walked down the steps, looking, in his jacket, like a child playing dress-up. Daniel waited until she was halfway across the clearing, then called, "Are you coming tomorrow?"

She spun around but didn't stop walking. "Am I welcome?" she called back.

Welcome? His smile was bittersweet. Oh, she was definitely welcome, and growing more so every day. "Of course," he said quietly, but she heard him.

"Then I'll be here." With a wave, she turned around again and disappeared into the woods. In a moment even the noise of her passage had faded away.

Daniel listened to the evening sounds, watched the sun set, then saw the light down the hill that meant Sarah was safely home. As he turned to go inside, he heard her question echo again. *Am I welcome?* Less than a week ago he had grudgingly invited her into his home, his life and his family. Now she had become a part of it, a part of *them*. For eighteen more days. Already he knew he would miss her when she was gone. How much worse, he wondered grimly, would it be when it actually happened?

October 15

Sarah arrived at the Ryan farm early Monday morning in a cheerful, lively mood after her walk. There had been little chance for exercise when Tony had been alive, and she'd forgotten what a difference it could make. She enjoyed the brief journey between their houses, savored the sights and sounds and smells of the woods, and she felt better because of it. She knew, of course, that as winter drew closer and the early-morning temperatures continued to drop, Daniel would probably insist that she drive—it would be so typical of him—but for now this was one of her pleasures.

As early as she was, Daniel was already busy in his workshop, sending a piece of wood that would soon be the seat in the final chair of his current project. Katie lay in the playpen, once again captivated by her own bare feet, but she sprang up, full of cheery smiles and babbles when she saw Sarah.

Daniel watched them exchange kisses and hugs before he turned away. Less than two weeks ago it had disturbed him to see Katie simply holding Sarah's hand. Their exuberant greeting bothered him now only in that he wished he shared his daughter's easy, emotional manner with others. With Sarah.

He gave a disgusted shake of his head. Yesterday he'd found himself envying Sarah's ex-husband. Today he was jealous of his own daughter! What was happening to him?

The answer was as simple, or as complex, as he wanted to make it. As simple as friendship, as the novelty of having someone else around, another adult, on a practically full-time basis—a pleasant change of pace from his usual solitary life. Or as complex as beginning again, as renewing his relationship with Sarah. As complex as getting involved. As falling in love.

He considered the options and chose simplicity. Friendship was easier to build, easier to discard. The end of a friendship would mean nothing compared to a badly chosen love. And Sarah would be a bad choice to love. The warm conversations, pleasant days and kisses aside, there were too many things about her he didn't know. Too many strikes against her. So she was beautiful, sweet and fragile, so she obviously cared a great deal for Katie, so she had just as obviously gone through some tough times that even now turned her eyes sad at unexpected moments. She had still given away their daughter. When Katie was tiny and had needed her mother's love more than anything in the world, Sarah had turned her back on her. Nothing could excuse that. Nothing could make him forgive that.

Sarah gathered Katie's socks and shoes in one hand and carefully lifted her from the playpen. She set the girl on the worktable, sat on the stool across from Daniel and began the task of putting the socks back on. Daniel hadn't spoken to her yet, she'd noticed, and he was working with a fierce concentration that she hated to disturb. She wouldn't have, if she hadn't felt that the ferocity was somehow aimed toward her. "Is the work that demanding, or are you trying to ignore me?"

He didn't look up, but his hands slowed. "Do you expect me to greet you the way Katie does?" he asked, trading the coarse sandpaper for a finer grade. "You forget, Katie knows nothing about you. *I* do."

The harshness in his voice hurt. She had thought they were past this anger and hostility, but apparently she had been wrong. She slid Katie's foot into one sneaker and tied the lace in a double knot, did the same with the other, then looked up at him. "You don't know anything about me, Daniel." Her voice sounded flat, weary. "You believe whatever suits your current mood."

Very carefully he laid down the wood, then the sandpaper, leaned his big hands on the table and leveled a cold, unforgiving look on her. "I know that you didn't want our daughter. I know that you sent her away to live with a stranger until it was more convenient for you."

"That's not true." She reached for Katie, squeezing her a little too tightly. When the child wailed, Sarah immediately loosened her grasp.

"Then what is the truth, Sarah? Why did you give her away?"

His stance was challenging, his voice ugly. Sarah knew that whatever she said, he was prepared to doubt her, to accuse and condemn her. If she told him that she'd had a son who was dying, he wouldn't feel it was enough to justify rejecting her daughter. The only "truth" he wanted to hear was *his* truth: that she'd been too selfish to keep Katie.

She slid off the stool to her feet, holding her shoulders erect, and said coolly, "It's none of your business." With that she carried Katie to the corner where they played, sat on the floor with her and turned her back on Daniel.

None of his business. Daniel's hands were trembling with rage. None of his business that she'd gotten pregnant with his baby and hadn't told him. None of his business that she'd given birth to his daughter without letting him know. None of his business that she'd sent Katie to him like an unwanted burden, a nuisance that was in her way. *None of his business.*

The desire to tell her that *everything* about Katie was his business was strong. That he had already taken action to ensure that Katie was *always* his business and would never again be hers. But he forced the taunt back. Telling her now would give her and her fancy lawyer seventeen days to pre-

pare their own case. It would be better to surprise her when
November first came. When he didn't return Katie to her.

He stole a glance at her, and that look did more to take
the edge off his anger than anything else could have done.
Her back was still to him, but it was no longer erect. Her
shoulders were rounded, her head bowed, in the classic
posture of defeat. If he listened closely, he would probably
hear traces of tears in her voice. She fought it, he knew, but
she cried easily—because her emotions were so close to the
surface? Because whatever had caused her to give up Katie
had left its mark on her, a wound that hadn't yet finished
healing?

He didn't want to feel sympathy for her, but he couldn't
help it. She had come in smiling and happy, and in a matter
of minutes he had reduced her to this, all because he didn't
like the way he was starting to feel about her.

He was no better at apologies than he was at affectionate
displays. He didn't know how to say that he was sorry for
judging her, but that he couldn't quit judging her until he
knew the truth. He didn't know what reassurance to give her
so that she would trust him with that truth. He didn't know
how to make her understand his frustration that she
wouldn't tell him anything, when he couldn't forgive her
without *something*.

When Katie gave her an unexpected kiss, Sarah forced a
smile for her daughter. "You're a sweetie, you know that?"

Pleased with her mother's smile, Katie rolled onto her
back and lifted one foot, tugging at her shoe. It hadn't taken
her long to discover that the way Sarah had tied the laces,
she couldn't remove her shoes.

Sarah gripped the shoe and gently wiggled Katie's leg
back and forth. "You're a manipulative child, aren't you?"
she chided. "You think a little thing like a kiss will make me
untie those knots, but you're wrong. I have my shoes on,
see?" Awkwardly she raised one foot to prove it. "And
Daddy has his shoes on. If you take yours off your feet will
get cold."

The child locked in on the one important word in Sarah's speech. "Off," she commanded.

Sarah picked up the stuffed bear from the floor to distract her. "Who is this?"

Katie snatched the bear. "Teddy." But she wasn't the slightest bit distracted. Hugging him with one arm, she used the other to tug at her shoe. "Off!"

Sarah got up and walked past Daniel without a glance, when she returned she was carrying a paper bag she'd brought with her. As Sarah had expected, Katie's interest in her shoes was replaced by the bag and its contents. Sarah had noticed plenty of toys, both handmade and manufactured ones, in the house and here in the workshop, but she hadn't seen any evidence of books. Perhaps Daniel wasn't aware of the value of reading to kids when they were young, or maybe it was something he didn't approve of or have time for or feel comfortable with. But she loved to read and intended to make sure that Katie did, too.

The books were old and worn, the pages showing signs of plenty of use. Sarah remembered the pleasure Tony had found in hearing the tales. Pleasure had come so rarely in his brief life that each source of it was treasured, and books had been some of his favorite treasures.

Daniel watched as Sarah settled comfortably in the corner, Katie on her lap, each holding one side of the storybook. If *he* had refused to let Katie remove her shoes, there would have been a screaming tantrum, but Sarah had simply directed her attention elsewhere. How had she known?

Because, came the obvious answer, she was that all-knowing, all-powerful being: a mother. But three months of caring for a newborn didn't make a woman a mother. It didn't prepare her for handling an active, stubborn, temperamental fourteen-month-old. But she *was* prepared. Almost as if she'd had experience.

His curiosity about her past was growing, but he'd blown any chance of learning anything today with his angry outburst. Anger wasn't the way to deal with Sarah; she'd just proven that with him and his demands, and with Katie and her shoes. He should have waited until they were talking companionably, as they had yesterday, until her defenses were down. Then he should have asked about her secrets without accusation or blame. But instead he had demanded an answer and gotten nothing except the knowledge that he'd hurt her.

He had to overcome his clumsiness. After all, he had never dealt with a woman on a regular basis. It was only natural that there would be lessons to learn. But he would learn them, would learn just the right touch to use with Sarah, and, sometime soon, he would learn her secrets. All of them.

"And the bear said..." Sarah's soft voice trailed away when she looked down at Katie. Her sturdy little body had been steadily relaxing, growing limp against her. Now the girl's eyes were closed, her arms hugging Teddy closely.

Sarah closed the book and laid it aside. She had never expected a child as active and lively as Katie to sit still for almost an hour while she read. She supposed it was the newness that had captivated her.

She was stiff from sitting so long on the hard floor with the twenty-five-pound weight of her daughter on her lap. She shifted Katie carefully, planning to rise to her knees, then her feet, and put Katie into the playpen. Before she'd made the first move, though, Daniel was there.

He lifted Katie as if she weighed nothing, holding her gently in one arm. He extended his other hand to Sarah, helping her to her feet. He didn't say a word to her as he turned and carried their daughter to the playpen.

Maybe he regretted the earlier incident, Sarah thought, stretching out the kinks. Or, more likely, he simply didn't trust her to get to her feet without waking or maybe even dropping Katie.

Daniel turned as Sarah bent from the waist, her fingertips brushing the wood floor. Her jeans stretched snugly with the movement, molding the curve of her hips and the long line of her legs. She was too slim to turn heads—her breasts too small, her hips too narrow, her legs too long and thin. Her figure was almost boyish—lean and straight, without curves or fullness. Why, then, did looking at her make him think of desire? Why, after no more than a glance, was he feeling the heat and the hunger... the need?

He didn't immediately go back to work, as Sarah had expected. He'd been sanding all morning, the tedious, monotonous sounds somehow soothing to her hurt feelings. He took such care with things that mattered to him—with his work and with Katie. He wouldn't stop sanding the pieces of wood that would become a chair until the finish was as smooth as satin. Until it was perfect. He was the best craftsman he could be, the best father he could be, the best man he could be.

Not that he didn't have faults. He was so stubborn, holding onto his anger and bitterness, refusing to give her the benefit of the doubt. He'd made up his mind about her nearly a year ago, and he was determined not to change it—not to let *her* change it. Would he ever accept her? she wondered as she traced patterns in the fine dust that had collected on the tabletop. Would he ever stop judging her? Would he ever have enough faith in her to believe, without proof, that she had made the right choice in sending Katie to him—the only choice?

She had to believe that he would, or their future—whether as lovers, friends, or just the parents of the same child—was hopeless. If he couldn't accept and believe in her, then there could be nothing between them, because she needed his acceptance. She needed his faith. And she was afraid that it wouldn't be long until she needed his love.

Daniel had dawdled in front of the cabinets that held his tools and supplies long enough. He came back to the table, a soft cloth in hand, and began rubbing the dust from a chair leg. "I shouldn't have yelled at you."

She smiled wryly. He'd made demands, issued insults and thrown out challenges, but he hadn't once raised his voice. But she understood that the statement was his own vulnerably awkward way of saying he was sorry. "It doesn't matter."

"Yes, it does. I'm not in the habit of losing my temper."

"Of course not, when you live alone and hardly ever see anyone." She smiled again, and this time he felt the warmth.

"Everyone gets angry occasionally. It's no big deal. Are these chairs all for the same customer?"

He let her get away with the subject change because he was a coward, he decided. He would rather discuss his work than his own shortcomings any time. "Yes, He's already got a table and a china cabinet to match these, plus a rocker and a desk and chair."

"Did you check your records recently, or did you just happen to remember that?"

He grinned at the skeptical tone of her voice. "I wish my memory was that good, but it's not. He reminded me about the other pieces when he ordered this set."

His occasional smiles softened the hard lines of his face, Sarah thought, made him look younger, nicer, less intimidating. It was too bad he wasn't more accustomed to smiles and laughter, like Katie was. Maybe their daughter could teach him.

"Do you have a lot of repeat customers?" She wanted to keep him talking, to learn more about him before he realized that he was sharing himself and self-consciously clammed up.

"Almost everyone who buys one piece orders again."

"Do you know how lucky you are to be able to make a living at something you enjoy, to run your business and your life on your own terms? Most people go through life with jobs they don't like or can't make a decent living at. Of course, you've got talent, too. All the luck in the world doesn't mean a thing if it's not backed up by talent and skill."

"Did you like your job?"

She climbed onto the stool, leaned her elbows on the table and cupped her chin in both hands. "I did," she replied, forgetting that the conversation was supposed to be about him. "I'd wanted to be a teacher since I was in grade school. I liked kids, and I loved teaching."

He supposed that was why she was always subtly teaching Katie. Her enthusiasm and her gentle manner must have made her popular with her students. "Why did you quit?"

She sighed deeply. "There were problems."

One of those, he had already guessed, was her divorce. She'd told him last week that she had quit teaching three years ago. Yesterday she'd told him that her husband had divorced her a year before she'd met *him*, which would have been three years ago. Had she been so emotionally devastated by the divorce that she'd had to give up the job she loved?

He didn't like either idea—that Brent Lawson had hurt her so badly, or that she had loved him so much. Not that it was any of his business. He hadn't even known her then. Still . . . "If you liked children so much, why didn't you and your husband have any?"

She had decided earlier that she wouldn't lie to Daniel. He was an honest man, and he deserved honesty in return. But she had also decided that she wouldn't tell him about Tony. She wouldn't give him the ammunition to hurt her the way others had in the past. But if that meant lying to him, then . . . She ignored the stab of guilt. If that meant lying to him, then she would lie.

"Brent *was* a child," she said, her voice distant, her eyes lowered to avoid Daniel's gaze. "Having a baby would have meant growing up, acting his age, accepting responsibility not just for himself, but for the baby, too." That was true, as far as it went. Brent hadn't wanted a baby, hadn't wanted to give up any of his precious time or his amusements or his expensive toys and trips.

Daniel couldn't understand the kind of man she was describing. Daniel had been on his own since he was sixteen— had cooked his own meals, washed his own clothes, kept his own house. He had supported himself first by farming, then with the business. Sometimes he felt he'd always been grown up, had never been a child. Then there were men like Brent Lawson.

Sarah followed the line of his thoughts by the puzzlement in his eyes. "Very few men mature as quickly as you did," she pointed out. "But then, very few men are left on their own at sixteen. Was it difficult?"

His automatic response was to say no, but he considered it for a moment. Life hadn't been easy after his mother had

left...but it hadn't been particularly easy before then, either.
"I was close to my father," he began slowly. "I spent most
of my time after school doing chores with him. He died
when I was eleven, and I had to take his place. I was big and
strong for my age, and it was easier for my mother to let me
take charge than to do it herself. By the time I was sixteen,
I guess she thought I didn't need her anymore. She got
married and moved away."

"Didn't you resent her for that?"

Again he considered his answer before giving it. "People
think that if you live way up in the mountains, you have to
be strong and self-sufficient."

Like him, Sarah thought, refusing to give in to the smile
that tugged at her mouth.

"I am. My father was. My grandparents were. But not my
mother. She's the kind of woman who needs someone to
take care of her." He began assembling the chair, his movements slow and steady. Patsy Ryan had needed someone to
care for her, and so did Sarah Lawson, but they were nothing alike. Patsy's need was a flaw inside her; she was too
weak to live on her own, to be independent. Sarah, on the
other hand, could do anything she set her mind to. The need
to care for her was *his*, a product of his old-fashioned masculine attitude.

"So she depended on your father, then you. And as soon
as she thought you were old enough to be on your own, she
found someone else to lean on." After all, a son couldn't
provide the same comforts that a husband could. Sarah
shook her head in dismay. "I can't imagine a woman aban-
doning her son like that."

Daniel looked sharply at her, and his mouth opened, then
closed in a tight line. She considered it great progress that he
didn't make the natural retort, "Can't you? *You* abandoned your daughter." But he thought it. She could tell in
every hard-set line in his face that he thought it.

"She was right," he continued after a moment. "I *was*
old enough to be on my own. I didn't need her. I didn't need
anyone. I still don't."

"So you've told me," she said dryly. "And you know what, Daniel? I don't believe you. You have too much to give to be satisfied with no one but yourself. You need Katie. You need Zachary Adam's friendship. And you need a woman, a wife. Someone who loves you."

"And where am I going to find that?" His tone was sarcastic, edged with a sharp bite. "With this face, I'm no prize."

Sarah was surprised not at the sentiment, but that he could state it so bluntly to her. She gave a shake of her head. "Believe me, Daniel, any woman with experience with men will take a good man over a handsome one any time." When he didn't look convinced, she continued. "Brent was handsome, and it turned out that he wasn't worth his weight in feathers. I'll never get involved with someone like him again."

And yet she had loved this man "not worth his weight in feathers." There must have been something more to him, something substantial. And he must have done something pretty awful to make her forget it. "Do you want to get married again?"

"I don't know." Right after her divorce, she would have said absolutely not. She hadn't thought she would ever trust another man. Then she'd met Daniel, and the trust had come instantly, instinctively, along with the attraction. If he ever chose to marry, he would be a good husband. Whether he married out of loneliness or love, he would commit himself fully to the woman he'd chosen. "I don't know too many people who have been happily married. It's frightening."

"My grandparents were." His memories of them were vague, since he'd been only seven when they died, one within two months of the other. But he remembered the happiness, the warmth, the love. "They were married for forty-two years, and they were happy."

"My mother's parents were married a long time, too, but I never thought of them as being happy. He was a mean old man, and she was even meaner." She gave a soft laugh. "Maybe that was just their way of showing affection."

He liked Sarah's way better—the easy touches, the hugs...the kisses. If she knew what he wanted to do every time she kissed him, she would probably never kiss him again. Then he considered her earlier statement. *Any woman with experience...will take a good man over a handsome one any time.* Maybe she did know. After all, it was almost impossible for him to hide. Maybe she didn't mind.

She got to her feet and wandered aimlessly around the room, looking at his tools, the wide variety of supplies, the few finished pieces that hadn't been shipped yet. It must be boring for her, he thought, half his mind on his work, the other half on her, during these long hours when Katie slept and all Sarah could do was talk to him. But she hid it well.

She picked up a level and tilted it from side to side, watching the colored liquid float back and forth. "I used to watch that show on PBS about renovating old houses," she said, returning the level to its place and sliding her hands into her pockets. There was a questioning note as she waited for acknowledgment from him. Then her face crinkled into a frown. "I guess without a television you wouldn't know about that. I think it's neat what they do—the carpenters and architects and electricians and landscapers. Barring acts of God and greedy developers, their work can last for years. So can yours. And so could mine."

She thoughtfully considered it before continuing. "Maybe that's why I liked teaching. The nine months or so that I was with those kids would affect the rest of their lives and, in some small way, their children's lives and *their* children's lives." She grinned. "Maybe I liked that sense of power."

She continued around the room, ending at the stool again. Full circle, Daniel thought, like their conversation. From their jobs to her marriage to his mother and back to their jobs. Complete.

Suddenly Sarah was out of things to say. It was time for Katie to wake up, she thought. Their daughter had such an incredible sense of timing. She always interceded just when things were getting uncomfortable or, and she smiled faintly with the memory of their first serious kiss, out of control.

But in the playpen across the room, Katie slept peacefully on.

When Katie finally awakened they left the workshop for the house, where Daniel fixed lunch while Sarah changed Katie's diaper and helped her wash up. Every few days she offered to help with the meal, but he always turned her down. She wasn't sure if he really didn't want her in his kitchen or if he was simply giving her that little extra time with Katie, but the fact was that he was a far better cook than she was. His meals were simple, but always tasty and hearty.

After lunch Daniel got his jacket from the rack but left Sarah's and Katie's hanging. "I'm going to put the finish on that chair," he said gruffly, his manner uneasy, his eyes carefully guarded. "It's a little cool to be opening the windows with Katie out there, so why don't you two stay in here?"

Except for those few minutes after their kiss, this was the first time he had agreed to leave Sarah alone with Katie, and she accepted it for what it was: a measure of his precious trust, hesitantly given, but given just the same. "All right."

He walked to the door, then looked back. "How do you do your laundry?"

Caretaker, she thought with a smile as she slid her hands into her pockets and rocked back and forth on her heels. "Where did that interesting question come from?"

"You don't drive all the way into town just to do it, do you?"

"Not that it's any of your business, but I do it in the sink." In spite of the tart tone of her voice, her grin was easy and relaxed. "My clothes are clean, I assure you."

He made an impatient gesture. "If you want to bring them up here, I can wash them with our clothes."

Sarah glanced at Katie, who was methodically pulling every toy from the basket near the fireplace, then back at Daniel, and shook her head. "No. You've provided the wood for my fireplace, you repaired my porch, you feed me lunch every day of the week. No more charity, Daniel."

He was glad she'd mentioned the firewood. He needed to check and make sure there was enough. Scowling at her, he pointed out, "You can't have enough laundry to make a difference."

She simply shook her head again.

Insisting that she accept his offer would only injure her pride and lead to a fight, he realized, so he did the next best thing. "Let's make a deal. You do Katie's laundry... and wash yours with it."

Tilting her head to one side, she considered it. "What about yours?"

His voice was gruff again. "I'll wash my own clothes."

"You can't have enough to make a difference," she mimicked. "All or nothing, Daniel."

He started to argue but remembered her pride. "All right."

"Then I'll accept your offer." Solemnly she stuck out her hand. When he grudgingly took it, she stepped forward and kissed his cheek. Sealed with a kiss. She could take a great deal of pleasure, she thought as she watched him go, in closing all her agreements with Daniel that way.

October 16

Tuesday was the half way point for Sarah. She'd been in Sweetwater sixteen days, and there were sixteen days left until the first. Until Katie came to live with her.

What a difference that would make in her life, she thought as she watched her daughter play with the wooden animals Daniel had made for her. It would mean finding a job and a new place to live, something she had to do pretty soon. It would mean being totally responsible for her daughter once more, doing everything that Daniel had done for the past eleven and a half months. It would mean being whole again.

She longed for that day with all her heart . . . and dreaded it just as much. Because it would also mean not seeing so much of Daniel.

She had come here knowing that she would like him, because she had liked him in Nashville. She had come knowing that she both admired and respected him. But she certainly hadn't come expecting to fall in love with him. And although she wasn't sure, she thought that was exactly what was happening.

She tried to remember falling in love with Brent, but her mind refused to cooperate. How could she call up memories of Brent, whose only asset was his handsome face, when Daniel, who had every quality a woman could want in a man *except* a handsome face, was working across the room?

The problem was, Daniel didn't *want* to fall in love, not with anyone. Certainly not with her. He'd made that clear enough in their time together. She knew that he needed a woman, but a lot of good that knowledge did her when he didn't *want* one.

She didn't want any more pain, didn't want any more broken dreams or heartache. The wise thing would be to pull back now, before she fell any deeper. Maybe she could do that if Katie weren't involved, but for the next sixteen days, avoiding Daniel would mean avoiding Katie.

Maybe her heart would somehow protect itself. Maybe he would change his mind. Maybe...

She sighed wearily. She had never imagined two years ago that spending the weekend with the big, quiet man from the mountains could have such far-reaching effects. *Maybe*, if she ever ventured close to another man again, maybe this time she would take protective measures—to save her body, her heart and her soul.

October 18

Daniel made a welcome change in their usual routine on Thursday when, shortly after Sarah arrived at the house, they climbed into his truck for the long drive into town. The reason he gave her for the trip was simple: he had to pay a few bills and pick up a special order from the hardware store. His other reason he kept to himself: he thought Sarah could use a break from the isolation of the mountaintop.

It was a beautiful day—the sky a rich blue with thick cottony clouds, the sun bright and warm and soothing, the trees glorious in their fall colors. Sarah admired everything she saw, wondering as she did why she'd never been able to find this kind of beauty to share with Tony. Had she been so obsessed with his illness and the struggle to keep them going that she'd failed to show him the pleasure in simple things like a warm sun or a crimson-leaved tree?

She had, she was afraid. But she wouldn't make that mistake with Katie. She would be the best mother a child could want. Then, with a glance at Daniel, she corrected her silent vow; she would be the best mother any father could want for his daughter. She wouldn't disappoint either of them.

Daniel parked down the street from the hardware store and turned off the engine. For a moment he just sat there before turning to face Sarah. "No one in town but Zach knows anything about you," he said flatly.

Sarah paused in the act of unfastening Katie's seat belt. He meant that he'd told no one about Katie's mother—who she was, where he'd met her, what their relationship was. Showing up like this, the three of them together, would give the gossips a field day. "So they'll wonder who I am."

"One look at you and Katie and they'll *know* who you are. She looks just like you."

Katie began wriggling free of the loosened belt, drawing Sarah's attention back to her. She unfastened the last buckle, but didn't pick the child up. "Are you ashamed of me, Daniel?" she asked, her voice low and uneven with hurt.

He smiled. If the situation was reversed and she was about to make an unofficial announcement to all her friends and neighbors that he was the father of her child, he would expect some shame on her part. Her friends' reaction to him would be no different from that of the redheaded lawyer— unpleasant surprise, dismay, dislike, maybe even a little fear. But the situation wasn't reversed, and he wasn't expecting any adverse reactions from his neighbors and acquaintances. He just wanted her to be prepared for the looks and the hushed whispers.

He reached for her hand and squeezed it lightly. "No, I'm not ashamed of you," he assured her. "It's just . . . people are going to talk. When your lawyer brought Katie here to live with me, everyone was dying of curiosity about you, but no one had the courage to ask. After they see how pretty you are, they're going to be nosier than ever."

As soon as the last word was out, he grew strangely silent. Had he really taken her hand so easily, complimented her so casually? True, he had only said what he'd thought all along but had never risked saying aloud. Still . . .

He let go of her and picked up Katie instead. "Are you ready?"

Sarah nodded. After everything she'd been through in the past three years, curious stares from complete strangers couldn't affect her. Hushed whispers and lingering second glances wouldn't bother her.

The first people they met were two old men sitting on the bench in front of the hardware store. They were dressed the same, in heavy boots and denim overalls and heavy jackets, with identical caps reading Weaver's Feed and Grain. Sarah recognized one of them as Leon Peters, her landlord, seventy years old and slower than molasses, according to Daniel. The other man looked about the same age.

In the city they could have walked past the two men without a word, but not in Sweetwater, Daniel thought with regret. In the city no one would know what kind of relationship he and Sarah had had two years ago, and no one would care. Sometimes he wished for that kind of anonymity.

Sarah said hello to Leon Peters, then Daniel introduced her to Henry Walters. The old man's faded blue eyes studied first her, then Katie, then Daniel. Although he didn't say a word, he seemed satisfied with what he saw. She resisted the urge to confirm it for him. Yes, she wanted to say, Daniel and I were lovers, and Katie is our daughter, and if I'm lucky, maybe we'll be lovers again. But she said nothing.

"Saw you two in the park last week," Leon remarked, sounding as old and worn out as he looked.

The day that Sarah had kissed him, Daniel remembered. "That must have been . . . Tuesday, I reckon."

Leon might be old, Daniel thought uneasily, but his mind was as sharp as ever.

"Looked like you was old friends," the man continued.

Sarah saw the discomfort on Daniel's face and stepped into the one-sided conversation. "We *are* old friends, Mr. Peters. Isn't it a beautiful day?"

"Yeah, that it is. Be getting cold soon, but not until we have our festival." He gestured to the square across the street. "They could use a little help from someone as strong as young Daniel."

Sarah glanced across the street, where a half dozen men were erecting wooden booths for the Harvest Festival. Although she wouldn't mind spending a little time in the park herself—there were children about Katie's size playing there—she wasn't about to volunteer Daniel for work. "I imagine they could. It was nice meeting you, Mr. Walters," she said brightly. "And nice seeing you again, Mr. Peters."

Daniel and Katie followed her into the store. "Young Daniel. Have they always called you that?" she asked as she looked around. "Or was there an old Daniel at one time?"

"Two of them—my father and my grandfather. I'm named after them."

"So you'll be young Daniel until you have a young Daniel of your own."

His expression grew grim. "There won't be any other children." Having another baby would mean marriage. While he could never hold it against Katie that he and Sarah hadn't been married when she was born, he could make sure that it never happened that way again. And he'd already told Sarah that he didn't want a wife, so that meant no more children, either.

Her smile was sweet and innocent. "You just might be surprised, Daniel. Go on and pick up your things. I'll just have a look around."

Daniel talked to the clerk about his order, the weather and this weekend's festival while carefully deflecting the man's subtle questions about Sarah. His business completed, he held Katie in one arm, the box of porcelain and brass drawer pulls in the other, and turned to look for Sarah. He found her in the corner, examining a display of tools with idle curiosity, but before he could approach her, the door swung open and Zachary Adams walked in.

The lawyer, dressed in jeans and a sweatshirt, was obviously looking for Daniel, and he grinned when he saw him. "Hey, Daniel, Katie."

Katie smiled precociously. "Sach!" she squealed with delight, wriggling out of her father's arms and leaping toward the lawyer. Zachary caught her just as Daniel grabbed her legs. With a grimace, Daniel released her into his friend's embrace.

"Hey, sweetheart." Zachary nuzzled her, making her giggle, then looked at her father. "How are things going on the mountaintop?"

Daniel glanced toward the corner where Sarah had been, but there was no sign of her. "All right," he said cautiously.

"Have you been letting Sarah see Katie?"

His reply came from the girl herself, who laid her fingertips over his mouth. "Not Sair. Mama." She cupped her chubby hands over his cheeks and commanded, "Say 'Mama.'"

Zachary obliged her before turning his attention back to her father. "Listen, Daniel, have you changed your mind about your plans for—" His voice trailed away as Sarah came around the corner to stand beside Daniel.

Her smile was warm and friendly. "Hello, Mr. Adams."

"Miss Lawson." He sounded off balance, as if surprised by her presence. "Uh, listen, Daniel, if you're not in any hurry, why don't you come across to the square and help us with the booths for this weekend?"

Daniel was hesitant. He'd never taken part in the town's celebrations or its preparations. It wasn't that he minded the work, just that no one had ever bothered to ask him. He glanced down at Sarah, one brow raised questioningly.

"I noticed earlier that there were a couple of kids over there," she said softly. "Maybe Katie could play with them while you're working."

That was just the right thing to say to make him agree. Nearly three weeks ago he had promised to find his daughter some playmates, but so far he'd done nothing. Today he could. "Let me put this box in the truck first." He left the store, and the other three followed him, Katie perched on Zachary's shoulders.

"You two seem to be on pretty good terms," the lawyer remarked as they strolled, out of Daniel's earshot, along the uneven sidewalk.

"We're working on it."

"Keep one thing in mind, Sarah. In spite of his size and his looks, Daniel is a very..."

She slowly, evenly, met his eyes and finished his statement. "Sensitive man. He's a very gentle man. His life has been rough, and his relationships have been rough, too."

Zachary acknowledged her correctness with a nod. "I suppose it's occurred to you that there's an easy way out of this situation you're in. If two people want the same thing, the only logical solution is to share it—in this case, through marriage. Don't even consider using Daniel that way."

"Why the warning?" she asked curiously. "Only last week you helped convince him to let me see Katie. Today you're concerned about how I might use him. Why?"

Zachary hesitated before answering, trying to decide just how much would be saying too much. "Because today I saw the way he looks at you."

His statement left her quiet and thoughtful when they joined Daniel at the truck. She studied him for a moment, searching for some sign of what the lawyer had meant. Was there a new softness in his eyes when he looked at her? Was he smiling more often, more sweetly, than before? Or was her hope so strong that she was seeing things that weren't there? She didn't find any answers in his face.

It was a busy morning in the small park. In addition to the half dozen men working, there were two women and, playing around them, five children, the oldest one about five.

Daniel helped himself to tools from the bed of the pickup parked on the grass, then looked from the women on the benches to Sarah. "Will you be all right?"

She nodded.

"Watch out for the woman in the red sweater," Zachary advised as he handed Katie over. "She's got the sharpest tongue in Sweetwater County. Come on, I'll introduce you to them."

The woman named Linda seemed genuinely nice, Sarah thought, and aching to know about her and Daniel. Betsy, the one in the red sweater, was another matter. Even without Zachary's warning, she would have been wary of the other woman.

"So you're Katie's mother," Betsy announced less than ten minutes after they'd met.

Sarah was sitting on the ground, a suddenly shy Katie cradled in her lap. Linda had encouraged her to join the other children, but she was more comfortable watching from the safety of her mother's embrace. "Yes," Sarah replied evenly. "I am."

"Which means you had a . . . fling with Daniel Ryan."

Underneath Katie's small jacket, Sarah's hands clenched into fists. The woman made it sound dirty. There were so many ways to describe the weekend she and Daniel had shared, but they all made it sound dirty. Cheap. Meaningless. She wanted to tell her that it hadn't been that way. It had been special, important, precious, and Daniel was special, too. But she didn't say anything, just hugged Katie a little bit closer.

"Betsy!" Linda scolded. She smiled apologetically at Sarah. "Don't pay any attention to her. She's like this with everyone. How old is your little girl?"

"Fourteen months. Which ones are yours?" But she didn't need to ask. There were two little boys, ruggedly tussling on the ground, and a girl, maybe two years old, who wholeheartedly joined in. Then, across from them, were two prissy older girls, both dressed in dainty dresses, matching jackets and lace-edged socks, playing quietly. They had to be Betsy's children.

Linda confirmed her guess, then called her daughter over. "This is Melinda." She flushed as she said the name. "My husband insisted on naming her after me, and for two years I've been apologizing for it. I've got to get over that before I give her some sort of complex." She brushed a smudge of dirt from her daughter's face, tugged at the elastic-waist jeans she wore, then turned her towards Sarah. "Melinda, this is Miss Sarah, and that's her daughter, Katie. Why don't you see if Katie would like to play with your dolls?"

The girl, with a delicate ivory complexion and straight black hair, crouched in front of them, solemnly studying Katie. At last she reached out and touched Katie's soft curls. "Pretty baby."

Katie shoved her hand away. "Not baby. Katie."

Melinda offered one of her dolls, but Katie refused to take it. With a shrug, the older girl dropped it on the ground and returned to the fight with her brothers. Sarah echoed the shrug. "She's not used to other kids."

"Obviously not, living way out there in the middle of nowhere with no one but that—" Betsy caught herself, gave Sarah a condescending smile and finished, "With no one but her father. Not even her mother. Why is that, Sarah?"

She could brush the other woman off. She could ignore her. Or she could answer her. She politely responded, "That's really none of your business."

"Have you come to stay, or are you just visiting?" the woman persisted.

"That's enough, Betsy," Linda interrupted, her voice sharp, as if commanding one of her children. "I know you take pleasure in being so unpleasant, but not today."

Showing no sign of embarrassment, Betsy rose to her feet. "Come along, girls. We're going now."

Sarah turned to follow their progress. As she was turning back, her gaze met Daniel's. She knew he couldn't have overheard the conversation, but he still looked...concerned. Maybe Zachary's warning about Betsy's sharp tongue, coupled with her sudden departure, was enough for him to guess at what had been said. She smiled reassuringly at him before tuning back to Linda. "I'm sorry if I intruded here."

Linda's laugh was hearty. "Oh, no, don't be. I wasn't exactly thrilled when I got here today and found Betsy. You know, I've known her all my life, and I can't remember a time when she wasn't snooty and obnoxious. It's just gotten worse since her husband, Harold, was elected mayor in the last election." She scooted to the end of the bench. "Why don't you and Katie sit up here?"

Sarah leaned down to check on the child. She was curiously watching the other kids play but wasn't ready yet to join them. She might not reach that point this first time, Sarah knew, but she hoped that wouldn't be the case. She didn't want Daniel to worry if Katie wouldn't interact with the other children.

They moved to the bench, but from here Katie didn't have a clear view of the others. She was constantly shifting, leaning around Sarah, peeking over her shoulder. Soon her natural curiosity got the better of her, and she scooted to the ground.

"She's precious," Linda commented. "Of course, all kids are at that age. It's when they get to be the size of my boys there that they turn into little monsters. Are you going to be here long?"

At Sarah's wary look, Linda raised her hand in defense. "I'm not prying. It's just that the Baptist church sponsors a weekly play day for kids who aren't in school yet. We meet each Wednesday from nine until three. The mothers take turns helping out one day a month. Then you have one day free during the other three weeks to do your shopping or whatever. If you're interested, give me a call. We're the only Schmidts in the phone book."

"Thanks. I'll talk to Daniel about it." Sarah watched Katie, who was inching toward the other children, then turned her attention to Daniel. He was by far the biggest man in the group—stronger, more efficient, a better carpenter. With his help, the remaining booths went up in record time.

"Hello, Daniel," Linda said when he and Zachary joined them. "You all are coming to the festival Saturday, aren't you?"

He looked to Sarah for the answer and found it in the brightening of her soft brown eyes. She wouldn't say so now, but she wanted to come, wanted to bring Katie. "We'll be here," he replied gruffly. "Sarah, I've got to do a couple of things. Do you want to wait here with Katie?"

She checked on their daughter's progress and found her sitting next to Melinda, curiously studying her. "We'll wait. How long will you be?"

"Not more than half an hour. Then we'll have lunch before we go home." Then he would ask her what the sharp-tongued Betsy had said. Then they would be alone again, the way he liked it—just Katie, Sarah and him.

Zachary walked across the square with him, stopping when they were assured of privacy. "I haven't heard from the private detective yet, but he promised that we'd have the report a week from today. Do you want me to bring it out when I get it?"

"Yes—no." The truth was, he wasn't sure he wanted to know what would be in the report. What if it was worse than he'd suspected? What if she had lied to him? But the news could be better than he'd suspected, too. She could have had a reason for sending Katie away, a reason that he needed to know.

But either way, good news or bad, the report represented a breach of trust. Sarah talked about honor and trust; she considered him a good, decent man. Yet he had hired a private detective to snoop into her past, to tell him the secrets that she couldn't trust him with. What did that say about his honor, his decency?

"I'll come into town next week," he said uneasily.

"You do still want to go ahead and sue for custody."

Daniel nodded.

"It's not too late to change your mind. Sarah would never have to know anything about this."

How much did Zachary suspect? Daniel wondered. That he wanted Sarah with a fierceness that left him weak? That he was starting to care for her? That sometimes, when he was tired, when his defenses were down, he *needed* her?

"I haven't changed my mind, Zach," he said emotionlessly. "I'm not giving up Katie." If Sarah left, he would deal with that. But he would *not* lose his daughter, too.

The half hour passed quickly for Sarah. She enjoyed Linda Schmidt's company, but she was glad to see Daniel pull up at the corner. She called Katie, who was finally playing with Melinda, and hand in hand they walked out to the curb.

"We have a diner and a restaurant," Daniel said, watching Sarah fasten first Katie's seat belt, then her own. "Where do you want to have lunch?"

She sighed. "If you don't mind, Daniel, I'd just as soon go home."

Because that was what he preferred, too, he didn't argue but headed the truck out of town. They'd driven nearly ten miles before he broke the silence. "What did that woman say to you?"

"What woman?"

"Betsy." He gave the name a dark inflection.

"Oh. Nothing worth repeating." She saw the doubt in his expression and shrugged. "She wanted to know why I gave Katie up."

"Did you tell her it's none of her damn business?" he growled. Even though he had often asked the same question, he was offended that someone else had asked it too.

"It's not worth getting annoyed over. *She's* not worth it. She's just a petty woman who needs to feel superior to everyone else. The other woman, Linda, was nice. I liked her." She told him about the day-care program Linda had mentioned, then went on to describe Katie's reaction to the boisterous kids. As they neared her house, she broke off. "Can we stop here and get my laundry? While you're working this afternoon, I can take care of that."

It took her only a few minutes to stuff her dirty clothes into a cloth bag. While he waited outside, Daniel checked the stack of firewood. He would bring more this weekend, he promised himself. Then she returned, and they continued up the mountain.

After lunch, Katie took a nap, and Daniel went to work. Sarah gathered their dirty clothes from the hampers upstairs and sorted them in the hallway outside the small laundry room. It seemed such a wifely thing to do—washing the laundry while the baby slept and the husband worked. But she wasn't Daniel's wife, and he didn't want to be *any* woman's husband. Some of her pleasure in the task disappeared at that thought.

. . . today I saw the way he looks at you.

Was there any merit to whatever change Zachary thought he was seeing in Daniel? She wanted to believe that there was, but hoped that her desperate longing wasn't blinding her to the truth. Because there was no doubt that she was falling in love with Daniel. Every day that she spent with him, every night that she spent without him, she fell a little bit deeper, a little bit more hopelessly, in love.

She carried the first pile of clothes into the laundry room, dropped it on the floor, then reached to the shelf above her for the detergent. Standing on her toes, she stretched, but the shelf was still a good six inches above her head. It was built for someone much taller, she acknowledged as she carefully hauled herself onto the dryer. Her fingers were closing around the cardboard box when there was a sound behind her, followed by Daniel's voice, mildly curious. "What are you doing?"

She turned around and slid into a sitting position. "I didn't hear you come in," she said with a guilty grin.

"I see." He didn't ask the question again. One quick glance confirmed that the supply shelf was far too high for her. He made a mental note to correct that as he moved closer.

It occurred to Sarah that he might not appreciate her using the dryer as a chair, and she started to slide to the floor, but Daniel was there—big, close, solid. He leaned forward, close enough for her to feel the heat from his body, and lifted the detergent from the shelf. He set it on top of the washer, then added the fabric softener and bleach. His task done, though, he didn't move away. He simply stood there and looked at her.

He had come to take a package of meat from the freezer for dinner, to ask her to stay and eat with them, to tell her that he and Katie would take her home later. But now his purpose was forgotten. Now all he could do was look at her.

She was so pretty. Every time he saw her, he was struck anew by her beauty. What could such a delicately pretty woman see in a man like him, except the fact that he was her key to their daughter? Was that what drew her to him? Maybe, he conceded. Probably. But he didn't want to think about that now. Didn't want to believe that this sweet, innocent-looking woman was capable of using him that way.

Didn't want to question her motives or her reasons. Didn't want to consider anything at all except how he wanted her.

It had been easier in Nashville. There had been no child, no shared past, no emotional ties, no distrust or anger or hurt. Then it had simply been a lonely man with an instant attraction for a beautiful lonely woman. An instant attraction that he'd tried to convince himself was no more than lust. But mere lust couldn't survive two years apart. Not like this. Not this strong.

He touched her slowly. If she wanted to move away, if she wanted to avoid his hand, she could—that was her right. But he knew she wouldn't. She would accept his touch...his kiss...his caress. Would she accept *him*?

His hand was big. Warm. Callused. And gentle. Sarah was surprised anew by how gentle this big man could be. She needed that gentleness, needed it to heal long months of pain and sorrow. Needed it the way she needed him.

His fingers moved to her cheek, his palm hard and rough against her jaw. He savored the sensations, from the heel of his hand to the tips of his fingers, before moving his hand lower, sliding over her jaw, down her throat, where her pulse beat visibly. Was it arousal, nervousness or fear that caused her heart to race so? he wondered. Surely not fear. Surely she knew that he could never hurt her, could never take anything she didn't offer willingly.

Arousal? His head found it hard to believe he could arouse a woman like Sarah with no more than a touch, but his heart wanted to believe it. He *didn't* want to believe that she was nervous because she had to endure this intimacy.

"Sarah?" His voice was thick with desire. With need. With unspoken pleas. *Don't stop me. Don't turn away.* And at the same time, *Please stop me before it's too late.* Before she became too important. Before he cared too much.

She swayed unsteadily toward him. It was the only invitation he needed. His left hand remained where it was, measuring her pulse, and the right one moved into her hair, sliding through the honey-colored silk to rest on her scalp. His mouth covered hers. There were no tentative gestures, no cautious sips, no gentle searches. There was hunger, quick and insatiable. Heat, simmering and dangerous. Need, heavy and hard and blunt edged.

He tasted... Sarah's eyes fluttered shut. Like air. Like water. Like everything she needed to live. He was making her ache with such sweet pain. Her breasts were tingling, her nipples growing erect, and lower...

She wriggled, trying to ease the ache between her thighs, and slid to the floor. The movement put her in intimate contact with the muscular strength of his body. With the masculine strength of his desire.

She had wanted before, but not like this. She had needed before, but never this kind of need—this swirling, dizzying, toe-curling need. She had hungered before, but not as if she were starving. Not until it hurt. Craving more, she reached for him, twined her arms around his neck and clung to him.

Her breasts were flat against his chest, her belly soft beneath his hardness. Daniel shuddered as she snuggled closer, as if trying to crawl inside his skin. Closer than any woman had ever been. Closer than he could bear without doing something they both might regret later. He tore his mouth from hers, dragged her arms from his neck and retreated to the doorway. "No, Sarah."

He sounded drugged—thick voiced, dazed. The way *she* felt, Sarah thought with a smile. "Why not?"

"It would be..."

"Fun?" Her smile grew wider. "Katie's asleep, the laundry can wait, and you can spare a few hours from your work."

He studied her for a long time, with that same solemn look that Katie had given the other kids. "It's that easy for you, isn't it? You get aroused, you go to bed. It doesn't matter who, or where, or when, or even why, does it?"

She looked as if he'd struck her. Her face drained of color, her lower lip trembled, and her eyes were round with hurt. How could he kiss her like that one minute and say something so cruel the next? Protectively folding her arms over her chest, she said softly, "If you think I'm a slut, Daniel, at least have the courage to say it. Don't hide behind inferences. Or is 'slut' too difficult a word for an old-fashioned man like you?''

There was derision in her last words. Knowing that he deserved it didn't make it any easier to bear. "I don't want to go to bed with you," he said coldly. It was a lie—a defensive one, but also a painfully obvious one, he admitted. She deserved better than that, better than him.

She let her gaze drop lower, pointedly, insolently, to his groin and the proof of his lie. "Well, you sure could have fooled me. But I guess good men don't go to bed with sluts, do they?'' She started toward him. Her voice had lost its softness and was sharp and thick with pain. "I'm going for a walk. I'll be back before Katie's up.''

But Daniel blocked the door. He couldn't let her go, couldn't let her think he was such a bastard. Without a word, he threaded both hands into her hair, lowered his head and kissed her again.

So gentle. So sweet. Sarah was drowning in sensation. Her anger and wounded feelings vanished, overcome by the sudden breathtaking resurgence of desire.

A simple kiss of apology, that was all he'd intended. A kiss to say what he couldn't put into words. But he couldn't end it, couldn't let her go, couldn't stop his hand from gliding down her throat, down to her breast. He laid his hand flat, completely covering her small breast, and felt her nipple hard against his palm. Her T-shirt, like most of her clothes, was worn thin, allowing him to feel everything. To feel too much.

Sarah arched her back, pressing against him, and a whimper escaped her. At the soft, helpless sound, Daniel released her. He brushed his hand gently over her hair. "Wanting is easy Sarah," he murmured. "I imagine I've always wanted you . . . and I imagine I always will. But that doesn't make it right.''

"But this *is* right, Daniel," she protested. "Can't you *feel* it?''

"No." It was another lie, but the end justified the means, he reminded himself. He had already betrayed her trust by hiring a private detective, by instructing Zachary to surprise her with the lawsuit, by breaking his word to her. But making love to her when he was doing those things—that would be the biggest betrayal, and the biggest lie, of all. "You're talking about sex, Sarah. About lust."

"No, Daniel," she disagreed. "I'm talking about a whole lot more. But if you don't understand that, then there *is* something wrong here."

He saw the dampness in her eyes, heard the quaver in her voice. He wanted to draw her close again, to hold her and kiss her and love her until all the sadness was gone. But he couldn't. In two more weeks she expected to get Katie back. Instead she was going to get served with notice of his lawsuit. If nothing more happened between them, she would simply hate him on that day. If more *did* happen, she would despise him until the day she died with every ounce of feeling she possessed. Worse, she would blame herself, too, for letting him use her that way. "I'm sorry, Sarah."

It was the first time he'd said those words to her, but they gave her no pleasure, brought her no healing. She wasn't sure anything could ease the pain of knowing that he didn't find her suitable to satisfy his baser desires. Maybe she had been right earlier, for he certainly hadn't denied it. Maybe good men didn't go to bed with sluts.

She turned back to the laundry, knowing he was watching her, trembling so badly that she spilled the cup of detergent across the washer. "Just for the record, Daniel," she said, her voice low and uneven, "I've been with only two men—my ex-husband, and you. I don't think it's very fair of you to condemn me on that basis."

Was it true? he wondered, at the same time knowing that it was. He had known two years ago that her experience with men had been limited. She had been awkward, shy, not used to undressing in front of a man, to sharing the intimacies between a man and a woman. She had never been the easy, shameless, immoral woman he'd made her in his bitter memories. *Never.*

"Sarah..." He sadly shook his head. "I don't want to hurt you."

Keeping her back to him, she swept the spilled powder into the tub, then began loading the clothes. "There are a hundred different ways to hurt someone, Daniel. I have no doubt that you'll find every one of them."

"Sarah, please..." His voice was strained now. "I don't want to lose your friendship."

Friendship, she silently, tearfully scoffed. She wanted love, marriage, a lifetime together, and he was offering friendship—two weeks' worth. Until he got her out of his life. Taking a deep breath, she closed the washer and turned to face him. "I can't give that up. Except for Beth, you're the only friend I have." She tried to smile, but her mouth was trembling too much. "You'd better get back to work now."

"Sarah—"

"*Please?*" She was going to break down and cry, and she didn't want to do it in front of him. He would worry and feel responsible and try to take care of her, and that would just make everything so much worse. She didn't want his caretaking anymore, not if that was all he was willing to give.

Because he could see that she was on the edge, he gave in and left the house. If he stayed, he would have to soothe her, and if he did that, he would end up making love to her. And in two weeks he would lose her, totally, completely, without a chance in hell of getting her back.

He'd forgotten the dinner invitation, his reason for searching her out, he realized as he walked across the hard ground. It was just as well. He didn't think the pain in his belly was going to go away in time for him to eat dinner, anyway.

October 19

It was cold on Friday night after the sun went down, but that didn't stop Daniel from going out to sit on the porch, his flannel-lined jacket buttoned up tightly, his hands shoved deeply into his pockets. Katie was asleep upstairs, tucked beneath a baby-sized quilt, sharing her pillow with Teddy, and Sarah had gone home more than two hours ago.

She hadn't forgiven him for yesterday's scene in the laundry room. She had talked to him, had smiled and laughed and acted as if everything were normal, but something had been missing—some spark of life, of happiness. She was pretending, the same way he was pretending he didn't want an affair with her. He supposed it said something for their honesty that neither of them was very good at that kind of lie.

Honesty. Once it had meant everything to him. His father had taught him as a small child to always be honest, always tell the truth, and for the better part of thirty-four years, he'd done just that. And now, with the only person who mattered in his life besides Katie, practically everything he said or did was a lie.

In less than two weeks, it would be over. His sigh was heavily tinged with relief... and regret. Zachary would file the lawsuit, and Sarah would know how Daniel had deceived her, and whether or not he wanted her wouldn't matter anymore, because she would never have anything more to do with him.

Unless he changed his mind.

He stopped rocking and propped his feet on the rail. Eyes closed, he considered the possibility. Change his mind? Let Katie go off to live wherever Sarah found a job? Settle for being a part-time father, for seeing his daughter every other weekend and maybe in the summer? Stand back and watch while some man took *his* place in Katie's life?

Never.

So what other options did he have? What solution would allow him to have Katie, and Sarah, too?

Marriage.

He said it out loud, testing its sound, its flavor. Marriage. He and Sarah had talked about it often enough—her failed marriage, his lack of desire for one, her parents', his parents' and their grandparents' marriages. It was the obvious solution to his problem. Through marriage, Katie would remain with him without the trauma of a court battle. Through marriage, he would gain a wife, a beautiful wife, and the chance to have other children. Through marriage, he could have Sarah, could be with her and make love to her without guilt or shame.

How many times had he told her that he didn't want a wife? How many times had he lied to her? But if they were married, the lies would stop. There would be no deceptions, no misleading, no dishonesty. There would be no lawsuit. If she agreed in the next thirteen days to marry him, she would never even have to know what he had planned. His guilt would be absolved; his needs would be satisfied; his daughter would be protected. All with one brief, simple courthouse ceremony.

He grimly rolled his head from side to side. What reason did he have to believe that Sarah would even consider marriage to him? She spent time with him because of their

daughter; she wanted to go to bed with him because of...
His frown deepened. Physical urges. That was as good a way
to describe the need as any other. If she hadn't lied to him
yesterday, it had been nearly two years for her. That was a
long time for any need to go unsatisfied. She wanted an affair for thirteen days, at the end of which she expected to
get Katie back, pack up and leave. To deal with his guilt, with
the honor that she was so certain he possessed, he had to
have more. He had to have a commitment, a promise, a future. He had to have marriage.

He could approach it bluntly, openly. We both want Katie, so let's get married and raise her together. And pray that
she didn't find such a proposal as calculating and cold-
blooded as he did.

Or he could woo her. He could take the affection that
she'd already shown him and try to turn it into something
more. Not love. He'd never received love from anyone but
Katie, and he had long ago learned not to expect it. He
didn't need Sarah's love to have a good marriage. But
warmth, caring, friendship—surely those were things she
could give, things he could live with.

But what if *she* needed love? Could he give her that? It
pained him to look too closely at the answer, that maybe he
already did love her. How could he let himself love a woman
who had never intended to be part of his life? How could he
love a woman who never would have seen him again after
that weekend if she hadn't been unlucky enough to get
pregnant? Affection, caring, friendship—that was what he
felt. And, of course, desire. The same physical urges that
drove her. That was *all*, he insisted. And he believed it. Tonight, in the cold, quiet dark that surrounded him, he let
himself believe the lie.

October 20

Sarah was tugging her jeans on when Daniel arrived to pick her up for the festival Saturday morning. She fastened them quickly, then pulled on a plain white shirt, buttoning it as she walked to the open door. "I'll be ready in a minute," she called.

From his position beside the truck, Daniel nodded in response. She returned to the bathroom, where she tucked her shirt into her jeans and refastened them. Without makeup or perfume or jewelry, there wasn't much left for her to do besides comb her hair. For a moment she indulged her feminine vanity, wishing she could look her best for Daniel. If he saw that she could be pretty with makeup, earrings, a necklace, perfume, maybe some nicer clothes, would he be impressed? Would he be more attracted to her?

She didn't think so. He'd said Thursday morning that she was pretty... but Thursday afternoon he'd told her that he didn't want her, that it would be wrong for him to want her. The problem wasn't with her appearance, she admitted glumly. It was what was inside her, or what Daniel believed was inside. He thought she was easy, without morals, without shame. He thought she was the kind of woman who could give up her baby because she found the child inconvenient. He couldn't see past his judgments and condemnations to the woman who loved her daughter more than life itself, to the woman who loved *him*.

And she couldn't help him. She couldn't tell him her secrets just so he would forgive and accept her. She couldn't play on her son's tragedy to gain Daniel's approval. She wanted his trust and faith to be given freely, not on the condition that she provide him with satisfactory reasons for the actions. Such justification wasn't fair to Tony, and it wasn't fair to her.

Sighing softly, she practiced a smile in the mirror. For twelve more days she would be Daniel's friend, because that was all he would accept from her. Then she would have Katie, and he would be out of her life. He would be Katie's father and nothing else. Like thousands of divorced mothers, she would see him briefly when he came to get Katie and when he brought her home, and they would be awkwardly, painfully polite to each other, for their daughter's sake.

And she would never fall in love with anyone else again.

She took some money from her purse and stuffed it, along with her keys, deeply into one pocket. After locking the door, she went outside to join them.

Katie was still in her car seat, chattering softly to herself. Her conversation was serious, Sarah thought with a grin. Her dark blue eyes were somber, her full pouty mouth unsmiling.

Slowly Sarah walked past the truck to watch Daniel. He was unloading firewood, adding it neatly to the small stack that remained from the first load. When he finished, he turned to face her. In a matter of seconds her easy grin was transformed into a forbidding frown. She looked from him to the stacked wood, then back again, and the frown grew colder.

No more charity, she'd told him a few days ago. He met her frown with one of his own, daring her to challenge him. If her pride was hurt, that was too bad, but he'd be damned if he'd let her spend the nights down here in an unheated house with nothing but a pile of blankets to keep her warm.

Friendship was one thing, Sarah thought despairingly, but this was too much. She didn't want anything that he gave only because he felt obligated. She didn't want him taking care of her when he couldn't care *about* her. "Take it back."

"No."

She moved closer, until she had to tilt her head back to see him. "I don't want it."

"But you'll use it." If he had to come down here every night and every morning, he would make sure she used it.

"Daniel—"

"Sarah." He brushed his hand over her hair. It was just a gesture, easy and meaningless, but two weeks ago he couldn't have made it. "You can't make me take it back."

He was right. He was so much bigger and stronger than she was that she couldn't *make* him do anything. "At least let me pay you for it. How much would that amount of wood cost?"

He opened his mouth to tell her that he didn't want her money, that she couldn't afford it, anyway; then he saw the hopelessness in her eyes. She expected him to refuse payment, to make her pay instead with her pride, so he named a price. It was less than the market value of the firewood, but he saw her flinch.

She mentally reviewed her bank balance and silently groaned. "I'll write you a check—"

"After you find a job." *If* she found a job. If she agreed to his proposal—if he found the courage to make it—maybe she would choose not to work. Maybe she would stay home with him and Katie and be a full-time wife and mother. "Okay?"

Relieved, she nodded. "Thank you, Daniel."

"Are you ready?"

With another nod, she returned to the truck. She was looking forward to this trip into town today. On Thursday, while Daniel had worked on the booths, Linda Schmidt had described how they would be decorated, the rides that would be set up for the kids, the crafts and foods and games that would be available, and it had sounded like a wonderful way to spend a day with Katie and Daniel. In spite of his rejection later that afternoon, she was still determined to have a good time.

Traffic was heavy on the highway into town. The streets that formed the town square were blocked off, and rides, games and picnic tables filled both lanes. They had to park several blocks from the square on a quiet side street filled with lovely old houses.

"I like Sweetwater," Sarah commented as they walked, their pace slow to accommodate Katie's chubby legs. "It seems like a nice place to raise a kid." When she got no response, she dared a sidelong glance at him. His expression was solemn, his mind miles away. "I have to come into town next week. To look for a job and a place to live."

He looked at her then. The end of the month was approaching, her lease on the farmhouse was running out, and, he would bet, so was her money. If everything worked out, she could move directly from the farmhouse into his house, and she wouldn't have to worry about money. All she would have to do was what she'd been doing for the past week and a half—take care of Katie. He would take care of everything else.

Misinterpreting his grim mood, she hastened to reassure him. "I meant what I said before, Daniel. You'll be able to see her as often as you want."

"Tell me, Sarah." They had almost reached the square, and he stopped to get her answer before they approached the crowd ahead. "Is there anything you wouldn't do for Katie?"

She gave it a long moment's consideration, then shook her head. "No. She's my daughter."

Daniel nodded once, and they began walking again.

She's my daughter. The simple statement told him everything. She would do anything in the world for Katie. She would love her, help her, support her, fight for her. She would defend her, teach her, encourage her. She would, if convinced that it was in Katie's best interests, even marry for her. That was all he needed to know.

* * *

The sights and sounds of the eighteenth annual Harvest Festival were too much for Katie to take in. From her perch on Daniel's shoulders she stared wide-eyed and open-mouthed at everything, not certain which sight she liked best.

"This is wonderful," Sarah said after a weaving walk around the square. "When I was a kid, my mom loved to go to fairs—not the big state fairs, but little county ones, where everyone knew each other, and the merry-go-round was the most sophisticated ride. She especially loved the crafts—the quilts and clothes and the lace. She always said she was going to learn to do some of them . . . but she never had time."

A faint sadness came into her eyes, and Daniel wished the childlike wonder would return. It made her look so young, so carefree and happy, and he liked it when she looked happy. "It must have been hard for her, supporting the two of you."

She nodded. "She worked hard. My father didn't pay child support, of course. Men are like that."

"Not all of them." He couldn't understand a man who would abandon his children any more than he could understand a woman who did. "I would have supported you and Katie if I'd known."

Unexpectedly, she wrapped her arm around his waist and gave him a hug. "I know." Knowing instinctively that he was blushing at her public display, she stepped away. "Cotton candy!" she exclaimed, spying bags of the pink-and-blue confection hanging from the sign of a booth. "Can Katie have some?"

Before he could answer, she was halfway to the booth, pulling money from her pocket. She picked up a bag of each color and held them up for Katie to see. "Pink or blue, Katie?"

She pointed to the blue, then leaned down from Daniel's shoulders to claim it. With a laugh, Sarah shook her head, clasping the bag tighter. "A little at a time, sweetheart. I don't want you to get sick." After paying and returning the change to her pocket, she headed toward an empty bench in the park, where Daniel put the girl down.

Sarah tore off a chunk of the wispy spun sugar and handed it to Katie, who wasn't quite sure what to do with it until her mother showed her. "Has she ever had candy?" Sarah asked suspiciously after seeing Katie's surprised but enthusiastic response to the treat.

Daniel gave a shake of his head. He'd never developed much of a taste for sweets himself, so it had never occurred to him to buy them for Katie.

Laughing, Sarah pulled another big piece from the paper cone. "Oh, Daniel, you're entirely too good, you know that? Every child should have a father like you." Her tone was teasing, but the compliment was sincere. When she had first found out almost two years ago that she was pregnant, she had wondered why God was so angry with her—first Tony, then the pregnancy. But she had been blessed in one respect; she couldn't have found a better man to have a baby with if she had searched all her life.

When Katie finished the cotton candy, her hands and face were coated with a sticky blue crust. She grinned, first at her mother, then her father. "More candy, Daddy."

He directed a dry look in Sarah's direction. "Now see what you've done?"

Sarah wetted a napkin at the nearby drinking fountain, then returned to scrub the girl clean, amid demands for more candy. "We've created a monster," she teased.

"*We* created a child," Daniel corrected. "*You* created the monster."

Sarah looked up from her kneeling position, the look on her face soft and wondrous. Was that the first time he'd ever acknowledged her role in producing Katie? he wondered ruefully and guessed from her reaction that it was. Katie was no longer his daughter, or Sarah's, but *theirs*. A joint production, a joint responsibility. That would be one of his selling points, if he needed any, when he asked her to marry him.

For just a moment he sat motionless. He was really going to do it, wasn't he? Last night he'd gone to bed thinking about it, certain that it was the most foolish idea he'd ever had. But he was going to do it. Daniel Ryan, who had boasted that he would never get married, that he didn't want a wife and, more importantly, didn't need one, was going to propose to Sarah Lawson.

Sarah Ryan. He liked the sound of that—light, happy, beautiful. Like her. And he liked the idea of being married. Even if there was no love involved, what did it matter? Good marriages were built on other things—respect, friendship, affection, understanding, trust. Love was a bonus. They could be satisfied without it.

"Go, Mama," Katie pleaded, trying to pull Sarah to her feet. "Go, Daddy."

Daniel stood up and offered a hand to pull Sarah up. For a long moment his fingers remained laced with hers; then, slowly, he pulled away. "Go, Sarah," he softly imitated their daughter.

It was, Sarah decided, the most wonderful day of her life. She rode the merry-go-round, standing beside Katie's horse, for countless whirls while Daniel watched them from the sidewalk. They ate cotton candy and hot dogs and warm, salty pretzels, and drank tall icy cups of Coke. They visited each crafts booth and watched the games and took Katie to the petting zoo, with chickens, ducks, rabbits, a pony and a lamb. By the time they got her out of the small enclosure, she was pleading with her father to take the lamb home with them.

And she met people—Zachary Adams's parents and grandparents, Linda Schmidt's family, and Leon Peters's wife, along with practically every other person in Sweetwater County. She wondered if all these people made it a point to greet Daniel every time they saw him, or if her presence had something to do it. She sadly suspected that it did. The introductions were awkward for him at first as he wasn't sure quite how to refer to her. He settled quickly on giving just her name, accompanied with his usual scowl. No one dared to question him further.

"You've got to quit doing that," she remarked, shifting the sleeping Katie to her other shoulder.

"Doing what?"

"Frowning at everyone who comes over. You're going to make them think you're disagreeable."

"I *am* disagreeable," he said, giving her a suitable frown. It only made her laugh.

"They're just curious. You can't blame them. You show up one day with a baby that's obviously yours, and a year later I come, and she's obviously mine, too. They just want the details."

"I'm not annoyed with them." It was true. Although at one time he would have resented such prying into his life, he knew these people. They weren't malicious, just nosy.

Before he could continue, there was another interruption, this one from Zachary. "Is Katie going to enter the contest this evening?"

"What contest?" Sarah asked, shifting again. She had turned down Daniel's offer to carry Katie, enjoying the feel of the small warm body cuddled snugly against her too much to give it up, but now the added weight was getting heavy fast.

Zachary gently brushed a curl of Katie's hair from her face. "The costume contest." At Sarah's blank look, he explained further, "They have a contest for the best costume after the sun goes down. Fortunately, the festival is always held close to Halloween so it's not a problem for the parents."

"We didn't know, so we don't have anything for her." She glanced from him to the big man beside her. "Daniel . . . ?"

He didn't need to hear her request to know what she wanted. He stepped closer and carefully took Katie from her. The little girl settled into the familiar cradle of her father's arms with a soft sleepy sigh and a gentle snore. "We'd probably better head home soon, Sarah."

She nodded. "Zachary, your town does a good job of throwing a party."

"It gets better every year." He looked from her to Daniel, then back again, his gaze speculative. "Maybe you can see for yourself next year."

Her smile was slow. "Maybe I can."

The sun was setting, turning the sky a dozen shades of rose, purple and blue, as they started toward the pickup. Sarah walked a few feet from Daniel's side, humming along with the band set up in the middle of the square. Soon the stars would be out, the sky would turn dark, and the lights would come on. There would be a dance tonight, with baby-sitting services provided in the church, while the older children rode one last ride, played one last game. Even though it would be chilly without the sun's warmth, the people wouldn't mind. They would simply put on the jackets and coats they'd left in their cars and enjoy every last minute of pleasure that the Harvest Festival offered.

"Do you dance, Daniel?" She twirled around, moving ahead of him, swaying gracefully in time to the fading music. "I like to dance. I like music. I'd like to dance with you." She would like to feel his arms around her, would like the chance to touch him, to feel his body move against hers. She would like to dance with him until he shared her hunger, until his need was so strong that he forgot who she was, forgot what he thought she was and loved her anyway.

Her cotton shirt was loose, but each swirl flattened the fabric against her, outlining her small breasts, her erect nipples. He watched, wanting to stop her, wanting her to never stop, and he kept his hands clasped tightly together underneath the baby to stop himself from reaching for her.

She spun one last time, coming to a breathless stop beside the truck. Daniel stood in front of her. She told herself that she wouldn't touch him, but her hands came up of their own accord to rest on his broad, strong shoulders. She ordered herself not to caress him, but the action came automatically, one hand gliding down his chest, the other sliding to the back of his neck. She absolutely would not kiss him, she silently scolded, but her mouth was hungry for the taste of him. Even knowing that the sweetness of the kiss would only be followed by pain, she wanted it, needed it.

"No, Sarah," she murmured to herself as she moved a step closer.

Daniel moved Katie to his shoulder, caught a handful of the billowy white shirt and pulled Sarah to him. "Yes, Sarah," he growled, and his mouth covered hers.

Her body went briefly limp against him before it grew taut with hunger, wicked and wild. She kissed him as hungrily, as greedily, as he kissed her, and struggled for more, trying to satisfy a lifetime's need with just one kiss.

It took the sound of an approaching car to penetrate the haze that enveloped Daniel's mind. He broke off the kiss, then rubbed his mouth back and forth over hers, taking one last taste. Looking down, he realized that he was gripping the fabric of her shirt as if it were a lifeline, and he forced his fingers to slowly relax and let go.

"Sarah—"

She quickly laid her fingers over his mouth. "No. Don't say anything, please." She needed to savor the lingering pleasure of his kiss without his rejection, without his regrets.

Was she afraid he would once again lie and tell her that he didn't want her? he wondered as he opened the truck door. Or afraid he might say he did?

She moved around the truck and climbed in as he was fastening Katie's seat belt. Bending, she kissed their daughter's forehead. "Do you think she'll sleep all night?"

"Probably, since she missed both naps. She had a good time."

"Kids love things like this." Sarah settled comfortably in the seat and adjusted her seat belt. She rolled her head to the right so she could see the stars, which were beginning to appear above them. "Did you?"

"Have a good time?" He paused a moment. "Yeah, I did."

"Maybe next time..." She was about to say that they could stay and dance through the night, but her voice faded away. There probably wouldn't be a next time for them, not together. Once everything was settled with Katie, he probably wouldn't want to see Sarah again except when he came to pick up their daughter. After such a lovely day, that thought made her especially sad.

Daniel looked at her and saw her sadness, but he didn't question it. He was feeling a little melancholy himself. Maybe it was knowing that he was going to take her home, then go to his own house. To his own bed. Without her.

When they got to her house, Daniel left Katie, still sleeping, in the truck and went inside with Sarah long enough to build a fire. When he was done, he looked disparagingly at the lumpy sofa and its heavy layer of blankets but offered no criticism. "Do you have enough blankets?"

From her position next to the door, she nodded.

"Are you sure? I told you, my grandparents were married for forty-two years, and my grandmother quilted for all forty-two of them. I can loan you some."

"I'm sure." As if to make a liar of her, a shiver passed through her as he came near. But it wasn't a chill. It was weakness, she thought, that made her desperately want a man who desired her but didn't *want* her. Or maybe it was less complicated than that. Maybe it was love.

He stopped in front of her. "We'll see you tomorrow?"

Again she nodded.

"Lock the door as soon as I leave."

She bobbed her head once more, and he muttered a vicious curse, yanked her to him and kissed her hard and fast and more than a little desperately. As quickly as it had started, it ended, and he was gone, the screen door banging behind him. "Good night, Daniel," she whispered, watching him go.

October 21

Sarah lay on her back, her eyes closed, listening, smelling, feeling her surroundings. Below her the ground's hardness was padded with a quilt of muslin and calico, lovingly handmade more than forty years ago by Daniel's grandmother. Above her, individual rays of afternoon sunshine, breaking through the leaves, touched her face, bringing a few degrees' warmth to her skin. There was a breeze so light she barely felt it, its passage through the trees marked by a soft, rustling whisper.

On one side there was a distant rush, like wind, but steady, constant. The creek that Daniel had told her about, that appeared out of nowhere and tumbled over the smooth, rounded rocks down the mountainside. It tasted cold, he'd told her, and sweet—hence the name, Sweetwater. Very original, she had teased, and he'd laughed.

On her left there was a louder rustle, this one crashing, starting, stopping, scuffing. Katie, she knew, exploring everything she could find in this quiet, shadowed clearing, watched by Daniel like the sharp-eyed bird that had fled the tree above her when they'd intruded.

She took a deep breath, held it, let it out, then breathed in again. The single big scent that she had labeled as "the woods" was made up of a myriad different scents: the dampness of the forest floor; the sweet, piney aroma of the trees; the woody smell of broken branches and fallen trees; the moist flavor of water; the heady, memory-filled smell of crackling brown leaves; the fresh, pungent aroma of... Her forehead wrinkled into a frown as she searched for the right words. *Green.* That was it. The smell came from the weeds, the pines, the few sprigs of grass that grew in the rich soil. It was the smell of the color green.

There was a faint tickling above her upper lip, and she concentrated on it. It was soft, green, sweet. "A pine needle."

Opening her eyes, she saw the slender green needle in Daniel's hand and smiled triumphantly. "You were right," she said as he drew the needle over her cheek to her jaw. "If you concentrate, you can hear and feel and see so much." See with your eyes shut—that was what he'd told her. If she wanted to appreciate the woods, she should see them with her eyes shut.

He was lying beside her, his head supported on one big hand. While she had been concentrating, so had he—on her. He had studied her face and the lines of her body. He had watched the movement of her eyes beneath their lids, the smile, the frown, the triumph. Someday he would like to do the same exercise with her, but instead of awareness of her surroundings, he would like to teach her awareness of her body. He would like to remove her clothes and lie beside her and touch her, tease her, caress her, while she concentrated on each touch, each response, each need.

His own response, quick, hard, thick, prompted him to roll onto his stomach, his head pillowed on his arm. Since he'd decided to marry her, since he'd given himself respectable intentions toward her, his desire was intruding more frequently, stronger, harder to control, impossible to hide. He had progressed from wanting and needing to craving, yearning, aching. It hurt to look at her, to touch her, but it was a good pain. A pleasing one. An erotic one.

He laid his arm over her chest, his elbow on her stomach, his hand on her chin. On each side of his arm were her breasts, small, firm, their peaked tips visible through the cotton shirt. As much as he craved contact with them, he made no effort to touch them. That would come later, when Katie was asleep. When nothing could disturb them, when nothing could draw him away from rediscovering the pleasures of Sarah's body.

Her eyes closed again, Sarah felt Daniel's finger, rough and blunt edged, rubbing across her lips. She opened her mouth to him, capturing his fingertip between the tiny sharp edges of her teeth, bathing it with her tongue. He pulled away and clasped her chin in his hand, then leaned over her. "Open your mouth," he demanded, giving her only an instant to obey before his was on hers, his tongue stabbing inside, his lips bruising, his teeth hard.

She drew his tongue deeper, until there was no more, until they had joined as thoroughly as they could. Her hands clenched into tight fists around the muslin-and-calico quilt, as if it could save her from the madness that swirled through her, but her head knew that nothing could save her but Daniel. He had taken her into the madness, and only he could bring her safely out.

Questions rushed through his mind. Would the ground be too hard for Sarah's slim, fragile body? Would Katie take her nap early today? Could he make it back to the house in the condition he was in? Could he wait that long?

Her breathing was fast, his ragged, when he rolled away from her. His blood was pulsing and his heart thundering, while hers fluttered erratically. The only visible evidence of her arousal, her hardened nipples, subsided, while the painfully swollen bulge that tightened his jeans seemed a permanent condition.

Sarah was the first to speak. Staring at the autumn-colored canopy of leaves above her, she gave a soft sigh and murmured, "Oh, my."

Oh, my, indeed, Daniel thought with a grimace as he adjusted his jeans. Soon he would satisfy his cravings—the one in his body, and the one in his soul. Very soon.

* * *

When they made their way out of the woods by the last rays of daylight, Daniel insisted that Sarah stay for supper. The stew was already cooked, and afterward she could bathe Katie, read her a bedtime story and tuck her into bed. Sarah wondered if he knew how much the mother in her missed doing those little things for their daughter. She also wondered if he understood the significance of what he was saying. If she stayed long enough to put Katie to bed, she would have to spend the night. It would be too dark to walk home alone—not, she knew, that he would ever let her—and he wouldn't leave Katie in the house alone long enough to take her home.

He understood, all right. It was too difficult for him to say flatly, openly, "Stay with me." He trusted that Sarah knew him well enough to find the second, more intimate invitation hidden behind the innocence of the supper invitation. He also trusted that she wanted him enough to accept.

He was right.

After dinner they played with Katie; then Sarah took her upstairs for her bath, while Daniel did the dishes. She had forgotten how much fun bath time with a toddler could be, and how messy. After Katie was bathed, shampooed and dressed in pajamas, Sarah spent another five minutes cleaning the bathroom.

"Put your clothes in the hamper," she said, handing Katie her dirty clothes rolled in a manageable ball.

The child accepted the bundle, then looked blankly at her mother. Laughing, Sarah crossed the room to the wooden box. "This is a hamper. See, you lift the lid and put the clothes inside, then shut it."

After the demonstration, Katie lifted the lid, threw her clothes in and shut it. A moment later, she opened it, threw in a wet towel and let the lid bang down again. The loud noise pleased her, so she picked up the soft gray rug from the floor.

"No," Sarah scolded gently, replacing the rug and removing the towel, then hanging it over the shower rod. "No rugs, no wet towels." She saw her daughter's sly blue eyes spy her discarded tennis shoes and shook her head. "No shoes, either, Katie. Just clothes. Come on, let's go read."

It was a new experience for Katie, being readied for bed by her mother, but when it came time for the actual tucking in, it was her father she turned to. Sarah didn't feel even a twinge of dismay. She hoped that there would always be certain times and certain rituals that Katie preferred to share with her father.

"Good night, sweetheart." Sarah gave her a kiss, then began gathering the storybooks, while Daniel took the baby upstairs. She stacked the books in a neat pile and added them to one of the bookcases, then returned to the sofa, stretching out along its length.

When Daniel came down a few minutes later, he found her there, a pillow beneath her head, her eyes closed, her breathing steady, her arms at her side. He wondered briefly if she'd fallen asleep, then saw the movement of her eyes behind closed lids.

"Can you hear the hissing of the logs?" she asked, playing the game once more. "And there's water dripping somewhere."

Without a word, without a sound, he knelt beside the sofa, facing her. She was still for a moment, feeling, listening for the even sounds of his breathing; then, slowly, she moved her hand upward, making contact with his chest, then still higher, until it cupped the beard-roughened skin of his jaw.

Without speaking he returned her hand to the cushion, then leaned forward, his movements agonizingly slow. She could sense his motion, could see the shadow that fell over her, could soon feel the heat from his body. Then his mouth touched hers. His lips were hard but gentle, coaxing, teasing. His tongue, when it probed between her teeth, was insistent, demanding entry, thrusting inside her. He tasted like heat, smoky and dark, simmering, building, like a fever starting to climb. There were other flavors, too—hunger too strong to ignore; desire, thick and unmanageable; and need, strong, razor edged, painful.

She breathed in, filling her lungs with his scent. He smelled like welcoming bright sunshine and enticing dark shadows, like sweet pine and fragrant wood smoke. She smelled the baby scents of their daughter and the tang of need, every bit as intoxicating, as sharp, as it tasted.

Daniel ended the kiss, teased her lips with his tongue, then began another kiss. This time he gave her even more, adding sweet, gentle-rough caresses. His fingers stroked her face, her hair, her throat. They slid underneath the rolled-up sleeves and the open-necked collar of her shirt, their tough, callused surfaces gliding smoothly over her flesh. She was so soft, he marveled, so satiny, silky soft. It seemed sinful for hands as rough as his to touch skin as fine as hers, but he did it anyway and savored every second.

Sarah had had enough of the game. Her arms left the sofa to wrap around his neck, tugging, pulling him until there wasn't so much as a breath between them. She took her own chance to explore, to thrust her tongue hungrily into the warm dark wetness of his mouth.

Gently he freed her mouth and sat back, his solemn dark blue eyes studying her flushed face, her parted lips, her dazed eyes. She wanted him. He could see it in her face, in the rapid pulse at the base of her throat, in the swollen tips of her breasts. It made him feel powerful . . . and incredibly tender. If he disappointed her, if he hurt her . . .

She raised one hand to his chest, feeling the thudding of his heart through the flannel. Still holding his gaze, she unfastened the first button of his shirt, then the second and the third, all the way down to the cool brass of his belt buckle; then she slid her hand underneath the fabric. His chest was smooth, without a single curl to hide the sculpted perfection of well-defined muscles. She found his nipple, round, flat, responsive, and drew one blunt fingernail over it until it was as hard and no doubt as achy as her own. With a sly, lazy smile she located the other one and treated it to the same teasing strokes. Still smiling, she let her hand glide lower, over his stomach, flat and rock solid, across his belt and the rough denim of his jeans, and she found something else rock solid.

Her smile disappeared, only to reappear on the smooth, sensuous lines of Daniel's mouth. "Have you forgotten? I'm a big man," he murmured.

She traced the denim-clad outline of his arousal—long, heated, hard, thick. "Yes," she agreed, her voice less than a murmur. "You are."

Reaching out, he cupped her chin in his hand. "I won't hurt you, Sarah."

She knew that. He had such strength that he could crush her, could literally break her, but that strength was tempered with gentleness, tenderness, goodness. He would never use it against her.

She continued to stroke him, her fingers gentle and erotic, increasing his need and, curiously, her own. Each time she touched him, her own desire grew, her own ache grew. She needed him against her, over her, inside her, filling her. "Make love to me, Daniel," she whispered. Pleaded.

He almost smiled, but the action was lost before it was completed. He lifted her hand and pressed it to his mouth, biting the soft flesh of her palm, leaving the dampness of his tongue on her skin. Then he stood quickly and easily and lifted her effortlessly in his arms.

She had never been carried to bed before. Sarah laced her fingers around his neck and left a trail of kisses down his throat all the way up the stairs. This was a lovely benefit of his size and incredible strength, she thought as he laid her on his bed; then she thought once again of his arousal and silently repeated the appropriate word. Incredible.

Daniel left her on the bed and made his way across the dark room to the fireplace. Kindling and logs were already laid; all they needed was a match. He found the box of matches, struck one and held the flame to the dried wood. For a moment, as the fire caught and grew, he stood there, thinking of Sarah in the bed behind him, of the awkwardly swollen ache in his groin, of the bigger ache in his heart. She could soothe them both, could satisfy them both—the first again and again, the second for the rest of his life.

The wood was burning brightly now, giving heat, painting the room with its golden light. Daniel turned his back on it while he removed his boots and socks, the braided rug muffling their fall. His shirt was already open. It took just a tug and the unfastening of one button to free it, and then it fell, too. His hands hesitated at the belt buckle; then, with a shrug, he began undoing it. She had seen him naked before, and only moments ago she had caressed him so thoroughly that there couldn't be anything left to surprise her.

He was wrong. On the bed, a pillow tugged over to support her head, Sarah watched him undress. For a moment after removing the last of his clothes, he stood in front of the fire, and she stared at him, motionless, speechless. She had never realized how perfect, how beautiful, he was. His body was all long sleek lines, each muscle perfectly formed, each curve precise, everything flowing together to produce perfection. Beauty.

He came to the bed, and the mattress sank as he lay on his side next to her. Slowly he brought his hand to her face, gliding his index finger across her jaw, over her cheek, down her nose to her mouth. As she'd done that afternoon, she opened her mouth to him, sucking the tip of his finger inside, biting the scarred flesh, bathing it. Lower, against her hip, she felt his manhood surge as the sensations spread up, out and down.

He replaced his finger in her mouth with his tongue, slowly moving it in and out, deeper, hungrier. At the same time he touched her, for the first time *really* touched her. His hand found the small mound of her breast and dragged the soft cotton shirt back and forth over her nipple with each caress until, in spite of his consuming kiss, she moaned. He stroked her belly, as flat as his own but so narrow that he could span it with one hand. And he reached lower, between her thighs, pressing firmly against her as he slid his hand back and forth. When she whimpered and arched her hips to ease the ache he was feeding deep inside her, he shifted one muscular leg to rest over hers, holding her captive to his caresses.

Sarah wrenched her mouth free and gasped his name. "Daniel, please..."

His only response was a smile—faint, masculine, smug. Still smiling, he brought his hand back to her shirt and began unfastening buttons. She was naked underneath it, for her breasts were small and needed no support. But there was nothing wrong with small, he thought as he tugged the shirt from beneath her and tossed it aside. Not when they were nicely rounded and crested with hard rosy-colored nipples. His tongue lazily tasted one, then he sucked it into his mouth and the playing ended. He suckled her breasts hungrily, greedily, making her shudder with need. At the same time his hands found the snap and zipper of her jeans, and quickly, almost savagely, he stripped them and her panties away.

His touch gentle once more, he stroked through the soft golden-honey curls between her thighs and found the hot moistness that awaited him. His fingers probed inside, testing, making her writhe. She was so small, he realized. He had teased her for being surprised by his size; after all, he was a big man. Now the tables were turned. Although she was a small, slender, delicate woman, he was stunned by just how small. How could he join with her without hurting her?

As if she sensed his indecision, she reached for him. "Daniel, I need you," she whispered, her voice as thick and heavy as his need. "I want to feel you inside me, please..."

"I don't want to hurt you." His voice was rough, almost a growl. They had come so far that he couldn't bear the thought of stopping, but the idea of causing her physical pain for his own satisfaction was even more unbearable.

"The waiting is hurting. It won't hurt when you're inside me."

He wasn't convinced, but he vowed to be as gentle, as tender, as he could. He moved between her legs, guided himself to her, and slowly, cautiously, filled her. His eyes, dark and wary, were on her face, searching for any sign of pain or discomfort, but they found nothing but the loveliest, sweetest smile of pleasure he'd ever seen.

Somehow they fit. He pushed deeper, and she took him, all of him, until soft brown curls met softer blond. Through some mystery that he would never understand—and would, thankfully, never question—they were perfectly mated.

Sarah cupped her hands to his face, the dark stubble of his beard pricking her palms, and pulled him to her for a kiss. His tongue thrust into her mouth, mimicking the rhythm of his hips, and she welcomed it, the way she welcomed him. She moved with him, meeting him, giving herself over to him. The soft helpless sounds she made—of pleasure, he knew, not pain—excited him, driving him faster, deeper, his great muscles flexing and straining, until he suddenly became still. There was an instant of nothingness, then release exploded through him. He held her tightly, filling her, dimly aware of the broken cries of her own fulfillment; then he sank heavily, weakly, against her.

He didn't know how much time had passed before he found the strength to raise his head. He looked down at Sarah, still beneath him, still joined with him. Her eyes were closed, her hands clasped around his waist, her smile gentle. "Let me move...."

Murmuring in dissent, she tightened her arms around him.

"I'm too heavy for you."

She couldn't deny that—he *was* heavy. He was also the sweetest, most welcome burden she'd ever borne.

"Sarah...honey..."

Her eyes opened at that. "You've never called me honey before."

Trying to support himself on one hand so she wouldn't be crushed, he reached behind his back and untangled her hands, then moved to her side. His hand automatically reached for her breast, savoring its softness. "Your hair is the color of honey," he murmured. "Rich...sweet... thick... And your eyes..."

She reached for him, too, snuggling close to his warmth, sliding her thigh neatly between his, and Daniel forgot what he was saying. The feel of her leg, long and surprisingly hard muscled, pressing against the most vulnerable part of his

body made him forget everything except this woman, and
his need. Would it ever be satisfied?

Sarah felt him changing shape, growing long and hard
once more, and she pressed a hot wet kiss to his nipple.
"Again, Daniel?" she asked, huskily teasing. "Do you
think if we ignore it, it will go away?" While she waited for
his answer, her hand slid down his stomach until it reached
him, and her fingers gently and lovingly closed around him.

His head was tilted back, his eyes squeezed shut, his teeth
clenched. "You're not—"

Her hand slipped lower still to cup him, and he gasped.
"You're not ignoring it," he growled like a big angry cat. A
tiger, she thought, or maybe a wildcat.

She sounded like a cat, too, a greedy one. "No," she
purred. "I'm not. One more time, Daniel?"

She rubbed him tighter, and he groaned deep in his chest.
Easily he turned her on her back and shifted between her
legs, and easily, so easily, he entered her, smooth and deep
and tight.

Sarah felt her body working to accommodate him, felt the
mere presence of him start the fever again. Soon, she knew,
in a matter of minutes, there would be such sensation, such
an overflow of feeling, that coherent speech would be impossible. Before that happened, there was one thing she
wanted to say.

"Daniel Ryan, you are—" Her breath caught as he withdrew from her heat, then slowly, inch by inch, returned. He
withdrew again, and the ache created by his absence was
spreading quickly, completely engulfing her. With one long,
heavy, swift thrust, he filled her again, and she sighed.
"Incredible," she whispered. "You are incredible."

October 22

Daniel woke at his usual early hour Monday morning, but for the first time in his life, he was in no hurry to get out of bed. He glanced at the bedside clock, saw that it was almost seven and knew he had another hour before Katie would begin stirring.

Disciplining himself, he turned his attention to the window opposite the bed. The sky was dark, and he heard the faint splatter of rain on the glass. He welcomed the rain, cold and dreary as it was. He welcomed any excuse to stay in bed an hour longer.

He glanced at the clock again. He'd been awake two minutes and hadn't yet looked at the woman snuggled so closely beside him. That was two minutes too long. Without the faintest hint of regret at his weakness, he turned to her, gently shifting her so he could study her. Sarah responded to the movement with a soft sleepy sigh, but didn't wake.

God, she was beautiful. To wake up next to her every day would be worth any price he had to pay. If she married him, he would have that privilege without paying a thing. He would have the right to look at and touch her, to kiss her, to

claim her in public as his own. And he would have the right
to love her, like last night.

The thought of their lovemaking flowed through him like
a sweet dream, spreading warmth to every part of his body.
He felt his sex stir with faint longing and gave a heavy sigh.
He couldn't wake her after a long, restless night simply to
start again. She had to be tired...although she certainly
didn't look it. In fact, he thought curiously, she looked more
rested, more relaxed, than he'd ever seen her. Even in sleep,
a smile touched her lips, turning the corners up. He wondered if she was dreaming, and if the dream included him,
then chided himself for such thoughts.

Sarah opened her eyes to narrow slits, saw the broad ex-
panse of tanned chest in front of her, closed them again and
smiled. Her sleep-filled mind hadn't deceived her, after all.
She *was* in Daniel's bed, snuggled up close to the naked hard
length of his body— Her mind drew up short, and her leg
shifted to investigate. Yes, definitely hard. Incredibly hard.

"Are you asleep? Or just pretending?" he asked gruffly,
sensing a change in her.

Her smile grew broader and brighter as she opened her
eyes to the sight of his face. "Good morning." Sliding
higher in the bed, she pressed a kiss to his chin. The heavy
growth of beard was rough and raspy and made him look
wicked, she thought and decided immediately that she liked
it.

Good morning. The simple greeting took on new meaning for Daniel today. It *was* a good morning, for no reason
other than that it followed last night. He softly, awkwardly, repeated it to her.

"Daniel..." Sarah rose to her knees, taking the covers
with her. She pushed him back, and he let her, mostly to see
what she would do. There were a lot of ways to make love,
and he was willing to learn every one.

She nudged his legs apart and knelt between them. She
was in an excellent position to study him, and she did so
slowly, leisurely, taking in every long muscle, every strong
and perfectly proportioned part of him, including— The
sound of a cry next door interrupted her concentration.

"Does Katie usually get up this early?" she asked, disappointment clear in her voice.

Before she'd finished the question, Daniel was on his feet, pulling on the jeans he'd discarded the night before. "She never wakes up this early, and she never cries when she does wake up," he said grimly, fastening the row of metal buttons.

Sarah watched him leave the room, then ventured from the bed herself. The air was cold, raising chill bumps all over her body before she reached her goal, Daniel's flannel shirt. She shivered into it and buttoned it, folded back the sleeves until her hands were exposed, then set about rebuilding the fire while she waited for him to return.

When he came back, he brought the baby and a thermometer. He left the door open, and Sarah felt the heat filtering in. He deliberately kept his room cold, she realized, but the rest of the house was warm for Katie.

She watched from the fireplace as he sat down on the bed and removed Katie's pajamas and her diaper. She should join them, she thought, swallowing hard. A good mother would be as concerned as Daniel, would want to help care for her baby, her little voice taunted. A good mother wouldn't stand all the way across the room, doing nothing.

But if she went closer—close enough to see Katie's face, to feel her skin—she might see that something was wrong, that her daughter was sick, and the fear that held her across the room might overwhelm her. The social worker at the hospital had warned her more than a year ago that one of the consequences of Tony's illness would be an overreaction to any illness, no matter how minor, in Katie, but Sarah had never had to deal with it. In the three months that she had lived with her, Katie had been perfectly healthy. Now...

The thermometer confirmed Daniel's suspicion. "She has a fever. Will you change her diaper while I get the Tylenol?"

Sarah forced herself across to the bed, climbing onto the mattress next to Katie. "Hi, sweetie," she whispered, bending to brush her lips over the girl's forehead. It *was* hot, she admitted. But kids got fevers—colds, teething, an upset stomach—practically anything could cause a fever. It didn't mean it was serious. Dear God, it couldn't be serious.

Katie didn't even smile for her. It was obvious that she felt ill, even to Sarah, who didn't want to believe it. After coughing a few times, she simply lay where Daniel had left her, staring at the soft blue flannel of her father's shirt, not caring about the woman who wore it.

Sarah changed the diaper quickly, expertly re-dressed her in the fuzzy pink pajamas, then picked her up, cradling her in her lap. Katie remained there until Daniel returned and gave her the prescribed number of drops of medicine, then she immediately reached for him. This time Sarah *did* feel a twinge of dismay. A little girl should want her mother when she was sick, not her father. But this little girl didn't even understand the concept of mother. As far as *she* was concerned, "Mama" was just another name, like Katie or Zachary or Teddy. All she really understood was Daddy.

"Dr. Hamilton's office opens at eight," Daniel said, holding Katie to his shoulder. "If we get ready now, we'll be there right on time."

Sarah uneasily edged farther back on the bed. "Do you really think she needs to see the doctor? You haven't even given the medicine time to work." Was the look he gave her a little odd? she wondered, hoping it wasn't, knowing it was.

"Her temperature's a hundred and one, she has a cough, and she's more than a little lethargic." There was a sharp edge to his voice, one that he tried to temper. "All you have to do is get dressed, Sarah. We can stop by your house on the way, and you can change or whatever, okay?"

She nodded reluctantly and slid off the bed. It took her only a few minutes to find her clothes, rumpled after a night on the floor, then she dressed and took Katie downstairs while Daniel got ready. When he came down, wearing fresh clothes and cleanly shaven, he got a rain slicker from the closet and wordlessly offered it to Sarah. Already tugging on his denim jacket, she shook her head. "Keep it for Katie."

He went outside to warm the truck, then came back for them. Carrying Katie, the slicker draped over her, he also held Sarah's arm, guiding her across the slippery ground.

It hadn't taken long enough to get to her house, she thought. Daniel pulled into the driveway before she'd found an excuse for not going into town with them. She paused for a moment, looking at him over Katie's head, wondering if she could blurt out her fear and escape without explanations, without emotional harm. She knew she couldn't. "It'll just take me a few minutes," she murmured as she opened the door.

She wasn't afraid for Katie, she told herself, sprinting through the rain to the porch. She was certain it was just a cold or maybe the flu, something the doctor could easily treat. She was afraid for herself. Afraid of the memories that taking a sick child to the doctor would bring back. Afraid of the way she would handle them on this dreary, rainy day. Afraid she would break down and tell Daniel everything, and he...

Her house was even colder than Daniel's bedroom had been. She stripped off her clothes in exchange for clean ones, brushed her teeth, washed her face, combed her hair. She paused only briefly to meet her own eyes in the mirror. Had last night changed anything? Now that they were lovers, how would Daniel react to her story about Tony and why she'd sent Katie away? Would he temper his disgust or lessen his blame because they'd become intimate again? Or had last night been strictly physical, not touching his emotions at all?

There were no answers in her eyes and no time to find them elsewhere. Pulling his jacket on again, she got her purse and left the house.

Sarah was as quiet as Katie on the way into town, Daniel noticed. Was she concerned about their daughter's illness? Annoyed because he hadn't asked her opinion? Hurt because Katie had turned to him for comfort instead of her? He didn't know. And right now, he admitted frankly, he didn't care. Those were things he could worry about later, after Katie had been taken care of.

Dr. Hamilton's office was in the front portion of a lovely old Victorian house two blocks off the main street. Sarah assumed that he and his family lived in the rest of the house. At the click of Katie's seat belt coming undone, she turned to look at Daniel. "I'm not going in."

He stopped and stared. "What?"

"I'm not going in with you."

"Your daughter is sick. Don't you even care?" The edge was back, but this time he made no effort to soften it.

"Of course I care." She was struggling to keep her voice under control, to stop the telltale wavering that meant tears would soon follow. "She needs you and the doctor. Not me. I . . . uh, thought I would make a phone call, then meet you back here."

His eyes were hard and unforgiving as he stared at her. "Damn it, Sarah, you're her *mother*."

The way he said the last word made her go cold all the way through. She'd heard that particular inflection before. *How could you give her away? You're her mother. A mother would find some way to keep her baby, no matter what it cost. What kind of mother are you, anyway?*

She didn't have many defenses against him, but she mustered the few she possessed and turned a cool, distant look on him. "Take her inside, Daniel. I'll be here when you're done."

He lifted Katie out, then slammed the door with such force that the truck rocked. Sarah watched until they were inside the house, then tucked some change into her pocket and slipped from the truck.

It was two and a half blocks through the rain to the nearest pay phone, and it was just that—a phone, no booth. Sarah dropped in some change and dialed Beth's number.

"Are you all right?" her friend demanded after a moment. "You sound awful."

"I'm fine," Sarah lied.

"Come on, is that place finally getting to you? I couldn't stand living in such a tiny, boring little town. Or is it *him*? Has he driven you crazy yet? I honestly can't imagine what it was you saw in him two years ago. I mean, I realize that things were tough for you and you were lonely, but—"

The wind changed direction, and so did Sarah, seeking a position where the rain would hit her back. "I like Sweetwater," she said, softly interrupting her friend. "And I love Daniel."

She had known her revelation would slow Beth down, but she hadn't expected these long moments of complete silence. She kept waiting for some response, then finally prompted, "Beth?"

"Sorry," came the dry rejoinder. "I was just trying to imagine—as big as he is, and as scrawny as you are—how in the world the two of you manage to—"

Sarah interrupted. "We manage very well, thanks."

"Then you've told him about Tony." The lawyer couldn't see the hard, cold man she'd met a few weeks ago in Zachary Adams's office conveniently forgetting his opinion of Sarah as a mother who had given away her child. Only a full explanation of the reasons would satisfy him.

"No."

Beth was silent again. "Well then, you're *going* to tell him about Tony, right? I mean, the guy's got a right to know—after all, it affected him, too. You can't expect him to build a life with you without knowing about something as important as your son's death."

Sarah's sign was long and heavy. "I said that *I* love *him.* I never said anything about how he feels about me."

Even without her voice breaking at the end, Beth would have recognized the tears. They'd been through too much together in the past three years for her to miss them. "Oh, Sarah," she sighed. "The man is nothing but trouble. Come home and forget about him for the next ten days. Then we'll go get Katie together, and you won't ever have to see him again."

"I can't do that," she whispered. "Beth, I can't,"

Her friend sighed again. "Is there anything I can do, like maybe talk some sense into the idiot?"

The suggestion brought a reluctant smile to Sarah's face. If anyone could talk sense into Daniel, it certainly wouldn't be Beth. To say that they hadn't hit it off was like saying the South was a little warm in July. "Will you be here on the first?"

"We have an appointment with Ryan in Zachary Adams's office at one o'clock. How about if I come early and take you to lunch first?"

"That sounds fine. Beth?"

"Yeah, Sarah?"

"You're the best friend I have—"

Uncomfortable with emotional displays, Beth interrupted with a flippant response. "The only one right now, kid. You're in enemy territory there."

"You've done a lot for me and Tony and Katie, even though we'll be old and gray before I can pay you." She rubbed her hand over her wet cheeks. Beth had always insisted that she wanted no money, but Sarah had been equally insistent about paying her...someday. "Anyway..." She swallowed past the lump in her throat. "I love you, too. I'll see you next week." She hung up quickly, before her friend could respond with a joke, and headed back toward the doctor's house.

Daniel and Katie were waiting in the truck. Dr. Hamilton had seen her immediately, had made a quick exam and taken a chest X ray, then given Daniel a prescription for antibiotics. The whole visit had taken less than fifteen minutes. Fifteen minutes that Sarah hadn't been willing to give them.

Her behavior bewildered him. He knew she loved Katie every bit as much as he did, but she certainly hadn't shown it this morning. Would it have cost her so much to go in, meet the doctor and hold Katie's hand through the exam, as he had done?

There was an annoying niggling at the back of his mind, something he needed to remember, something to do with Sarah and doctors... Before he could bring it to mind, though, he saw her walking along the sidewalk, head ducked, drenched by the rain, and whatever anger he had left faded. She looked so sad. Lost. There were questions he needed to ask, answers he needed to hear, but they could wait. When they were home and Katie was resting, when Sarah was dry and warm—then, he promised himself, they would talk. He tucked Katie's blanket over her, then got out of the truck, unmindful of the rain, and met Sarah on the other side.

Sarah wondered why he'd gotten out in this miserable weather to meet her. So Katie wouldn't witness his anger? She raised her head slowly, feeling the sting of the rain-drops, and looked into his face, expecting to see cold, harsh derision. Instead there was a mix of expressions—bewilderment, curiosity, concern. When he opened his arms, she walked right into them, pressing her face against his chest. She knew the demand for explanations would come later, but for now, she gratefully accepted his offer of comfort.

"Are you okay now?" he asked, bending his head so his mouth was near her ear.

Nodding, she looked up into his face, blinking away the sting of the rain. "Daniel, I'm sor—"

Before the word was out, he'd stopped it with his mouth, kissing it away gently, sweetly, tenderly. When he lifted his head, his eyes, grave and solemn, met hers. "I need to go to the drugstore; then we'll go home, all right?"

She nodded once. Home. That was where she wanted to be.

Forty minutes later they were back at the house. Daniel shrugged out of his coat, shifting Katie with his movements, then draped it over the coatrack. "Go upstairs to the bedroom and find something dry to wear," he told Sarah. "I'll put Katie to bed. Then we can talk."

She agreed and led the way upstairs. In his room she added another log to the fire, then removed her wet clothes, leaving them on the stone hearth while she dried herself. In his closet she found a soft gold-plaid flannel shirt that she put on; then, with the quilt from the bed, she curled up in the single chair near the fireplace, taking advantage of the quiet time to look around the room.

Like Daniel, the furniture was massive and solid. The four-poster bed, the dresser, the chest and the chair were solid pine, made with his own hands—she recognized the workmanship. The cushions where she sat were pale blue and white, and the quilt she'd taken from the bed was navy blue with small splashes of the same colors. There were windows on two walls, and the stone fireplace filled half of the third. The mantel above it was filled with photographs.

Sarah tugged the quilt closer while she studied the pictures. They were in no special order, just a random chronicle of Katie's life, from the time she had come to live with Daniel until recently. Katie, so tiny and sweet, sleeping peacefully beside her Raggedy Ann. Smiling to show off her two new teeth. Dressed in red velvet and white lace, unimpressed by the Christmas gifts around her but smiling for her father anyway. Asleep, laughing, smiling, pouting, playing, loving. Now Sarah knew why there were no photos of their daughter in the living room. Daniel kept them here, where he could see them at night before sleeping and first thing in the morning after waking.

He came into the room, drying his hair with a towel. He had already discarded his shirt in the bathroom; now he needed dry jeans. He changed quickly, then added the damp jeans to her pile of clothes. She looked startled by his appearance, he noticed, as if she were still engrossed in the different faces of their daughter.

Lifting her up, he sat in the chair, then settled her across his lap, pulling her head to his chest. "You didn't get a chance to see the pictures last night, did you?" he asked, his voice a comforting rumble deep in his chest.

"My attention was on something else." She rubbed her cheek over the rain-cooled skin of his chest, then hesitantly asked, "How is Katie?"

"She'll sleep for a while. It's just a cold, Dr. Hamilton said." He thought for an instant of the memory of Sarah and a doctor, but let it slide from his mind. There would be time for that later.

"Daniel?"

"Hmm." He brushed his lips over her hair. It tasted cold, damp, sweet.

"I'm not a bad mother."

Daniel's arms tightened around her. She made the claim quietly, wearily, as if she'd had to defend it too many times in the past. As if she didn't expect to be believed. As if she sometimes didn't believe herself. "I know."

"It wasn't easy sending Katie away. I used to have nightmares that you wouldn't give her back when it was time, or that she would never forgive me."

He sat still and stiff beneath her. He reminded himself that he *wasn't* going to keep Katie from her—he was going to unite them as a family—so there was no reason for the guilt. There was curiosity mixed in, too, and hopefulness. Was she finally going to trust him with her past?

"I wasn't even sure that you would want her," she continued, her voice soft, her gaze distant. "But I remembered how you'd looked when you talked about wanting children. As if babies were special, a gift to be treasured. And I knew that you would be a gentle, loving father."

He stroked her hair, still damp but drying into honey-gold wisps. "Why did you do it, Sarah?" he whispered. "You love her. You're her mother. Why did you send her away?"

Behind his words, she heard the echo of this morning's angry, condemning taunt. *Damn it, Sarah, you're her mother.* "I did what I had to do," she said with a sigh. "Nothing can change it. Nothing can make it right...or wrong." She moved, pushing the quilt back. With the fire burning brightly, the room was warm. With Daniel's body next to hers, *she* was warm.

Daniel accepted that she wasn't going to give him any answers this morning. It was enough to know that, whatever her reasons, sending Katie to live with him had cost her dearly.

They sat for long moments, enveloped in silence—warm, close, comforting silence, like the heat from the fire, the heat from their bodies. He held her and stroked wherever his hands happened to rest—her hair, her arm, her hip. Eventually, after what seemed like a lifetime to Sarah, his hand moved gently, hesitantly, beneath the gold-plaid shirt.

The muscles in her belly rippled and grew taut as he rubbed his hand across it. Although he couldn't feel them now, last night he'd traced the thin faint pregnancy lines that marked her skin. How had she looked pregnant, he wondered, with her belly big and rounded with his baby? Had her breasts gotten full and swollen with milk? Had she suffered from morning sickness, backaches and swollen ankles? Had she had anyone to turn to for help? The next time would be different, he vowed. He would be with her, would help her, would take care of her. The next time she would have *him*.

Her midriff was as smooth as silk and just as warm. Although she'd gained a few pounds in the past couple of weeks, she was still too thin. He could feel her ribs, too prominent beneath her skin. But he had no complaints about her breasts. They were small, soft, sweet, perfect.

"Sarah . . . about last night . . ."

Her eyes were shut, her breathing uneven. When his thumb and forefinger closed around her nipple, she stopped breathing completely for a moment, then dragged in a harsh, sweet breath. "Don't regret it, Daniel," she whispered.

"I don't. But . . ." He slid his hand back to her belly, stretching his fingers from one jutting hipbone on the left to its mate on the right. "You're not taking birth control pills, are you?" It was a meaningless question, one he already knew the answer to.

"No." She was stunned by how completely she'd overlooked the risk of pregnancy—not wise for a thirty-one-year-old woman whose two pregnancies had both been unplanned.

"While I was in the drugstore, I—" His face was flushed a dull red. It wasn't an easy subject to discuss under the best of circumstances, but doing it after the fact made it even harder. "But it might be too late."

She opened her eyes then and looked directly into his. "What would you do if it was too late?"

He answered without hesitation, without qualification. "I'd take care of you." After a moment he asked uncertainly, "What would *you* do?"

Sarah began unbuttoning the shirt she wore and guided his hand back to her breast. "I would force you to marry me," she said with a fierceness that added weight to her threat. "It couldn't be helped that Katie was born illegitimate, but it won't happen again, Daniel."

He looked vaguely annoyed as he stroked her breast. "I just *said* I would do that, so you couldn't 'force' me."

"You said—"

"I said that I would take care of you. That means marriage."

She shook her head. The sensations his big rough fingers were sending through her were making it hard to speak, hard to think clearly. "To some men that means living together...or helping to support the baby...or paying for an abortion..."

He lifted her so that his mouth could make contact with her straining nipple. He nipped at it, bathed it with his tongue, sucked it greedily. "I'm not most men," he reminded her when he laid her on his lap again. There, warm against her bare thigh, she could feel the hard, thick length of his desire straining against the confining jeans.

"Daniel?"

"Hmm." He moved his hand to her other breast while his mouth nuzzled wisps of hair away from her ear. His soft response shivered through her, and she turned her head, trying to capture his mouth even as she spoke. "I want you, Daniel. I want you inside me. I want you to love me like you did last night and never stop."

"Yes." That was what he wanted, too. To never stop.

They moved to the bed, removing his clothes along the way. She wore his shirt, the buttons loose to allow him intimate access. While he took care of protection, she teased and tormented him with her hands and her mouth, making him feel her need, making him taste his own need, and when he took her, it was sudden, rough, demanding, yet curiously gentle. In spite of the ferocity of his need, in spite of her writhing, driving pleas, he never hurt her. He pushed her to the limit, but never crossed the line. Just further proof,

Sarah thought in the quiet aftermath, of what an incredibly special man she'd found.

"Do you have to work this afternoon?" she asked when he turned away to check the time. Idly she traced her fingertip down the smooth curve of his spine, over taut skin and powerful muscle.

Daniel lay down again and mimicked her actions, his finger gliding over her skin, leaving a heated trail behind. "That depends."

She was too sated to respond even when he reached the soft golden curls at her thighs. "On Katie?"

"And you."

"What about me?"

He nudged her leg aside, bending her knee. He lifted her other leg and trapped it between his thighs. The position left her completely vulnerable to him. "Do you want to take care of Katie?"

"Sure." She shivered when his hand returned to touch her. His finger glided through the curls, relaxing her; then, without warning, he stroked the most sensitive part of her, heated and swollen, and made her gasp.

"Or would you rather split the baby sitting with me—" he stroked again, this time dipping inside her and ending on the sensitive nub of flesh "—and spend the rest of the day taking care of me?"

She couldn't answer. Her body was throbbing from too much stimulation, yet not enough. She was mindless, aching, hungry for release from this lovely new pain, but not certain she could survive it. Her fingers twisted into the jumble of covers beneath them, and her hips arched in silent pleading. Then the view behind her tightly closed eyes turned purple, navy, black, until it exploded, accompanied by a drawn-out helpless whimper, into a bright, blinding display of colors.

Daniel watched the shudders that racked her body, then the smile of lazy satisfaction that came to her lips. He could grow addicted to it, he thought—to this power to make her cry and plead, to make her writhe, to satisfy her pleas. To satisfy her need. To fill her body and her heart and her soul until there would never be a place for another man as long as she lived.

As he watched, her smile changed from satisfaction to threat. "You'll pay for that," she whispered, her voice husky and promising. "When I find the strength . . . you'll pay."

October 24

Tomorrow would be the twenty-fifth, the day the private detective's report on Sarah was due. Daniel had told Zachary that he would drive into town on Thursday or Friday to meet with him, but he was dreading it. Soon he would know the past that Sarah had deliberately kept hidden from him. Soon he would find out from a stranger all the things that she didn't want him to know. It was wrong...but as long as she refused to tell him herself, as long as she refused to trust him, it was his only choice. Still, it was wrong.

Maybe today she would talk to him. Maybe if he asked the right questions...if he even knew what they were.

"You look like you're a million miles away," Sarah remarked.

He looked up and saw that she was watching him from across the worktable. The sleeves of her pale blue sweatshirt were pushed up to her elbows, and she was sanding the narrow bar of wood that he'd given her, occasionally running her hand over it the way she'd seen him do. Her hair was disheveled, her clothes coated with fine dust, but she was beautiful. And he wanted her.

Not just physically, although that need was still there. They'd spent all of Monday and most of Tuesday in bed, and she'd slept beside him each of the past three nights. There was still hunger, but its edges weren't so sharp now. No, he needed more than the feel of her small delicate body beneath his, joined with his. He needed to see her smile, to hear her laugh, to watch her with Katie. He needed to talk to her, to work with her, to spend the quiet evenings beside her. He needed to know that she would be with him today, next week, next month, next year.

His frown grew dark and fierce. What he was describing was love, and he was *not*, God help him, going to love her. Not yet. She had too many secrets, too many mysteries. He would offer her friendship. He would take care of her. He would care for her. But until all his questions were answered, until he was satisfied with her answers, he wouldn't let himself love her.

Sarah suspected from his stony expression and long silence what he was thinking, and she dreaded it. She didn't want to fight with him, she never wanted to, but when he finally spoke, his voice low and dark and rumbly, she knew they would.

"Why did you give Katie away?"

"Daniel—"

"Why did you do it? Didn't you care about her? Didn't you love her?"

"Of course I did, but—"

"Then why in God's name did you send her away? You were her mother! A baby needs her mother! A baby deserves a good mother!"

Sarah turned her back to him and stared out the window. It was still rainy and dreary and cold. With Daniel's last words, she was starting to feel that way inside.

Maybe it was time to tell him everything. Maybe, by some miracle, he would understand that she'd done what was best for everyone. Maybe he would see that sending Katie away had broken her heart. Or maybe he would continue to believe that no good mother would ever give up her daughter.

Maybe he would continue to judge her. Maybe *he* would break her heart all over again.

When she turned to look at him again, Daniel knew that she'd thrown up another wall against him. Frustration made his hands tighten around the length of wood he held until he thought it would snap.

"You have no right to judge me, Daniel. You don't know what my life was like—"

"And whose fault is that?" he interrupted. "How many times have I asked for an explanation?"

"None. You demand, Daniel, you don't ask. You demand to know why I was such a horrible mother to your daughter, but you don't want to know the truth. You just want something to support what you already believe."

"That's not true."

"Yes, it is. The day Katie came to live with you, you tried and condemned me, and nothing that's happened since then makes any difference."

"No—"

"Yes! Have you ever once considered the possibility that I had no choice in what I did? Has it ever occurred to you that giving her away affected me more than anyone, that it hurt me more than anyone? Have you even once thought that I could give her up and still be a good mother?"

Daniel stared guiltily at his hands, but he didn't relent. "I need to know."

"Why? Is your conscience bothering you for sleeping with me? Of course, the first time you didn't know what kind of woman I am, but this time you do know, and you want me anyway. Does that disgust you, Daniel? Does that offend your precious honor?"

"Stop it, Sarah," he muttered, rising to his feet.

"It's all right, Daniel," she continued recklessly, tears glittering in her eyes. "Men are attracted to women like me all the time. It's part of our allure—that we're not respectable, we're not good enough, that we're nothing but tr—"

"Shut up!" His voice was an angry crack of thunder that, across the room, stirred the sleepy quiet around Katie and made her whimper. Pushing the stool aside, he started to-

ward the door. He had to get out. He couldn't stay here and
listen to her talk that way, couldn't hear her say such things
about herself and know that, because of him, she believed
them.

Sarah waited until he'd pulled his coat on and jerked the
door open before she spoke again. "You want to hear the
best part. Daniel?" she asked sadly. "I love you anyway,
knowing that you think I'm an awful mother and an awful
person. Knowing that you think you deserve someone better, knowing that you sleep with me only because I'm available and easy... I still love you."

He stopped suddenly, his fingers tightening around the
cold metal knob, her words whispering around him. *I still
love you.* He had waited all his life to hear those words, and
for a moment he felt nothing but joy—sweet, warm, comforting. It smoothed the rough edges of his anger, and for
just a moment, it let him believe. After years of being as
alone as a man could be, now he had Sarah. Now he had her
love.

He turned back into the room and slammed the door.
Disturbed by the noise, Katie lifted her head and looked
around, frowning sourly at Sarah for bothering her nap,
then went right back to sleep.

Daniel advanced on Sarah, grasped a handful of dust-
covered sweatshirt and jerked her close. Her cry was swallowed by his mouth as he kissed her with all the passion and
anger and sorrow and joy he felt at that moment. "You're
wrong," he muttered, brushing his lips over hers. "I don't
think you're awful..." He nipped at her bottom lip. "And
I don't think I deserve someone better than you...." He
kissed her again, swiftly, hungrily. "And I make love with
you because the need for you has crawled inside my soul...."
He raised his head a few inches and stared into her eyes.
"And you don't love me."

He was saying that he didn't want her love, Sarah
thought. Because he could never return it? So she could
blame it on the argument and her emotional state, and they
would both pretend that the declaration had never been
made? It was an easy way out—a few moments' discom-

fort, then it was over. But she wasn't taking it. "I do love you, Daniel. If you don't want me to say it, I won't. But not saying it won't change the way I feel."

He felt what that polite little speech cost her pride, knew the deeper price she would pay if he asked her not to mention her love. He raised his hand to her face, stroking her soft skin. "Sarah..." There was nothing he could say. He couldn't accept her love, nor could he reject it. Either one could break her heart...and maybe his. Gently he pulled her close.

He held her for a long time. It was the way he solved his problems, Sarah realized. He apologized with kisses. He smoothed away arguments with embraces. He was a physical man, and he relied on physical means to express what he was feeling. It made him a hard man to read, but she could learn, if he gave her a chance.

Daniel pushed her back and brushed his fingers through her hair. "Why don't you take Katie to the house and get lunch?" he asked gruffly. "I'll be up in a while."

"But she's not—" Sarah glanced over her shoulder to see Katie standing in the playpen, her arms filled with dolls, and watching her parents with a grin. "All right."

He didn't release her immediately. "Sarah...thank you." For Katie. For herself. For her love. He couldn't give her love in return, not yet, not until he knew the whole story of what she had done, but for the first time in his life, however briefly, he'd had the pleasure of hearing those words.

She lifted Katie out of the playpen. "What time do you want lunch?" she asked as she dressed the child in her jacket and knit cap.

"Give me half an hour," Daniel said with a glance at the clock on the wall. That would be long enough to think about this morning's discussion. It would also be about as long as he could stand being away from them.

"Bye, Daddy," Katie called from Sarah's shoulder as they stepped outside.

He watched them go before he started cleaning the workshop. Ordinarily it was a job he saved for the end of the week, but he needed something to occupy his hands, something that didn't require the full concentration of his mind.

I do love you, Daniel.

Was it true? Who knew but Sarah? He certainly didn't. He didn't even know if he wanted to believe it. Then he scoffed at that. He'd waited all his life for someone to love him. Now that Sarah was trying, instead of accepting it gratefully, he was doubting her sincerity, trying to convince both her and himself that she didn't really mean what she'd said.

She had accused him of judging her, and she'd been right. She had accused him of condemning her when he knew nothing about her life, and she'd been right about that, too. Under the circumstances, he ought to be more than grateful that she thought she loved him, he thought wryly. He ought to get down on his knees and thank God—because everything was working out the way he'd planned.

His actions slowed as the full implication of Sarah's love sank in. His plans for marriage were virtually assured now. If Sarah loved him, she would almost certainly agree to marry him. That would mean they would be a family, that he could take care of her, that Katie would be with him always. It would mean a new life for him, filled with people who loved and needed and depended on him.

And it would mean using Sarah's love to accomplish his goals, twisting it, taking advantage of it, so he could have what he wanted.

No, it wasn't like that, he argued silently, guiltily. Marriage would be good for her, too—*he* would be good for her. It was the only solution to their situation, and it was one that would benefit both of them—all *three* of them. Sarah would be happy as his wife. He would spend the rest of his life making sure of that.

He swept the dust and wood shavings into a corner, leaned the broom against the wall and started toward the door. Only fifteen of his allotted thirty minutes had passed, but that was long enough. He was going inside. To his family.

* * *

The rain ended after dinner, after Katie was in bed and the kitchen was cleaned, after the lights were turned low and the fireplace stoked. The absence of the drops pelting the roof and the windows created a sudden silence that made Sarah sit straighter to listen. "The rain has finally stopped. I was beginning to think it never would." Sighing softly, she settled in once more, leaning against Daniel's chest, the top of her head providing a place for his chin to rest. His arms were draped loosely around her, his hands clasped on her belly.

He gazed at the fire, watching it sizzle and flare. His feet, in thick white socks, were stretched toward the hearth, absorbing the heat from the flames. He felt lazy and comfortable until Sarah spoke again.

"I need to go into town tomorrow."

"Why?" He had planned to ask her to take care of Katie while he went to Zachary's office. He had planned to lie to her, to tell her that he needed supplies. He didn't want her to know that he was meeting his lawyer. He especially didn't want her to know that it was about *her*.

"It's only a week until the end of the month, and I haven't made any plans. Remember, I told you I have to look for a job and a place to live." She should have done it days ago, but she hadn't been able to motivate herself. As long as Daniel welcomed her into his life, she could pretend that everything would work out, that maybe once in her life there would be a happily-ever-after. She had been living in dreams, not facing reality. She'd done that for a while with Tony—had pretended that there would be a cure, a miracle, a transplant, or that the whole thing was simply a mistake and her son wasn't sick after all. Finally she'd been forced to face the facts: he *was* sick; there *were* no miracles; and, for him at least, there *was* no transplant. No donor. No chance.

It was once again time to face facts. She had enough money to last a few more weeks, another month at most. She had to find a job. She had to find a place to live. Maybe Daniel would still welcome her once she and Katie had moved out; maybe someday he would even learn to love her, but those were dreams for the future. She had to live in the present.

"Can't it wait until next week?" By then the lies would be over—the private detective's report read and filed away, the plans to sue for custody of Katie forgotten, and the guilt dealt with. By then he would have asked her to marry him, and she would have no need to find a job or a place to live.

Sarah laughed softly. "You've never looked for a job in the real world, have you Daniel? If I'm lucky, I'll get something right away that will at least support us, while I look for a teaching job."

"Money's no problem."

Again she laughed. "Maybe for you, it isn't, but most folks live paycheck to paycheck—and it's been a month since my last one."

"I'll support Katie, and you, too."

"No," she said firmly. "I'll appreciate your help with Katie, but you're not responsible for me, Daniel."

He was trying to be—couldn't she see that? he thought in frustration. But how could she, when he'd given her no hint of his plans for their future? The only time they had talked about marriage to each other, pregnancy had been one of the conditions. He wanted to marry her whether or not she was pregnant, whether or not she loved him, whether *he* loved *her*. They were meant to be a family, the three of them and whatever children they had in the future.

He had eight more days to make her see that. He prayed it would be enough.

October 25

As usual, Daniel was awake long before Sarah on Thursday morning. He left the bed long enough to open the door so the room would get warm for her; then he returned to lie beside her, his arms holding her close.

Every night she made love with him with unbelievable passion, and every morning she looked so tiny and fragile in his arms. He wondered what magic kept him from hurting her physically and wished it could protect her against emotional hurts, too. He had hurt her yesterday in the workshop—had made her cry, had made her say terrible things about herself. But last night she had come to him anyway, had loved him as fiercely, as sweetly, as she had every night before. Because she had forgiven him. Because she loved him.

But what would happen if the day came when she couldn't forgive him, when she stopped loving him? What would his life be like without Sarah? Cold. Grim. Bleak. Like it had been before, only worse. Then he'd had only his dream of what a woman's love could be like. Missing something he'd never had couldn't begin to compare to missing something he'd had and lost.

He wouldn't lose her, he vowed fiercely. He would be the best husband, the best father, the best friend any woman could ever want. He would give her everything she ever wanted, would *be* everything she'd ever wanted, and she would stay with him for as long as he needed her. For forever.

When he hugged her tightly, Sarah stirred, then woke. "What time is it?" she asked sleepily.

"A little after seven."

She snuggled closer to his warmth, rubbing her cheek against his chest. "Is the sun shining?"

"Yes."

"Is Katie still asleep?"

"I guess."

"Good." She laid her hand on his side, sliding it back and forth. She loved touching him. His skin was warm, stretched taut over powerful muscles and as flawless as a piece of fine wood after endless sanding and smoothing. She also loved his responses to her touch. Sometimes, like now, he relaxed, giving himself over to the soothing sensations. Other times, when she used just the tips of her fingers in a barely-there caress, his muscles twitched reflexively, and his skin rippled with chill bumps. Always he responded by becoming aroused, sometimes swiftly, sometimes slowly, but always thoroughly, hard, throbbing. Always satisfying.

"Does Sweetwater have a newspaper?" she asked, rubbing the hard curve of his spine. When her hand reached his neck, she felt the tension there and began massaging it away.

"A weekly. It comes out every Wednesday."

"You don't mind my going into town, do you?" After all, she had taken over most of Katie's care, along with fixing lunch and even occasionally helping him in the workshop.

It took him a long time to answer. Too long. "No... I don't mind." He wouldn't stand in her way by asking her to wait. The only excuse he could give would be his own errand, his meeting with Zachary, and that could wait until tomorrow. "When do you want to leave?"

"I guess about nine. I'd better go to the house and get ready—"

"You can get ready here. Tell me what you need, and I'll get it while you're in the shower."

She started to argue but decided it wasn't worth the effort. Besides, the idea of getting bathed and dressed in the ice-cold farmhouse didn't sound very appealing at this time of the morning. She told him what to get, then started to burrow close again, but he was already sitting up. "Maybe it could wait a little while," she suggested, drawing her hand down his back to his hip.

He sat still for a moment, considering it, then lay down once again. Rolling onto his side, he studied her for a long time before touching her, his hand flattening itself over her belly. "You're pretty." It wasn't a compliment as much as a simple statement of fact. There was such a sweet, innocent beauty in her face, her body, her soul. If she was the kind of woman who could selfishly give up her own child, wouldn't it somehow show? Wouldn't it leave a mark that would destroy the sweetness, the innocence, the beauty?

Sarah's gaze held his. If she returned the compliment and told him he was handsome, he wouldn't believe her, and in the literal sense of the word, it wasn't true. He looked hard and rough and rugged, but not handsome. Still, she found more beauty in the lines a hard, lonely life had etched into his face than she could ever see in a typically handsome man like Zachary Adams or Brent Lawson.

"I like waking up with you." He moved his hand slowly until it was underneath her breast, his fingers following the curve of the small mound. "I've never had this kind of relationship with a woman before. If I ever gave it any thought, I guess I knew the nights would be special... but I didn't know the mornings would be, too."

"I like waking up with you, too."

His grin was quick and a little uneasy before it faded.

She lifted her hand until her palm cupped his beard-roughened cheek. "I do like it." She rubbed her hand back and forth. "I like it a lot."

He caught the tip of her stroking finger between his teeth and bathed it sensuously with his tongue. When he finally released it, he touched his mouth to hers.

Sarah wrapped her arms around his, pulling until his body was warm and hard over the length of hers. As she shifted her hips to accommodate him, as he found his place, heated and welcoming inside her, she whispered in his ear, "I *love* waking up with you, Daniel."

Katie was annoyed at being ignored by her parents. By the time Daniel, dressed in hastily buttoned jeans, lifted her from the crib, she was in the middle of a full-fledged temper tantrum.

"Ignore her," Sarah advised when he came back to his room carrying Katie. She waited until he'd set the baby on the rug before wrapping her arms around him. "She's spoiled rotten, you know."

"I don't think so," he said stiffly, his blue eyes made darker by their frown.

Sarah laughed softly. "You look like a mother bear whose cubs are in danger. I'm not criticizing you or her. I'm just saying that she's so good-natured because she always gets what she wants when she wants it. She has two full-grown adults who jump when she cries. When she sees that screaming isn't getting her what she wants—namely your attention—she'll shut up and try some other method."

It was less than five minutes before Daniel felt a tug on his pants leg. Smiling in spite of her red-rimmed eyes, Katie lifted her arms. Nestled in his arms between him and Sarah, she was as happy as could be. She gave him a kiss, offered her mother one, too, then demanded in her sweetest voice to *go.*

"She's not going to like your leaving without her," Daniel remarked, leaving her in Sarah's arms while he finished dressing.

"Well, she'll have to get used to it. Once I get a job..." Breaking off, she sat down on the floor and busied herself with removing Katie's pajamas. Once she had a job, they would be living elsewhere, and there would be no lazy mornings in bed with Daniel. Dear God, she was going to miss him! To not be able to share his bed or his meals, to touch him or to simply look at him—how could she give that up? But, unless he offered her something—marriage, an extended affair, *anything*—what choice did she have?

Daniel's hands had become still on his shirt. Now he finished buttoning it, tucked it into his jeans, then fastened his belt. "Once you get a job, what?" he asked guardedly.

"She'll have to get used to not always going along. She'll be going to a day-care center or a baby-sitter. I would really prefer a day-care center, so that she'll have a lot of other kids to play with. I really think she needs that kind of exposure. She's never really been around kids, but it's something she needs to do, so it'll be easier for her when she starts school, or when she has a younger brother or sister...." Once again her voice faded away.

Daniel slowly walked to the fireplace, stopping a few feet in front of them. All Sarah could see without raising her head were his bare feet and the creased denim of his jeans. "Are you planning to have another baby?" he asked, the sharp edges of his voice softened by caution.

She avoided looking at him. "I, uh..." She removed Katie's diaper and folded the sides together, neatly resticking the tapes. "Can we talk about this later, Daniel? I really need to get going."

"Sarah—"

"Later, please?" Without pausing, she rushed on. "Come on, Katie, let's get you dressed so I can take a shower and get myself ready. Don't forget my things from the farmhouse, Daniel."

With a flash of bare legs under her robe, she was up and gone, Katie toddling along at her side. Daniel remained where he was, staring at the place where she had been. Oh, they would talk about it later, all right. If she had any ideas at all about getting pregnant with another man's baby, she could be *damn* sure they would talk about it later.

The blue dress was fine wool, well made and came from one of Nashville's better stores, but none of that changed the fact that it was *plain*, Sarah thought woefully, studying herself in the bathroom mirror. On a day when she needed to cloak herself in confidence, all she had was this plain blue dress. She gave a sigh and straightened the thin matching belt at her waist. Well, it *was* all she had, so it had to do.

Daniel glanced up from his game with Katie when she came down the stairs. For a moment his expression was blank as he took in his first view of Sarah dressed the way she must have often looked for her husband—in expensive clothing, her hair sleekly combed, her battered tennis shoes replaced with low-heeled leather pumps that flattered her slender legs.

Then he smiled. "You *are* pretty."

It was a reaffirmation of what he'd told her earlier that morning—plain and simple and just what she needed to hear. "Thank you. Want to wish me luck?"

No. But he kept the word inside. "You'll find what you need." But not in town. Here, with him and Katie—that was all she would ever need. He would make sure of that.

He rose from the floor and helped Katie with her jacket. The only jacket Sarah had was his, he realized, and she certainly couldn't wear that with such a pretty dress. "Why don't you take my truck?" At least he could see that the cab was warm for her.

She gave a shake of her head. "My car's fine."

One raised eyebrow showed his opinion of that statement quite clearly. "Then wait here and let me go get it."

Her grin was quick and broad. "Your long legs probably wouldn't fit in my little car. I'll be fine, Daniel."

He wasn't convinced, but he let the subject drop. He took the denim jacket from the coatrack and draped it over her shoulders. "At least until you get to town," he insisted when she started to protest.

He drove her to the farmhouse and walked over to the small yellow car with her. It took several tries to start it, and Sarah saw his eyes roll upward just as the engine caught.

"I wish you'd take—"

She cut off his words. "I'll be back after lunch."

He started to speak, but just shook his head instead. "Do you need anything from town?"

"No." He ducked his head to kiss her. "Be careful."

"I will." She watched in the rearview mirror as he returned to the truck and climbed inside. He hadn't wished her good luck, she realized, not now and not even at the house when she'd asked him to. Maybe he didn't want her to find a job in Sweetwater. Maybe he wanted her to stay here with him. Then she smiled a little bit sadly. Or maybe he wanted her far away.

They had seven more days. Next Thursday would be the first, and she and Katie had to have someplace to go, some way to live. Seven more days, and what happened after that was Daniel's choice.

The small complex that housed the Sweetwater schools was Sarah's first stop, where she received directions to the administrator's office. Janet Hillier was a stern-looking gray-haired woman who reminded Sarah of a drill sergeant—always in control, tough but fair. She looked over the résumé Sarah had typed before leaving Nashville, then raised sharp blue eyes to give her the same thorough study. "You graduated from Tennessee State."

Sarah nodded.

"And you taught for six years."

Again she nodded.

"Why did you quit?"

She had been expecting this question, but she hadn't yet found the proper answer. She settled on the least innocuous. "Personal problems."

Mrs. Hillier wasn't impressed with the response. "I assume they've been resolved?" she asked dryly.

"Yes."

She read through the résumé again, then folded her hands on top of it. "We do have a teacher who will be quitting in early spring to have a baby. She teaches the fourth grade, but that would be no problem. However...may I be frank with you, Miss Lawson?"

Suspecting what was coming, Sarah managed only an uneasy nod.

"Sweetwater is a close community. Everyone knows everyone else's business." She paused for a moment. "It's also an old-fashioned community, Miss Lawson. We don't have the problems that schools in larger towns and cities have—the alcohol, the drugs, the bad behavior."

And the pregnancies—that was one the woman had left out. Sarah clenched her hands tightly together. If they didn't tolerate alcohol, drugs or pregnancies from their students, they certainly wouldn't tolerate any of the three from their teachers.

"Although your credentials are impeccable and your record shows the kind of stability we look for, frankly, Miss Lawson, I don't think I could get you approved by the board. The people here live by different standards than they do in the city. They have different values. That's largely why they live here—because they can raise their children in a wholesome, family-oriented environment."

"I see." Sarah's voice was cool and calm and the slightest bit unsteady. "And my daughter and I are short one member of the family to qualify."

"If Daniel lived elsewhere—"

Sarah bit back a bitter laugh. They really *did* know everyone else's business here.

"We could probably work something out. But he's a member of our own community. That makes a difference." Mrs. Hillier was silent for a moment, then she cautiously asked, "Is there any chance that you and Daniel will get married?"

Sarah got to her feet. "He doesn't want to get married," she replied honestly. "Thank you for your time, Mrs. Hillier."

"You might check over at the Baptist church," the older woman suggested. "They want to start a preschool program, and they're looking for someone to help with it."

"If the school won't have me," Sarah said with grim amusement, "the church certainly won't. But thanks, anyway."

"If anything changes..."

If Daniel married her. If she became respectable. The grimness moving into her eyes, Sarah murmured thanks once more, then left the office.

Back on Main Street, she picked up a copy of the newspaper and found a grand total of two help-wanted ads—one for the church, one specifying a man for the local feed and grain—along with one ad for a garage apartment for rent. Since it was her only other choice, why not see how a pastor justified rejecting her because of her illegitimate daughter? she decided.

He was very nice about it...and very adamant. "The church board made it clear that they want to hire either a mother or a single woman," he explained.

Sarah smiled wearily. "I fit on both counts, Reverend. I'm single, and I'm the mother of a fourteen-month-old girl."

"Well, yes, but—"

But she was an unmarried mother. She wasn't *respectable*.

She didn't waste any more of his time. At the first pay phone she came to, she called about the apartment and announced up front that she wasn't married and had a young daughter. The apartment was no longer available, the woman responded and hung up the phone.

After stuffing the newspaper in a trash bin, Sarah walked down the street until she reached the diner. It was still early for lunch, she acknowledged, but at least that meant she could eat in peace while she considered her next move.

The waitress gave her a long, critical look before slapping the menu down on the table in front of her. "Do you want coffee?" she asked ungraciously, the tone of her voice as critical as her look.

Maybe it had been a bad day for her, Sarah thought, or maybe she—like everyone else Sarah had had contact with today—didn't like immoral young women with illegitimate daughters. Or maybe, she thought with a sigh, she was simply reading too much into the waitress's unfriendly attitude.

"No, thanks." Sarah gave the plastic-coated menu a quick glance, then handed it back. "A chicken salad sandwich and iced tea, please."

The woman wrote the order on her pad, then tucked the pencil behind her ear. She studied Sarah for a moment longer before giving a shake of her head and turning away.

Sarah was shaking her own head in dismay when a pleasantly familiar voice asked, "Mind if I join you?"

It was Zachary Adams, dressed in faded jeans, a corduroy jacket and a blue-plaid shirt. She supposed the tie knotted loosely beneath the collar of the shirt made the outfit suitable office attire in Sweetwater. "Be my guest."

"Give me a roast beef sandwich and a Coke, Marcy," he called to the waitress as he slid into the booth opposite Sarah.

"Are you here alone?" He had expected to see Daniel today, not Sarah. It was just as well, though, because the report from the private detective hadn't yet arrived.

"Yeah. Daniel and Katie are at home. I've been job and house-hunting."

"Any luck?"

"Yeah—all bad." She waited until the waitress served their drinks before leaning forward. "Tell me, Zachary, has anyone in this town ever had an illegitimate child?"

"Not since my great-great-grandmother." He grinned boyishly. "They almost ran her out of town. But that was a long time ago, and all the Adamses since then have been totally respectable, so they've forgiven us."

Sarah didn't know whether to believe him or not, but at least he made her smile for a moment. Then she remembered her own situation and sighed. "They don't even know me, but they're not going to forgive me. The school has a position opening in the spring, but they can't hire an unwed mother. The church wants to start a preschool program, but they don't want an unwed mother, either. The landlady of the one apartment listed in the paper suddenly remembered that it wasn't available when I told her that I was single and had a baby. Even the waitress here acted as if she didn't want to serve me."

"Well, that's a different matter." Considering it, he frowned. "Maybe I should say it's a different side of the same matter. You see, Marcy wants to get married again."

"So?"

"There are three men in town who are single, over twenty and under sixty: Daniel, Terry Simmons and me. Now...Marcy doesn't like me and never has, and Terry is her ex-husband."

Sarah felt a distinct curl of jealousy in her stomach. "If she wants Daniel, why hasn't she gone after him?"

"She has, but it's kind of tough when he usually only comes into town once or twice a month. He's been showing up a lot lately, but you're usually with him, and I imagine that cramps her style a bit."

Sarah turned to look at the waitress again. She was in her early thirties, kind of pretty, and a lot shapelier under the tight pink uniform than Sarah herself was. Looking back at Zachary, she asked, "And what does Daniel think of her?"

He grinned at the unfamiliar edge in her voice. "If Daniel wanted her, Sarah, he wouldn't be spending all his time on the mountain with you. I assume you two are spending a lot of time together."

She met his gaze for a long solemn moment. "He's been letting me see Katie."

"Uh-huh." Zachary leaned back when the waitress served their lunch. When she was gone, he asked, "If you can't find a job here, what will you do?"

Sarah stirred sugar into her tea, took a bite of her sandwich and shrugged. "I don't know. Try the next town, and the next." She sighed wearily. "You know, the very things that make small-town life so appealing are shutting me out of it—the old-fashioned values, the mores, the close-knit community. I just want a good place close to Daniel to raise our daughter. I want to be able to support her and provide a home for her. But these people act like I should have a scarlet letter tattooed on my forehead."

"It's unfair," Zachary agreed, "but Sweetwater *is* a small town—one about twenty years out of step. Of course, you could sue for discrimination, but I wouldn't advise it. Even if you won, the town would never accept you."

"You're an attorney. How can you make a living when you never recommend lawsuits?" she asked with a laugh;

then, once again, she sobered. "You know what's even more unfair is that this doesn't affect Daniel. The fact that he's got an illegitimate daughter doesn't affect their opinion of *him*—*I'm* the one they blame. *He* was in that bed, too, and he never offered to marry me, but he still comes out of it with his reputation intact."

"Would you have accepted if he had proposed?"

Reluctantly she shook her head. "No, not then."

"But you would now." Zachary spoke quietly, his blue eyes locked on her face. She looked away quickly, but not before he saw the answer in her eyes.

"You know, maybe you shouldn't be sitting here. After all, you're Daniel's lawyer," she said in an awkward attempt at humor.

"I'm his friend first, his lawyer second. If you stick around, maybe I'll be your friend, too."

She offered him a shy smile. "Except for Daniel and Beth, I don't have too many friends."

"Beth." He grinned boyishly again. "We've talked about my client, now let's discuss your lawyer. Tell me about Beth Gibson."

"She's a good lawyer and a good friend. She's very bright, very tough...." Slowly Sarah smiled. "But those aren't the things you want to know about her, are they?"

"Let's start with whether or not she's married."

"No. Not involved with anyone, either." She'd known Beth since college and couldn't remember the redhead ever being seriously involved with anyone. There had been a few brief romances, but unlike Sarah, Beth had never wanted anything serious. Sometimes Sarah thought her friend didn't *believe* in serious relationships.

"I got the impression in dealing with her that she doesn't particularly like men."

"Beth handles a lot of divorces. Maybe she sees the bad side of men a lot more often than the rest of us do."

Zachary acknowledged that possibility with a nod. "When everything between you and Daniel is settled, I'd like to see her."

Sarah admired his honesty. Maybe he would change Beth's opinion of men in general. Or maybe she would cut him off at the knees with one look, as she was so capable of doing. "Why wait?"

"As long as she's your attorney and I'm Daniel's, our relationship is technically adversarial."

"Sometimes that's the best kind to have. Besides, things will be settled between Daniel and me in seven more days." One way or the other. She would have Katie, and maybe Daniel, too. Or maybe the end of their year-long arrangement would also mean the end of their relationship.

Zachary looked down, guiltily avoiding her gaze. "Yeah, next Thursday is the first." And, unless Daniel changed his mind, the beginning of a lifetime of heartache for Sarah, or Daniel, or both.

"Well, I'd better go. I want to talk to Daniel before I decide what to do next." Sarah reached for her tab, but Zachary picked it up first.

"My treat. It's not often that I get to have lunch with someone who doesn't want to talk about the crops, fishing or hunting. Give Katie a kiss for me."

"Sure. And thanks for lunch."

Daniel and Katie were in the workshop when Sarah got home. She went inside the house, quickly changed into jeans and a sweatshirt, then went to join them. Katie greeted her with a brilliant smile, a hug and several kisses that went a long way toward easing her depression over her failure to find a job.

"She's been watching for you all morning," Daniel remarked as he fitted a joint on an elegant ladder-back chair. "She couldn't figure out how you got away."

"I missed you, sweetie," Sarah said, holding Katie high and nuzzling her belly. "I don't know how I'm going to stand leaving you behind when I go to work."

Tension streaked through Daniel, but he kept it off his face by sheer force of will. "Did you find a job?"

"No." Her smile was bright and phony. "I missed you, too."

"What happened in town?"

She set Katie down and leaned her hip against the table. "I had lunch with Zachary Adams."

"Oh?"

He could put a lot into that little word without changing his voice or expression one bit, she thought with a genuine grin. "Yeah. And I met a friend of yours."

"Who was that?"

"Marcy." At his blank look, she felt relief easing over the jealousy. "The waitress at the diner? A pretty woman, I guess, if you go for that centerfold type."

When Daniel realized who she was talking about, he grinned, too, and the tension clenching his muscles began to ease. "If I did go for that type, I'd be flat out of luck with you, wouldn't I?"

Groaning dismally, Sarah looked down at her chest, then at him. "Don't use the word 'flat' in the same sentence with me, okay?" She traced her finger over the chair leg. "Where does this one go?"

"Nashville. What about a job? Was there anything available?"

Her smile faded completely. "Not for me." She turned away, intending to join Katie on the floor, but Daniel caught her arm in a gentle hold.

"What do you mean, not for you?"

"Nothing."

"Sarah."

He would feel responsible, she knew, and in spite of her complaint to Zachary about the unfairness of the town's attitudes toward her and Daniel regarding Katie, she didn't want him to blame himself.

"Sarah?" He lifted her chin so she had to look at him, and his eyes searched hers. "What did they tell you?"

"That I lack respectability." She swallowed hard and quickly continued. "I should have realized that. I mean, Sweetwater's a little place, and everyone knows everyone else's business, and of course they would be concerned about the kind of people they hire to teach their children. There are a lot of things that they don't approve of here, and you can't expect them to hire someone they don't approve of to spend six or seven hours a day with their kids, especially when they're so young and impressionable.''

Her flow of words came to a sudden stop when his hand fell away from her face. He walked away, stopping in front of the window, staring at the scene outside. ''Who told you that?'' he asked coldly.

Sarah told him about her two brief interviews. ''It's not their fault,'' she added in a flat, empty voice. ''If either of them had tried to hire an unmarried mother who doesn't even have custody of her baby, they probably would have lost their own jobs.''

He was furious, not with Janet Hillier or the reverend or the narrow-minded people of his town, but with himself. Because of him, Sarah was open to harsh judgment from everyone in town who knew about Katie. Because of him, she'd been made vulnerable to hurts inflicted by people who knew next to nothing about her. Because she wanted to stay close to him for Katie's sake. Because he hadn't yet found the courage to ask her to marry him. ''God, I'm sorry.''

Even though he couldn't see her, she shook her head. ''It's not your fault, Daniel. It's no one's fault. It's just the time and the place and the way things are.''

''It's *wrong*. They have no right to judge you.''

His anger and defensiveness on her behalf gave her a heady, warm feeling. She crossed the room and hugged him tightly. ''I love you, Daniel Ryan,'' she murmured, hiding her face in his shirt. ''I really do love you.''

October 26

Daniel used the excuse of business to go into town alone late Friday morning. Sarah never even suspected that he was lying to her, he thought regretfully. She trusted him, and he was betraying her with the lie, with this trip to Zachary's office to get the report from the private detective, with hiring the detective in the first place. His only consolation was that she would never know he had betrayed her. She would never have to face the insult of his lies. And he would never have to face the loss of her respect or her trust. *Or her love.*

Alicia Adams was preparing to leave the office when he arrived shortly before noon. She greeted him with a bright smile. "Zach said you might come by today. He's on the phone, but go on in. And tell him that I've left for lunch, okay?" She pulled her coat on, lifting her hair free of the collar. "By the way, how's Katie? I heard she's been sick."

"She's fine. It was just a cold."

"Is she with Sarah? She seems like a really nice lady, you know?" Without waiting for an answer, she picked up her purse and left the office, calling goodbye as the door swung shut.

A really nice lady, Daniel thought. Yes, she was definitely that. He tapped at the inner door, then stepped through. Zachary, the phone braced between his shoulder and ear while he wrote, waved him in. "No, that's no problem. If I don't see one of them soon, I can send a message out," he was saying. "I'm looking forward to seeing you again."

When he hung up, he tore a page off the notepad and offered it to Daniel. "That was Beth Gibson. She wants Sarah to give her a call sometime in the next few days."

Daniel accepted the paper warily, shoving it into his pocket as he sat down. He didn't trust the redheaded lawyer any more than he liked her, and he didn't like her at all. She had never understood Sarah's interest in him, had opposed giving Katie to him, had been against Sarah coming to live in Sweetwater. When she found out that he wanted to marry Sarah, she would probably do everything in her power to turn her against him.

"The report hasn't come yet, but I talked to the detective, a man by the name of Mintz. His office sent it express mail yesterday, so I should get it today. He didn't give me any details, but he said it was pretty interesting reading." He paused a moment to judge the effect of his next statement. "He said she's had some tough breaks."

Daniel already knew that. He'd seen it in her eyes, heard it in her voice. But the detective knew the details of those tough breaks. *He* didn't, not yet.

"Did Sarah tell you we had lunch together yesterday?"

Daniel nodded.

"She seemed pretty upset about her job interviews."

He nodded once more. Settling back in the chair, he crossed one ankle over the other knee and traced his finger absently back and forth over the hem of his jeans. "I, uh . . ." He looked at his friend across the desk. "I've changed my mind, Zach."

"About Sarah? About the kind of mother she is and suing for custody? I figured you had." At Daniel's fierce frown, Zachary shrugged and enumerated the reasons for his guess. "I saw you two together last week, and I talked to her for half an hour yesterday. She's practically living with you, she *is* Katie's mother, she's awfully pretty... and she's awfully fond of you."

Daniel clasped his hands together to still their nervous movement, but immediately began rubbing his thumb hard over his palm. "I'm going to ask her to marry me. If she agrees, I want to forget about the lawsuit. If she says no..." He fell silent. If she said no, Zachary would file the lawsuit and Sarah would know how Daniel had deceived her, and she would hate him. But he wouldn't lose Katie, too. He *couldn't*.

Zachary nodded once. "If she says no, we go ahead as planned on the first." He paused. "She doesn't suspect anything, does she?" He knew she didn't from their conversation yesterday, but he waited for Daniel's confirmation anyway.

"No." Saying it made him feel like a bastard. Just being here, he revised, made him feel that way.

"Well, if I'm any kind of judge of people, she'll accept your proposal, and you'll be able to forget that any of this ever happened."

"I hope—"

Daniel's response was interrupted by a voice from the waiting room. "Alicia's gone to lunch," Zachary called. "Come on in."

It was the mailman, and along with the usual mail, he was carrying a large flat envelope with an express label on it. Daniel was torn between the urge to snatch it from him and rip it open and the desire to tell him to take it back, that he didn't want it after all. These were Sarah's secrets. If he learned them, it should be from her, not from some stranger who had snooped into her life. But his need to know was greater than his respect for her privacy. He waited impatiently while Zachary signed for the envelope, then chatted with the mailman for a few moments.

Even as he talked, Zachary was slicing through the flap of the envelope. He drew out the papers as he said goodbye to the mailman.

It looked to be about fifteen, maybe twenty, pages thick, as far as Daniel could tell. That seemed like an awful lot to cover an average woman's life. He imagined that his entire thirty-four years could be summed up in one or two pages.

Zachary skimmed the pages as he turned them. Employment history, a list of residences, credit history. He gave a low whistle. "She's up to her ears in debt," he remarked. "She'll never get free. Hospital, pediatrician, obstetrician, anesthesiologist, nephrologist . . ." The detective had made notes beside each entry, specifying the specialty. He looked up, puzzled. "Katie didn't have any medical problems when you got her, did she?"

Daniel shook his head.

"The list goes on—name a specialty and it's on here." It was an exaggeration, but only slightly. "Internist, surgeon, hematologist, pathologist, radiologist. Has Sarah been sick?"

"Not that I know of." There were definitely no scars on her body, and she seemed healthy. Still, she *was* awfully thin and frail looking. And she didn't like doctors. She had refused to go with him to take Katie to Dr. Hamilton—a matter they still hadn't settled, he thought with a frown. He had let it go at the time, telling himself that he would bring it up later, but in reality he had been delaying the confrontation, unwilling to force the issue.

There was also that memory, in the back of his mind, of Sarah and a doctor. . . . His gaze dropped to his hands, but instead he saw her hand, small and delicate and oozing blood. It was the day she'd gotten that chunk of wood in her palm, he remembered now. When he'd suggested that she go to the doctor, she'd been adamant about him removing it instead. At the time he'd paid it no attention, but now, coupled with her later refusal to see Dr. Hamilton, it made sense. An illness that required the services of nine types of doctors could certainly result in a fear of the medical profession in general.

Zachary continued reading, sometimes aloud. "She was married for four years to Brent Lawson." He glanced up and saw that Daniel was already aware of that. "They divorced three years ago, two months after the birth of...their son, Tony.''

Daniel hadn't known that. He stared at the lawyer, who repeated the last few words. That wasn't possible. She and Brent had never had children—she'd told him so. Then he corrected that. She had told him that Brent was too immature, too childish himself. He hadn't wanted the responsibility of children. But he'd *had* a child. They'd had a child together, a son.

He looked at Zachary, trying to form a dozen questions, but not one came out. There was simply a stunned, helpless look on his face.

Quickly Zachary paged through the file. He glanced at one enclosure, a copy of the birth certificate for Anthony David Lawson. After handing it to Daniel, he continued to look. A moment later Daniel took the second sheet Zachary offered, and it answered one big question. It was a death certificate for Tony. For Sarah's son.

"He died in May. Five months ago." Zachary's voice was low, troubled. He didn't know what he'd expected to find out about Sarah Lawson, but this wasn't it.

Daniel's hands were trembling when he gave the two documents back to Zachary. He didn't want to know more...but he had to. He forced himself to sit still, his jaw clenched, his expression grim, and listen to the rest.

Sarah's baby had been born with an often-fatal disease, and her husband had walked out on her, had left her to watch their son die alone. She had sacrificed everything for Tony, including herself. Including, temporarily, Katie.

The guilt that he thought he'd banished with his decision to marry Sarah came back stronger than ever. He remembered the things he'd said to her, thought about her, the times he'd accused her of being a poor mother, of being selfish and caring only for herself. One day, right here in this office, he had asked her what kind of mother gave away her own child, and he remembered her answer clearly, remembered her pain when she'd said it. *One who has no other choices.* And he had cursed. There are always choices, he'd told her arrogantly. You were just too selfish to make the right one.

God, she ought to hate him for the way he'd treated her, the things he'd said to her. Between her son's illness and the bastard who had been her husband, she'd been through more than any woman should ever have to bear, and *he* had only made it worse. How could she ever forgive him for that?

After Zachary had covered the highlights of the report, he offered it to Daniel to read through. It took him longer than it should have because he was numbed by disbelief and dismay. When he finished, his heart ached for Sarah, for her little boy, for all of them.

The silence in the office was oppressive. Zachary stared at the papers lying on the desk, and Daniel simply stared. Finally the lawyer cleared his throat. "Do you want to take that with you?"

"No," Daniel had to clear his own throat. "She's more or less living with us. There's no place . . ." No place in his house or workshop that was off-limits to her. No place in his life.

"I'll keep it in your file." Zachary fell silent for several more long moments. "You said you don't want her to know about any of this, but, Daniel, you can't keep something like this secret. She'll know the minute she looks at you that something's wrong."

He knew Zachary was right. If he looked one-tenth as bad as he felt, Sarah would suspect right away. When he got on his knees and begged her forgiveness, she'd *know*. "I—I'll think of . . . something. . . ."

"It would be easier if she'd been open from the start, if she'd told you about the baby and her husband."

Daniel shook his head. "You saw those statements from her so-called friends and neighbors." They had condemned her actions, had said the same kinds of things he had. The difference was, they'd known about Tony. He hadn't. "She hardly knew me. When friends react that way, what can you expect from strangers?"

"So . . ." Zachary sighed. "What are you going to do?"

"Go home. Try to make things right. Hope that some-day she'll forgive me." He got to his feet, moving as if his body was tired. In truth, it was his spirit that was weary. "Thanks, Zach. I'll be in touch."

Alicia was returning from lunch as Daniel left. He didn't even hear her greeting. Outside, he stopped on the sidewalk and looked up at the sky. The sun was bright but offered little warmth. The wind sweeping down the street made him shiver inside his jacket.

He was tired, and he wanted to go home. To Sarah. But how could he face her yet? How could he walk in, knowing what she'd lived through, knowing that he had increased her burden with his judgmental behavior, and look her in the eye? How could he make up to her for what he'd done?

He climbed into the truck and headed home. He drove automatically, too deep in thought to concentrate on his actions. At the row of battered mailboxes four miles from his house, he pulled to the side and reached into the box on the end. Stuck in with his mail was a bill for Sarah from a doctor named Jackson. That was the surgeon, wasn't it? he thought, trying to remember as he stuffed the envelopes into his coat pocket, then deciding that it didn't matter. All that mattered was Sarah.

She was sitting on the porch when he got home, rocking in the afternoon sunshine. Katie was on her lap, and Teddy was on *her* lap. They all rocked lazily while Sarah read from the well-used storybook. Her greeting was a smile. Katie peeked over the top of the book, whispered, "Hi, Daddy," then held her finger to her lips, signaling quiet, before she resettled.

Daniel sat on the top step, turned so he could watch them. Sarah used her voice to make the story come alive, changing her pitch and tone with each character, growing loud and fierce, then soft and wispy. Her second-graders must have loved storytime in her class, he thought. They had prob-ably loved everything about her.

With each movement of the chair, the book she held shifted to hide her face from him. His gaze dropped to it, studying the brightly colored figures on the cover, the worn binding, the wrinkled edges. He had assumed that the books were part of her school supplies, meant to supplement whatever her last school had given her, but now he realized that the stories were too simple for second-graders. They were written for a younger audience, for toddlers like Katie. And Tony.

What had the boy looked like? Had there been any resemblance to his half sister? Had his life been comfortable, though brief? Had he missed his father or his baby sister? There had been too much information in the private detective's report, yet not enough. He wanted to know more about Anthony David Lawson. He wanted to *know* him.

The story finished, Katie wriggled down and ran over to hug her father. "Pink," she said, tugging until he looked at her sweater.

He tore his glance from Sarah and offered a half smile to Katie. "Yeah, honey, that's pink."

Impatiently she returned to Sarah, pulling at *her* sweater. "Mama pink, Katie pink," she said proudly.

Sarah left the rocker, swooped Katie into her arms, then sat down next to Daniel. "Now we need to find a pink shirt for Daddy, right?"

Following her mother's cue, the girl wrinkled her face into an exaggerated frown. "Noooo."

"No, daddies don't wear pink, do they?" After kissing Katie's cheek, Sarah reached over to squeeze Daniel's hand. It was a casual, familiar gesture. "How did your trip go? Get everything taken care of?"

"Yeah," he said quietly. He couldn't meet her eyes. His gaze was on Katie's feet, swinging merrily over the edge of the step. "She's stopped taking her shoes off all the time," he remarked, preferring such trivial matters to the ones that had been on his mind for the past two hours.

"It was just a matter of showing her who's more stubborn." Sarah looked faintly puzzled. "Daniel, is something wrong?"

"No." His denial came too quickly and too weakly.

"Did something happen in town?"

He shook his head. "I'm going to take care of some things. Why don't you and Katie go back inside?" Standing up, he stuck his hand into his pocket and found the week's mail. "Here's the mail. There's a letter in there for you. I'll be back—"

Sarah stood up when he did and accepted the envelopes. Then she moved in front of him, blocking his way. "Daniel, something's bothering you. Tell me what it is."

"Nothing, Sarah."

"Please..."

How could he lie when she was looking at him so earnestly? But how could he tell her the truth? "I'll be back later."

After a moment's hesitation, she moved aside and let him pass. She could have refused, could have argued or pleaded, but she couldn't force confidences that he didn't want to make. When he was ready to talk to her, he would. Until then, she would just have to wait.

She turned on the step and watched him walk off. When he turned away from the house toward the old barn, she called out, "We're having spaghetti for dinner tonight. Don't be late."

His only response was a faint nod that she would have missed if she hadn't been watching so closely; then he moved out of sight.

She sat down with a thump on the step and sorted through the mail, opening her single letter. Last month's payment had been credited, shown on the statement along with a computer-generated thank-you. The balance was slowly coming down, but it was still high. Multiplied nine times, plus the hospital bill, plus the fees for Beth's legal services, and her total debt was astronomical.

Absentmindedly she stuffed the statement back into its envelope and let her thoughts wander to Daniel. Was he still bothered by her experience in town yesterday? Or had something else happened? Had there been further comment on her unsuitability to work with the town's children?

With a sigh, she started to lay the mail aside when a piece of white paper, printed at the top with Zachary Adams's name and office address, fell from between two envelopes. The handwriting was a neat scrawl, and the message was to her. "Sarah, call Beth G. when you can—not urgent."

What did her friend want? Probably to see if Sarah's frame of mind was any better than it had been during their last conversation. She should have known better than to call Beth simply because she was upset. Like Daniel, Beth was a caretaker, a natural worrier. She would want to be certain that Sarah's distress was only temporary.

Well, she would call Beth tomorrow or Sunday, she decided as she stood up. Right now she had other things to do. "Come on, Katie," she invited, offering her hand to her daughter. "You and I are going to make spaghetti. Doesn't that sound like fun?"

Eating spaghetti was a new experience for Katie. Disdaining the silverware that she hadn't quite mastered, she dug into her dinner with both hands, coating her fingers, her face, her sweater and just about everything else with red sauce. By the time she finished, even her eyebrows and hair were liberally covered.

"Have you ever noticed that the dirtier she gets, the more she enjoys her food?" Sarah asked, staying well out of reach of their daughter's grasping hands.

Daniel looked at her as if he'd forgotten her presence. After a moment's blank stare, his gaze shifted to Katie. "That's nice," he mumbled before slipping back into his thoughts.

"Nice," Sarah repeated, shaking her head. There was definitely something else on his mind. He had come back to the house just as she was setting the table for dinner, and he hadn't spoken more than a dozen words to either of them. He hadn't eaten much dinner, either, and now he thought Katie's mess was *nice*. She tried again to gain his attention. "I found the message from Zachary."

Again he looked up. "What message?"

"To call Beth." Leaning back, she pulled the folded paper from her jeans pocket and displayed it for him before retucking it. "It was with the mail you took out of your pocket."

"Oh." He looked away again.

With a sigh, Sarah gave up. She got a dish towel from the kitchen counter and began wiping Katie's hands and face. She pulled the soiled sweater over the girls head, then patted her round belly. "Well, at least you got most of it inside you. Let me put something on this so the stains won't set. Then we'll take a bath, okay?"

"Okay."

Sarah took the sweater into the laundry room and was preparing to climb onto the dryer when an upward glance stopped her. Daniel had lowered the shelf so that everything she needed was within easy reach. Even the stain remover at the back of the shelf required no more effort than a tiptoed stretch to reach. After treating the stains on the sweater, she returned to the dining room. "Daniel, thank you," she said, her gratitude genuine.

He looked up from the spaghetti he was aimlessly twirling around his fork. "For what?"

"For moving the shelf in the laundry room so I can reach it." She passed behind him, bending to give him a kiss. "You really are sweet, you know."

"Yeah, sure," he muttered. He was a real sweetheart.

"I'm going to give Katie a bath while you finish eating, all right?" She scooped up their daughter and started toward the stairs. Halfway there, she turned back. "Daniel? We'll talk after she's in bed...won't we?" She tried to sound confident, but a note of uncertainty squeezed in. She had never seen him this way before, and she didn't know how to deal with him.

His sigh was heavy and seemed to shudder through him. "Yes," he said quietly. "We'll talk."

Still not reassured, Sarah took Katie upstairs. They splashed and played through her bath, then Sarah dressed her for bed. "Only one story tonight, sweetheart, okay? Then bedtime. Your daddy and I have some serious talking to do."

Was he tired of her? Did he want her out of his and Katie's lives? Had he decided to take Katie from her? Had he heard something in town that had turned him against her? The questions plagued her through the story of five mischievous puppies and nagged at her when she cleaned the kitchen while Daniel was putting Katie to bed. By the time he came down again, she was about to burst from curiosity and anxiety.

She was standing in front of the fireplace, her hands in her pockets. As slim as she was, dressed in the bulky sweater and jeans, with her short mussed hair, she looked almost boyish to Daniel—like a teenage girl not yet developed. But she wasn't a girl; she was a woman. A woman who was frustrated by, and fearful of, his moodiness. It showed in the concern in her doe's eyes, in her uneasy movements as she rocked on her heels, in the hesitant smile that quivered on her lips. "Well . . . can we talk now?" she asked him.

He stopped behind the rocker, his big hands gripping the back of the chair. His only answer was a nod.

Sarah waited for him to start, but when he said nothing, she sighed in despair. "Do you want me to leave, Daniel? Is that what's bothering you?"

Her conclusion surprised him into meeting her eyes. "No, of course not."

"Then what is it?"

"Tell me about Tony."

She turned as white as the crocheted collar on her sweater. Even her lips paled, until the only color in her face was her eyes, big and round and filled with the same shock that had rocketed through him six hours ago. "How did you . . . ?" Inside her pocket, her fingers closed around the crinkled note paper. She pulled it out, looked at it, then at Daniel. Beth. Just five days ago her friend had encouraged her to tell Daniel about Tony, had insisted that he had a right to know. But Sarah had never expected her to take steps to ensure that he found out. What had it taken—a brief phone call to Zachary Adams? An unimportant message for Sarah, accompanied by a casual, "Oh, by the way, let me do your client a favor. Tell him to ask Sarah about Tony." That would be enough—no details, no broken confidences. Just a little push in the right direction.

Or maybe Zachary had called her. He'd made his interest in Beth perfectly clear yesterday. Maybe he had called her to talk, to start a friendship, to ask for a date, and had asked for something, anything, that would help their clients settle things. And Beth, out of misplaced concern for Sarah, had given it.

She crumpled the note and threw it into the fireplace. It lay there a moment, untouched, then flared into bright, hot flames that died an instant later. It was like Tony's life. It had burned brightly for thirty-one months; then it had ended, over in an instant.

"Tony was my son. He's dead."

She wanted to sound detached, distant, but the plain, simple words and the lack of emotion conveyed exactly the opposite to Daniel. They hinted at the love, the sorrow, the grief, that she still lived with. That she would always live with. "Tell me about him," he repeated, his voice soft and unsteady.

She considered it for a moment, then her shoulders rose and fell with a weary sigh. Slowly she turned around to face him. "My marriage to Brent wasn't very strong after the first few years, and when I began talking about having a baby, it got worse. He didn't want the responsibility. He didn't want to put someone else first. When I got pregnant, he insisted that I'd done it deliberately, without his consent. I hadn't. I just seem to get pregnant...easily. I thought that after the baby was born, Brent would change his mind about him...but he didn't."

She was quiet for a moment, remembering. With another sigh, she went on. "Tony was a pretty baby. He had blond hair and brown eyes, and he was lively and healthy—or so we thought. Still, Brent didn't seem to care about him. All he could see was that there would be three of us to get by on his salary, for a while at least, instead of just two of us on both salaries. Then, the day we were supposed to leave the hospital, Tony became jaundiced, and the doctors wouldn't let him go home with us. There are a lot of reasons for jaundice. Some aren't too serious . . . some are."

For the first month or so, she told him, her voice soft and empty, Tony seemed all right, except for the yellowish hue of his skin. He ate normally, gained weight and was alert and active, like any other baby. She had taken a leave of absence to stay home with him, and she'd loved their time together. But Brent had resented him—the cost of his care, the demands he made on their time. He'd even resented Sarah's love for Tony.

The doctors weren't able to make a definite diagnosis right away. Some cases of jaundice resolved themselves within a few months, but when Tony's condition remained unchanged after eight weeks, they did surgery—a liver biopsy and dye studies of the liver and gallbladder. The diagnosis was biliary atresia, obstruction of the biliary system. It was a somewhat rare disease, with only two hopes for correction: surgery or transplant. The dye studies had already ruled out further surgery in Tony's case.

"The average survival rate without a transplant is eighteen months, and they told us that he would be sick most of that time. That was more than Brent was willing to take on. He hadn't wanted a baby in the first place, and he certainly hadn't wanted one who was going to require intensive and expensive care before he died a few months down the line." Sarah knew she sounded hard and cruel, but she didn't care. Brent had been hard and cruel. "So he moved out and filed for divorce. The judge ordered him to pay child support and to help with Tony's care, but he left the state instead. No one had the money or the time or the manpower to track him down."

She looked at Daniel, trying to judge his reaction. Soon she would get to the part about him—and Katie. Would that stunned look on his face remain, or would he be like so many of the others—judging, damning?

"Tony was a sweet baby. He learned to walk and talk, like other kids, but things were hard for him. He tired easily, and he was susceptible to other illnesses. He was in and out of the hospital on a regular basis, and as the disease progressed, he suffered a loss of appetite and hypertension. His abdomen was swollen and distended, and he was puffy looking, and that awful jaundice never went away. His only pleasure in life was reading. He loved to be read to, to look at the pictures. He would lie in my arms for hours at a time with his books.''

She didn't realize she was crying until a tear dripped onto her hand. She wiped her cheeks with her palm and continued, her voice still soft, but now filled with emotion, with painful memories. ''I never went back to the school. Tony needed constant care, and I couldn't afford a baby-sitter, even if I'd been able to find someone willing to take him. I sold the house, the car, everything I got in the divorce, and the social workers at the hospital helped us get every kind of aid available. It wasn't much, but we got by.''

Daniel's hands were gripping the chair back so hard that his fingers turned white. She wanted to go to him, to ease his hands away from the gleaming wood and hold them tightly in her own, but she couldn't. Not until she knew how he would react to the rest of her story.

''I was so tired. There was no one I could turn to for help. When you have a dying child, no one knows what to say, how to act, so they just stay away. I lost touch with almost all of my friends. Finally Beth offered to take care of him for a weekend. She gave me the keys to her apartment, told me to go out and have some fun, if I remembered how. And I met you. Two months later I found out I was pregnant again. I considered having an abortion. I considered giving the baby up for adoption.'' She risked another look at him. ''But I wanted her. I wanted her so much.''

The pregnancy had been difficult. Tony's condition had been deteriorating, and she had been exhausted all the time. It had gotten even worse after Katie's birth. Instead of providing around-the-clock care for one child, she now had to care for two. When Tony was hospitalized two months after Katie was born, Sarah hadn't even had the money for a baby-sitter for Katie so she could visit Tony. That was when she'd decided to contact Daniel.

"Why didn't you come to me from the start?" he asked, his voice low and trembling. "When you found out you were pregnant, why didn't you tell me? I could have helped you."

"I know that now." She sat down on the hearth, too tired to stand any longer, and let her head roll forward. When she looked up again, she continued. "But all I knew then was that I had a baby who was dying, and his own father couldn't handle that. Why should I have expected a stranger to care?"

It was a difficult question, one with no answer. "What about a transplant?"

"He was on the list, but no donor ever became available. Do you know what it's like, Daniel, to wait for a transplant? To pray that some other woman's baby will die so that yours can live?" Her voice broke, and the tears flowed freely at last. She covered her face with her hands and cried for Tony, for Katie, for Daniel—for herself.

He released the chair and crossed to her in two strides, lifting her easily into his arms. "It's all right, Sarah," he whispered, carrying her to the rocker, where he cradled her like a baby. "It's all right."

She cried until she was limp from exhaustion, until there were no tears left. Clutching a handful of his shirt, she rested against his chest, listening to the steady beat of his heart. "I loved Katie very much," she whispered. "But she had you. Tony didn't have anybody but me."

"He was lucky to have you." His voice was harsh, thick with emotion, but his hands as they rubbed her were sweetly gentle.

After a long silence, she spoke again. "I'm sorry."

"For what?" he asked in dismay.

"I should have told you sooner. I should have trusted you."

His fingers glided soothingly through her hair. "When did I give you reason to trust me with this? The things I said, the things I thought... I'm the one who owes *you* an apology. God, Sarah, I *am* sorry."

She laid her hand over his mouth. "You reached the only conclusions you could with the information you had. That was my fault. But it doesn't matter anymore. I'm glad you know. I'm glad I don't have to keep that part of my life secret anymore.''

After another silence, it was Daniel who spoke. "Sarah?"

"Hmm."

"Do you want another baby?"

She looked up into his face. Before her unpleasant experience in town yesterday, she had promised to finish this discussion with him later. Now, apparently, "later" had come. "Yes, I do," she replied softly. "Someday. When the time is right."

Daniel moved, depositing her in the chair and kneeling in front of her, his hands clenched around hers. He spoke in a low, tense rumble. "Make the time right, Sarah. Now."

She stared at him. He was clutching her hands tightly, but she didn't feel the pain. For one long moment she didn't feel anything but a curious emptiness waiting to be filled. "What?" she whispered at last.

"Marry me. Raise my daughter. Have my babies." He swallowed, took a deep breath and asked, "Will you marry me, Sarah?"

"Marry...you?" she echoed, still in a whisper.

"You need me, Sarah, and Katie needs me. We're all happier together than we are apart, because we're meant to be a family—not two people who sleep together, or two people whose only connection is their daughter." He broke off, struggling with the words. He had never said "I love you" to a woman before, but he had never loved before. Now was the time to say it, to acknowledge his love for Sarah—not affection, not desire, but *love*. But, God help him, when he desperately needed the words, even now, they wouldn't come. "I need you, Sarah."

She searched his face for a moment and found everything she needed to see. He might not use the word *love*, but he knew its meaning, and in his own gentle, caring way, she was certain that he did love her. "Yes," she agreed softly. "You do need me." Then she smiled the sweetest, dearest smile he'd ever seen. "I would be honored to marry you, Daniel."

October 27

Daniel lay on his back, staring at the ceiling in the firelit room, his hands clenched into fists at his sides, Sweat was collecting on his forehead, not from the heat—because in spite of the fire, it was still cool in the bedroom—but from the tension, from the force of will required to lie here perfectly still while Sarah—he clamped his teeth on a groan—was doing perfectly wicked things to his body.

Her small hand moved intimately between his thighs, stroking, caressing his hardness, while at the same time her tongue teased his nipple into a hardness of its own. She laughed softly, pleased with the power she held over him, but careful not to abuse it. With barely a twitch of his magnificent muscles, he could turn the tables and demonstrate the same power over her.

She left a damp trail of kisses down his chest, over his flat belly, across his hip. When her mouth touched him with an intimate, open kiss, his control broke, and he reached for her, lifting her up, settling her over his hips. She accepted his smooth, deep intrusion with a smile and a soft, sensuous sound of pure contentment. Leaning over, she brushed her mouth over his. "I love you, Daniel."

His response, as she'd known it would be, was to pull her close, to kiss her hungrily, with all the passion, all the love, he couldn't put into words. His tongue thrust into her mouth with a near-savagery that was tightly controlled, matching the furious pumping rhythm of his hips.

She tried to remain detached, in control, but he was filling her so sweetly, his hands tormenting her so gently, his mouth claiming hers so thoroughly. Uttering a low, helpless moan, she gave in to the sensations spiraling through her belly, gave in to the pure need and matched him, met him. When his body arched, shuddered and emptied its hot sweet flow, her body arched, too, strained by the convulsive tremors that started deep inside and swept through her.

When she collapsed against him, Daniel hardly felt her weight. She was so delicate, he marveled, stroking his fingers through her damp hair, over her slender neck, down her gleaming back. He could lie with her like this forever, their bodies heated and slick and still intimately joined.

Bracing her hands on his chest, she slowly lifted herself until she could gaze into his face. "Daniel . . . do you really want to marry me?"

Less than four hours had passed since his proposal—it was a little after midnight now, he saw with a glance at the clock—but she looked as if she still couldn't believe it. Well, he still couldn't believe she had said yes, either. "Yes, Sarah, I do."

"You're not just offering me respectability." She made it a statement, but there was a faint questioning note in her voice that pleaded for reassurance.

"No. I'm just offering me."

She looked relieved. "Good. I don't know if I care so much for respectability, but I love you." Her smile came back then. "Do you really want to have a baby with me?"

"You know I do."

The smile turned sexy and sensuous. "Good," she repeated as she moved her hips in a long, slow caress against him, the action meant to remind him of the precautions they'd skipped tonight. "Like I said earlier, I seem to get pregnant easily."

He lifted and rolled with her until his body sheltered hers in the warm soft jumble of the covers. "We have plenty of time to practice if you don't." Supporting his weight on his arms, he moved down, his tongue leaving a wet trail across her breast until it reached her nipple. He licked across it and watched the skin pucker, the peak harden. "Did your breasts swell when you were pregnant?"

She let her head sink into the pillow and her eyes close, the better to enjoy what he was doing. "Yeah, they did. Brent said that finally I looked—"

He traced a circle around her breast, then tasted her nipple once again. He could well imagine what her bastard of a husband had said. "Brent was a fool."

"Yes." The word was barely a whisper, because he was suckling her breast now, drawing her nipple between his teeth, sending the most pleasing nerve-quivering sensations racing through her body. Sliding her fingers into his thick dark hair, she held his head, reluctant to let him end the gentle torment.

At last he drew her hands away and laid them on the mattress at her sides, then moved lower on the bed. Her legs were trapped by his body, leaving her vulnerable to the torture of his tenderly stroking fingers, his gentle bites, his hungry kisses. He combed through the honey-colored curls, parting them, parting her, for the painfully slow, painfully sweet invasion of his fingers, and Sarah moaned.

Daniel rested his head on her hip, his eyes closed while he gathered strength. Farther down the bed, far out of her reach, his manhood was hardening again, swelling, aching for the sweet warmth inside her. He was as easily aroused by merely touching her as he was when *she* touched *him*. He could fill his place within her a thousand times and still crave more, still need her tight, heated welcome to feel complete. "Sometimes I think I didn't begin to live until I met you."

His voice was as thick and heavy as his need, and it flowed around her, securing her in its warmth. She opened her arms to him, beckoning him. "Love me again."

"Always, Sarah." He moved into position, sinking into her until the fit was snug and complete. "Always."

She was almost asleep when Daniel's voice tickled in her ear. Turning onto her side to face him, she snuggled closer to his chest. "Hmm."

"This disease Tony had . . ." He wrapped his arm around her, providing a pillow for her head. "Could our children have it?"

She blinked a couple of times to clear the sleepy daze from her mind. "It's not hereditary. It's a sort of birth defect, where the system just failed to develop properly. According to Tony's doctors, Brent and I could have had a dozen more children together, and the risks would have been practically nonexistent. There's no reason to believe it will affect any child that you and I have together."

"I'm sorry." It was a blanket apology—sorry that he had awakened her to ask, sorry that he'd had to refer once more to the sadness of her son's life, sorry that he'd judged her, sorry that she'd gone through such sorrow, sorry that Tony had had the disease in the first place.

Sarah understood and pressed a kiss to his shoulder. "Good night, Daniel."

Saturday was cold, the wind blowing over the mountaintop with a force that rattled the windowpanes. They spent the day inside, the living room fireplace filled with a crackling fire that spread its heat into the distant corners.

"Winter is definitely coming," Sarah said, lying on the couch so she could see the leaves, their stubborn hold broken by the fierce wind, sweeping across the clearing.

"We'll have some nice weather before the first snow."

She frowned at Daniel, who was lying at the opposite end of the couch, his legs tangled with hers, Katie sitting on his stomach. "How do you know we won't get snow now? Look at that sky, how dark and gray and cold it looks."

"It's not going to snow."

He said it so smugly that she couldn't stop her laugh. "I suppose Grandfather Ryan taught you how to predict the weather, didn't he? And I bet when you farmed, you planted by the phases of the moon, didn't you?"

"It's worked for years. It fed me, my father, my grandfather and all the Ryans who came before him."

"And it fed you well." With her foot, she rubbed over the powerful muscles in his thigh. "You're a walking advertisement for fresh air, hard work and homegrown food. I hope Daniel the fourth will take after you."

A son of his own to carry on the family name. He liked that idea, liked it immensely. But, hiding his pleasure behind barely opened eyes, he simply said, "If he's lucky, he'll look like you."

"If he's lucky," she corrected, "he'll be just like you. In every way." She moved her foot to tickle Katie's belly. The girl giggled and brushed it away, but continued to look at her book without so much as a glance for her mother. "You think you can ignore me, you little rascal?" Sarah tickled again, and this time Katie laughed out loud.

But when the laughter ended, she gave her mother an admonishing look, commanded, "No, Mama," then took her book to the rocker, safely out of Sarah's reach, where she continued to solemnly study the pictures.

"Those are Tony's books, aren't they?" Daniel asked.

"Yes."

"Do you have any pictures of him?"

"Yes."

"Where are they?"

She glanced out the window. "In an album in the trunk of my car." It was parked outside next to Daniel's truck.

"Can I see them?"

She hesitated only a moment. "The keys are in the pocket of my jacket."

He got up immediately and put his shoes on. There was a rush of cold air when he opened the front door, then another when he returned, a brown vinyl album in hand. Sarah sat up, making room for him beside her, then drew her knees to her chest, clasping her hands around them.

The first pictures could have been of any newborn baby—homely and wrinkled and normal. But gradually, as the baby grew older and the wrinkles smoothed out, he took on qualities that Daniel found familiar—the dark blond hair, the brown eyes, the delicate bone structure, like Sarah, and the sweet baby smile, like Katie. As he grew older, he also took on a faint yellow color, the jaundice that had been the first symptom of the disease that killed him.

There was one picture in the album of Brent Lawson, taken when Tony was about a month old, Sarah said. The man held the baby, but he kept him at a distance, not cradling him closely the way most fathers would have. He looked uncomfortable, almost annoyed that he'd been forced to sit still for this single photograph with his infant son. Daniel looked from the picture to Sarah. "Did you love him?"

She wished she could pretend that he meant Tony. It would be a much easier question to answer. But she had never taken the easy way out, and she wouldn't start now. "Yeah, I did. Even though we fought a lot, even though he was childish and immature and selfish, even though he resented Tony, I loved him. When he moved out and filed for divorce, I was angry and hurt, but I didn't want a divorce. It wasn't until later, when I realized how completely he'd abandoned Tony, that I really began to hate him."

"And now?"

"Now I feel nothing. He means nothing."

"Not even as your son's father."

She shrugged. "Tony had no father. All he had was me."

He turned back to the pictures, flipping the pages, seeing the signs of the disease's progression. All the holidays were represented—Christmas, Easter, the Fourth of July, his birthday, Halloween. Soon there were pictures of Sarah, heavily pregnant but thinner, burdened by the fullness of her belly and the sickly twenty-one-month-old boy who clung to her.

"One of the nurses at the hospital took those." Sarah touched the edge of one photo. "Katie was born about a week later."

"You look tired."

"I was. All the time." She smiled faintly at Katie. "She was active long before she was born. Her favorite times to kick were when I was trying to sleep. I had a constant back-ache from carrying both her and Tony.''

"You said he learned to walk."

"He did, and he tried, but walking up a flight of stairs left him exhausted." She turned the page and pointed to the top picture. "There's Katie's very first picture."

It was taken in the hospital nursery, with a bright-colored blanket bearing a placard with the name Lawson covering the sleepy eyed baby. Lawson was her legal name, Daniel thought absently, named for the bastard who'd run out on his own son, who certainly wouldn't have welcomed another man's daughter. His first action, once he and Sarah were married, would be to adopt Katie, to legally change her name to Ryan.

There were pictures of Katie and Tony together, the boy obviously pleased with his younger sister. Daniel studied them for some resemblance and found nothing but the structure of their faces. Tony looked more like his father than his mother, and Katie resembled her own father.

The photos of Katie ended at three months. Daniel recognized the last picture, not because he'd seen it before but because it had been taken on the last day that Sarah had had Katie. On *his* first day with her. The little dress and the blanket were tucked in the bottom drawer of the chest in her room, and the teddy bear was sitting in the rocker with her now.

"Did he miss her?" Daniel asked.

"Yeah. In the beginning he wanted to see her, to go with her, but . . . he got pretty sick after that, and . . ." Her voice trailed off, and Daniel closed the album, putting his arms around her, stroking her.

She didn't cry, although the tears burned her eyes. For a long time she sat in his embrace, absorbing his warmth, drawing from his strength.

Daniel brushed the hair from her forehead and kissed her there. "When do you want to get married?"

"Soon. Tomorrow. Today."

He kissed her again. "Do you want a church wedding?"

"It doesn't matter. There's only Beth to invite."

"I guess I'd invite Zachary." He sighed softly. "We can do it in the courthouse. It's not very romantic."

"That depends on who you're doing it with. The courthouse is fine. Or the church. The reverend would be happy to see that I'm correcting the error of my ways." She rested her cheek against his flannel shirt. "Now I'll be suitable for those jobs."

"I don't object to you working now, but after the next baby's born, I'd like you to stay home for a while," Daniel said hesitantly. "I make more money than we'll ever need."

Sarah thought of the bills she got each month and cringed. "I need to work at least part-time. I owe..." She sighed. "A lot of money. Tony's care was so expensive. Even with everything that was written off or done free of charge, his bills were still incredible. I know I'll never be able to pay them off, but I'd like to pay as much as I can."

He had seen the amounts listed on the detective's credit report. If business remained good, if he could make steady large payments, he could pay off the bills sometime in the foreseeable future, although he didn't want to think about how many years it would take. Once they'd had all the children they wanted and the kids were in school, Sarah could go back to work and could contribute her entire salary to the process.

Smiling, he gave a shake of his head. For the first time in his life, he was making plans for the future—five, ten, fifteen years ahead—with someone else. All the times he'd thought ahead, he'd seen himself alone, as he'd been for eighteen years. But now there were Sarah, Katie and all those babies they were going to have. Now there was his family.

"Do you want to let your mother know before we get married?" Sarah asked. It would be nice if his mother would come back to Tennessee for the wedding, if she would show Daniel that he meant enough for her to travel a few hundred miles. But the woman who'd made no effort to see her only grandchild probably wouldn't care about her son's wedding, either.

He was thinking about her failure to see Katie, too. "No," he replied, no hint of emotion in his voice. "I'll write and let her know later."

"I love you, Daniel." Sarah hugged him tightly, as if trying to force that love into him through the physical contact. "We'll be happy, all three of us. I promise we will."

He looked down at her with a gentle smile. "I *am* happy, Sarah. I—"

For a moment she thought he was going to say it: I love you. For a moment he thought he was, too, but the words caught, and instead he kissed her. He would learn someday, she thought as she accepted his kiss. Someday he would overcome this reticence and say those three sweet words. But she didn't have to hear them to believe them. She could feel his love in his touch, his kiss, his lovemaking. She could see it in his eyes, his smile, his actions.

But when the day came that he could say it . . . that would be the sweetest day of all.

October 28

On Sunday, for the first time in a week, Sarah woke up in bed alone. She rolled over to where Daniel usually lay, but the sheets were cold, signaling that he'd been up for quite a while. With a regretful sigh, she slid back into her own warm cocoon and fell asleep again.

Down the hall, in the room where his parents' bedroom furniture was now stored, Daniel sat on the bed, a clumsily carved wooden box in front of him. The box had been one of his first attempts at woodworking. One corner had never fitted together properly, the lid was warped, and the design he'd carved on the sides was awkward and childish. But his father had appreciated the Christmas gift from his ten-year-old son, had praised and encouraged him, and had honored the gift by placing all his important belongings in it. The next year his father had died, but his mother had left the box on the dresser, filled with papers, a few pieces of jewelry, some old photographs.

He lifted the lid and removed the pictures. There was one of his parents as newlyweds and another of the three of them when Daniel was two years old. There was another, old and faded, of his grandparents, their hair gray, their shoulders stooped from hard work, but still smiling, still holding hands. He laid them aside, then added the papers to the pile without looking at them. Any important papers were now kept in his file in Zachary's office. These were old copies, meaningless documents.

On the bottom was the jewelry, along with a pair of oval-shaped wire-rimmed glasses that had belonged to his grandfather. There was a pocket watch, the crystal broken for as long as he could remember, that had been his great-grandfather's. There was a brooch, ornately engraved, the silver tarnished now, that he'd seen pinned to his grandmother's church dress when he was little. And there was the ring.

It had come to Sweetwater with Leanora Ryan, the bride his grandfather had brought from Asheville nearly seventy years ago. It was a pearl mounted on a gold band—not a large pearl, but one of good quality. One that after years of neglect in this old wooden box still retained its soft luster. In his large palm it looked impossibly small, but it had fit his grandmother's finger. He was certain it would fit Sarah's.

Quickly he replaced the papers and the photos, fitted the lid on and set the whole box back on the dusty dresser. Hiding the ring within his hand, he left the room, closing the door behind him, and returned to his own room.

Sarah was still asleep, but she'd been moving restlessly. The covers had slipped below her arms, barely covering the soft swell of her breasts and leaving her left hand, resting on the pillow, exposed. Daniel sat down and waited to see if the movement would awaken her. When it didn't, he reached for her hand and carefully slid the gold ring onto her third finger. He'd been right. It was a perfect fit. After pressing a kiss to her hand, he replaced it on the pillow and left the room once again.

When Katie woke up, he dressed her and took her downstairs. "What do you want for breakfast?" he asked, setting her in her high chair while he circled the counter into the kitchen.

"Pancakes."

He frowned, thinking of the mess Katie and syrup could make. "You would. How about eggs?"

She shook her head.

"Bacon?"

Another shake.

"Cereal?"

"Pancakes," she repeated.

"All right. But after that our new rule goes into effect: you can only have pancakes when your mom's here to clean up after you."

"Mama go?"

"No, she's in bed. She's a sleepyhead." He found the pancake mix, set it on the counter with a bowl and milk, and reached for a cup. He was measuring the milk when, behind him, Katie giggled.

"Morning, s'eepyhead," she said in her sweet voice.

Sarah bent to kiss her mussed curls, then continued into the kitchen. She hadn't taken the time to dress, but had simply tied her robe around her waist and gone looking for Daniel. "Sleepyhead, huh?" she asked, sliding her arms around his waist. "Teaching my child to call me names because I sleep an hour late?"

Before he could respond, she pulled his head down and kissed him, her tongue sliding into his mouth, meeting his own tongue, searching as if to fill a hunger deep inside. When she finally released him, she took a deep breath, then extended her hand. "This is beautiful, Daniel."

He ran his fingertip over the ring. "It was my grandmother's. When she died, she left it to my mother, and when *she* remarried, she gave it to me. I want you to have it."

"You said your grandparents were happily married for forty-two years." She smiled, the love gleaming in her eyes. "Maybe we'll have the same luck."

"Maybe we will." After another kiss, he turned back to Katie's breakfast. "I'm fixing Katie some pancakes, but I'd like to go out for dinner. The restaurant in town isn't fancy, but the food's good, and the service is pretty good if you get there before church lets out. What do you think?''

She thought it sounded fine. And in addition to being a pleasant afternoon out, it would give her a chance to call Beth, to reassure her that everything was all right and to tell her, Sarah thought with a sly smile, about her change in plans. It would also give her a chance—her smile faded a bit—to take Beth to task for telling Zachary about Tony. Regardless of the intent—or the results—she'd had no right to go against Sarah's wishes.

They arrived at the restaurant shortly after noon. Sarah wore her blue dress again, and even Katie was in a dress, although she wasn't quite certain she liked the lace and the bows and the patent leather shoes that replaced her tennis shoes.

The Adams family was seated at a large table in the center of the dining room. When they saw Daniel and Sarah, they insisted that the three join them. Sarah ended up between Daniel and Zachary, while Katie got the seat of honor between Bonnie Adams and Zachary's grandmother.

After a moment's talk, Sarah turned to Daniel. ''I saw a pay phone out there,'' she murmured. ''I want to give Beth a call. Order for me, will you?''

''Do you need some change?''

''No, thanks. I'll call her collect, and she can put it on that bill I'm going to pay someday.'' She excused herself and left the dining room for the small foyer and the phone. It took a moment for the operator to put the call through; then Beth came on the line, sounding sleepy.

''I got a message from Zachary Adams that you wanted me to call. Is anything wrong?''

''Nope. I was just checking on you. Is everything okay at your end?''

''Everything's fine.'' She shivered as the door opened to admit more customers and a blast of cold air. ''I would have called sooner, but this is the first time I've come to town since Daniel gave me the message.''

"Well, the big day's only four days away. Are you getting excited?"

Sarah wrapped the phone cord around her finger. "Actually the big day is five days away."

"Five?"

"Friday. The second. Can you be here?"

The silence at Beth's end of the line was heavy. Finally she asked, "We're talking about two different big days, aren't we? I mean getting custody of Katie again. You mean . . ."

"Getting married to Daniel."

She waited for her friend's explosion, for all the arguments against marriage in general and marriage to Daniel in particular, but none of them came. Instead Beth asked, "Are you happy?"

"Yes."

"Do you love him?"

"Yes."

"Does he love you?"

This time it was Sarah's turn to be quiet. She waited until the customers coming through the door were inside the restaurant, then said, "He still hasn't said so, but—"

"But he's realized that marriage is his only chance of keeping Katie, and so what if he had to take you, too? At least he'll have someone to keep his bed warm." The instant the last word was out, Beth said, "I'm sorry, Sarah. God, I'm sorry. I know you told me last week that you loved him, but I didn't expect it to come to this, not so quickly— although I don't know why. I can't think of anyone in this world who needs love more than Daniel Ryan. And I don't know anyone who needs to give love more than you. I guess you two are a perfect pair. Forgive me?"

"Of course." Sarah hesitated a moment, then asked, "Beth feeling the way you do about Daniel, why did you tell Zachary about Tony?"

She could feel Beth's tension over the phone line. She knew the other woman well enough to know that she was sitting straighter, that her green eyes were flashing, her mind racing. "I didn't tell Adams *anything* about Tony. I called him Friday and asked if he could get a message to you to call me. That was *all*. Does he know about Tony?''

"Daniel does. I—I assumed that you told Zachary, and he told Daniel.''

"What exactly did Daniel find out?''

"I don't know.'' Sarah twisted the phone cord tighter until it was biting into her finger. "He saw Zachary Friday afternoon and got your message. He was upset when he came home, and when I finally got him to talk about what was bothering him, he said, 'Tell me about Tony.' ''

"You hadn't told anyone anything?''

"No. It's hardly something you bring up in casual conversation.''

"You didn't leave anything lying around—no papers, no pictures?''

Once again Sarah told her no.

"Damn! I bet they hired a P.I.''

"A private investigator?'' Sarah's voice broke on the last word. It was inconceivable. People like her didn't get investigated. That was for crooks, criminals, people who couldn't be trusted.

Beth swore again. "It fits—it all fits! He gave you access to Katie and got you to trust him, so you wouldn't be suspicious. Hell, any fool could see that you already thought Ryan was next to God because he took Katie, so he used you.''

"No.'' Conviction was strong in Sarah's voice. "Daniel wouldn't do that, Beth. You're too suspicious. You deal with people like Brent so much you forget that not all men are like him. Daniel isn't.''

"Sarah, open your eyes, sweetheart. Remember how adamant he was about keeping you away from Katie when you first moved there? For nine days he wouldn't let you near her except for one brief visit. He was convinced you were some sort of monster. Then suddenly after a talk with his lawyer, he opened his house and his heart to you. And now he's somehow found out about Tony, when you went to such pains to keep that secret.'' Beth sighed deeply. "Why the sudden change of heart? And how did he find out about Tony?''

Sarah was painfully silent.

"I'll bet you next month's vacation that he hired a private detective. If I'm wrong, you can go to the Bahamas in my place."

She unwrapped the cord, then stared at the pearl ring on her finger. "Why would he do that? He had to know that eventually I would tell him why I'd given Katie up."

"Did he question you about it a lot?"

"Well . . . yes."

Beth hated to say the next words, but she had to. "The only way I know of for him to find out about Tony is through a P.I. And the only reason I can think of for him to hire a private detective is to gather information to prove that you're an unfit mother in a custody suit for Katie."

Sarah blinked back the tears. "No. I don't believe that. He asked me to *marry* him, Beth. He gave me his grandmother's ring!"

"Sweetheart, I'm sorry." Beth swore softly. "Maybe I'm wrong, okay? Maybe—" But she couldn't think of any other plausible explanation. "Let me do some checking. I can find out pretty easily if someone's been snooping around. You can call me back tomorrow afternoon."

"No. I'll ask him." Daniel was an honest man. If she asked, he would tell her.... The thought trailed off. If he was guilty of what Beth suspected, then he *wasn't* an honest man; he'd been lying to her all along. What would stop him from lying again?

No! With every ounce of feeling in her heart, she knew that Beth was wrong. Daniel *loved* her. He hadn't said so simply because the words were foreign to him, but he had shown her. He had treated her as if she were the most precious gift he'd ever been given. He wouldn't go behind her back and hire a private detective. He wouldn't take advantage of her, wouldn't lead her on, while he was planning a lawsuit to take Katie from her. He wouldn't do that to her!

"I've got to go, Beth. I'll talk to you in a couple of days, okay? And I'll see you Thursday. Why don't you plan on spending the night and staying for the wedding Friday?"

"Sure, Sarah. If you need anything, let me know."

Sarah hung up the phone and reentered the dining room, making her way to the table, sliding into the chair next to Daniel.

"Why can't I ever get Beth Gibson to talk to me that long?" Zachary complained good-naturedly.

Her smile felt false. "Maybe you catch her at the wrong times."

"Or maybe you talk about the wrong subject," Daniel added darkly. He was studying Sarah's face, taking note of the stress lines around her mouth and eyes. He had known that the lawyer wouldn't be pleased by the news of their marriage, but he hadn't expected the effects of her efforts to change Sarah's mind to show so clearly. And that was only in a phone call. It would be even harder for Sarah when Beth showed up in person Thursday.

"That's a lovely ring," Alicia commented when Sarah reached for her tea. She looked expectantly from Sarah to Daniel, then back again, waiting for a response.

Sarah resisted the urge to hide her hand, and the ring, under the table, knowing it would only hurt Daniel. She just wasn't certain that she wanted to discuss their plans for marriage before she had a chance to clear up Beth's suspicions. But she knew Beth was wrong. Daniel wouldn't have her investigated, he wouldn't accuse her of being an unfit mother, and he certainly wouldn't marry her simply because it was his only chance of keeping Katie. He was too good a man to do such awful things. So what could it hurt to share their news?

The younger woman was waiting, and now the other two were watching curiously, and so was Zachary. Finally Sarah smiled. "Thank you. It belonged to Daniel's grandmother."

"And does it have some special significance?"

"You're nosy, Alicia," Zachary chided.

"It's all right." Sarah looked at Daniel. His hand was clenched around his fork as if he might break it, and he couldn't meet anyone's gaze. Dear God, she loved him more than she had ever loved anyone but her children. He *couldn't* be guilty of the awful things Beth suspected! Easing his fingers from the fork, she held his hand in hers, smiled at everyone around the table and announced, "Daniel and I are going to get married."

The simple dinner out turned into a celebration that eventually moved from the restaurant to the Adams' house. It was late afternoon before Daniel and Sarah said their goodbyes and headed home.

"Beth wasn't pleased, was she?" Daniel asked as he turned off the highway onto the narrow country road. He'd wanted to ask the question all afternoon, but he'd never gotten even a moment alone with Sarah. He wanted to know what the lawyer had said, wanted to know how to counter her arguments against him.

"Beth handles a lot of divorces. I'm not sure she believes in second chances or happily-ever-after." Sarah wiped a trace of chocolate from Katie's chin. Mrs. Adams had served a freshly baked chocolate cake, and Katie had thought she was in heaven. She had stuffed as much into her little belly as possible, and had smeared a fair amount on her outside, too.

"Are you having second thoughts?" he asked quietly. If she was, he would have to chase them away somehow, and the only way he knew how was physically, by loving her long and hard all night.

"I love you, Daniel," she said simply.

Reassured by her soft words, he let the rest of the drive pass in silence. When they got home, he carried Katie, who was almost asleep, balancing her on one shoulder while he inserted the key in the lock.

"Daniel?" Sarah had stopped on the top step, and her hands were clasped together. "I have to ask this—for Beth. I know it's not true, but I told her I would ask."

As the door swung open, he turned to look at her. "What?"

"How did you find out about Tony?" She was looking at him, but her gaze was focused on Katie instead of his face. "I thought she had told Zachary and he had told you, but she didn't. *She* thinks you hired a private detective to investigate me. She thinks you're going to try to take Katie away from me. I know it's not true, but—"

At the strangled noise he made, she lifted her eyes to his, and her heart began thudding in her chest. He looked so guilty. Dear God... Covering her mouth with one hand, she spun away, unable to face him any longer.

He set Katie on the floor, jarring her awake, and held her until she was steady. "Go lie down on the couch, sweetheart," he said, giving her a push in the right direction; then he took a step toward Sarah. When his hand touched her shoulder, she shuddered and jerked away.

"It *is* true, isn't it?" she asked, her voice thick and broken. "You lied to me. My God, all the lies . . . !"

"Sarah, listen to me," he pleaded, touching her again. This time she slapped his hand away.

"Listen to you? To more lies?" She hugged her arms across her stomach as if she might keep the pain inside. If it spread, if it got out, it would surely destroy her. "I trusted you. Daniel. I thought you were such a good, honorable man, and you *used* me!"

"That's not true, Sarah." Panic laced through him, making his hand tremble when he touched her once more. "Let me explain—"

She interrupted him with a hysterical laugh. "Explain? You think you can *explain* why you betrayed my trust in you?" She stepped back to dislodge his hand. "Did you hire a private detective?"

"Yes, but—"

"Are you planning to sue for custody of Katie?"

"Not anymore. Sarah—"

Not anymore. Beth was right. Sarah wanted to scream, to fall to her knees and sob out her sorrow, but she wouldn't do that, not in front of him. "And Zachary was in on it."

"Yes."

Her shoulders sagged under the burden of his admission. Squeezing her eyes shut, she slowly shook her head back and forth in silent denial. Then she looked at him again. "So Zachary handled the legal end, your detective handled the investigative end, and you . . . you handled me."

"No, Sarah, that's not the way it was. I—" He forced the words out, driven by fear, by desperation. "I *love* you."

The pain inside her grew hotter, sharper. They were the right words, but given at the wrong time for the wrong reason. "All this time I told myself that you loved me, that you didn't say it because the words were difficult for you," she whispered dully. "But it just wasn't true, was it? That's why you never said it. I made excuses for you at the same time that you were lying to me with every breath you took! Why, Daniel? *Why?*"

He sighed, feeling the chill spread through him. "I couldn't let Katie go," he said in a low unemotional voice. "She was all I had. If you took her away, you would have taken my life, too. I couldn't risk losing her."

"So you hired a detective to prove that I'm not *fit* to be her mother. And when you got his report and there was nothing in it to support that, you decided the only thing to do was marry me. You didn't have to convince me—you didn't even have to claim to love me." In spite of her vow not to cry in front of him, the tears, hot and stinging, were spilling down her cheeks. "Beth was right. Marriage was your only chance to keep Katie. So what if you had to take me, too?"

He grasped her shoulders and shook her. "Damn it, Sarah, stop it! You know that's not true! I *wanted* you— wanted to make love to you, to be with you, to spend the rest of my life with you. Yes, being married meant that we could both have Katie, but it also meant that I could have *you*, and that's just as important. I *need* you, Sarah. I love you."

His words couldn't penetrate the thick sorrow that surrounded her. "This past month I've been comparing you to Brent and telling myself how much better you are—a better man, a stronger man, a more loving man." She gave a sad shake of her head. "You're no better than he is. He was a bastard...but at least he was an honest bastard. I can't even say that much for you."

He took a step back, then another and another until the wall was behind his back. She hated her ex-husband; she'd told him so yesterday. Now she hated *him*, too. And the worst part of it was that he deserved it. For the things he'd done, the lies he'd told, the trust he'd betrayed, he deserved her hatred.

"Excuse me." She walked past him into the house, letting the screen door close with a thump behind her. Upstairs she found her laundry bag, neatly folded in the linen closet, and slowly, methodically filled it with her clothes. Back in the living room, she added the photo album and Tony's books, then knelt on the floor beside the couch. "I have to go now," she whispered to Katie, even though the child was asleep. "I can't see you for a couple of days, but Thursday I'm coming to get you, and we're going to go so far away from here that Tennessee won't mean a thing to you. *He* won't mean a thing. We'll be so happy together that we'll forget he even exists, I promise."

She brushed a kiss over Katie's cheek, smelling the rich chocolate from the cake. "I love you, sweetheart. I'll be back for you."

Drying the tears from her face, she stood up, removed the pearl ring and laid it in the center of his cleared desk, then got her keys from his coat pocket. Holding the laundry bag in both arms, she went outside. Daniel was standing where she'd left him, the look on his face one of heartache, of guilt, of loss.

"We're supposed to meet in Zachary's office to sign the papers at one o'clock on Thursday," she said, her voice dull and empty. "Bring her with you. Then file your lawsuit and we'll see who's not fit to take care of *my* daughter."

He didn't speak, didn't try to stop her, didn't try to hold her. He just stood where he was and watched the only woman he had ever loved walk away from him. Away from his house. Away from his life.

The bedroom was cold, and the skin of Daniel's chest and arms was unnaturally icy, but he made no effort to pull the quilt higher. It rested across his jeans-clad legs, where it had fallen when he'd lifted it to cover himself and had smelled Sarah's scent, warm and sensuous and innocent, all over it. The bed smelled of her, too, and so did the couch downstairs. That was why he was spending the night in the chair, staring at the cold fireplace.

There had been no lights on at the house down the hill. He had watched all evening for some sign of her, some sign that she was safe at home, but there'd been nothing. Maybe she had driven into town to call her lawyer and had spent the night there. Maybe she had returned to Nashville. Maybe she'd wanted to stay as far away from him as she reasonably could until Thursday.

He couldn't blame her. She hated him, but she couldn't hate him any more than he hated himself. He'd made excuses to justify what he was doing—how he was lying, how he was betraying her—but he'd known all along that there was no excuse, no justification. She was right to hate him, right never to forgive him . . . but dear God, he would get down on his knees and beg her if she would try.

She was the only woman who had ever seen past his size and his blunt manners to the man inside. She was the only woman who had ever loved him. Why hadn't he valued and treasured her love? Why had he risked losing it with lies and deceptions?

He gave a deep sigh, but it sounded more like a sob. It sounded, he thought miserably, like the final break in an already broken heart.

The room was cold with the kind of chill that made her teeth ache, that made her very bones throb with pain. Sarah

didn't need to peer out from beneath the covers to know that
the fire was out. The three logs that had been left on the
hearth had burned quickly. The rest of the wood, stacked
neatly out by the shed, had been soaked in last week's rain
and was still too wet to burn. When she had tried with one
log, it had sizzled a little, smoked a lot, then fizzled out.
And it was thirty degrees or colder outside.

Underneath all the covers she wore sweatpants, a sweatshirt, a sweater and several pairs of socks, and nevertheless
she was cold. But even if the room temperature had been in
the seventies, she would still have been cold. The worst of
the chill was coming from inside, from the emptiness Daniel's betrayal had created.

How could she have been so foolish, so naive? Daniel
must have realized from the beginning what a sucker she
was. All he'd had to do was take advantage of what she had
so stupidly offered. If not for Beth's suspicious nature, his
plan would have worked, too. Sarah would have married
him, would have loved him, would have been so idiotically
thankful to him, for the rest of her life. She would have lived
the next ten or twenty or fifty years—however long he'd
wanted her—believing in him, believing in his nonexistent
love.

Her eyes were dry now. She was finally all cried out.
There would be no more tears for Tony and Katie. No more
tears for Daniel. She was going to start believing in reality,
not dreams. In facts, not happy endings. In a few more days
her arrangement with Daniel would end, and she would take
Katie. And when he filed his lawsuit, she would defend
herself. She would protect her daughter.

Maybe they would run away, she mused. They would go
someplace warm—Florida, maybe, or California, or Mex-
ico. They would change their names and get lost someplace
where Daniel would never find them. And when Katie asked
about her father . . .

Sarah's sigh was broken. They wouldn't run away. She
would find a job nearby, and she would allow Daniel to see
Katie as often as he wanted, no matter how badly it hurt *her*.

And when Katie asked about her father, Sarah would tell her that he was a wonderful man who loved his daughter very, very much.

If only he could have loved *her*, too....

October 31

Beth Gibson was appalled by Sarah's appearance when she walked into the empty farmhouse Wednesday afternoon. She looked around the living room, saw the couch with all its covers that served as a bed, then wrapped her arms around Sarah's slim shoulders and hugged her. "I would have come sooner, but I had to be in court yesterday. You look awful. When's the last time you had anything to eat?"

"And good afternoon to you, too," Sarah said with a sniffle. Stepping back, she dragged her hand through hair that hadn't been combed in three days, then tugged at the sweatshirt that she'd worn for the past three days, too.

Beth walked over to the bed, lifting the heavy pad of blankets. One elegantly shaped eyebrow rising questioningly, she glanced at Sarah. "You sleep here?"

She rubbed her arms for warmth. "Yeah. The house came unfurnished except for that."

Taking note of Sarah's layers of clothes, Beth became aware of the chill in the room. "Did it also come unheated?"

"Well, there's the fireplace. I have plenty of wood, but it rained last week, and..." Sarah gestured to the barely singed log on the fireplace grate. "It's too wet to burn."

"And I thought the motel in town was bad. Sweetheart, what are you doing here?" Beth asked, the patience in her voice sorely strained.

Sarah drew the back of her hand across her nose, then shrugged. "I don't have anyplace else to go."

"If it's money—"

"You were right," Sarah interrupted before the other woman could offer her a loan. "About Daniel. And the private detective."

"I know." Beth took no pleasure in admitting it. "I talked to some of your old neighbors and some of the staff at the hospital. They were all questioned by a detective name Mintz, an ex-cop. He did a very thorough job." Huddling deeper in her fur jacket, she sat down on the couch and waited for Sarah to join her at the opposite end. "So Daniel admitted it."

Sarah nodded.

"I assume you called off the wedding, or you wouldn't be looking like this."

"What else could I do? He's told so many lies that I can't trust him anymore."

Beth tilted her head to one side, leaning on one perfectly manicured hand. "Did you ever consider, Sarah, that maybe he just got trapped by the circumstances?"

Huddled in the corner of the couch. Sarah watched her suspiciously. She knew she could count on Beth the friend for total support, but Beth the lawyer couldn't help but look at situations from every side. She always wanted to know not only what people did, but why they did it. Whatever her personal feelings for Daniel, she had the emotional distance to step back and study the reasons for everything he'd done. Well, Sarah didn't have that emotional distance, but she would listen, simply because it was easier to listen than to stop Beth's analysis.

"When he first decided not to give Katie back, he didn't know you. What information he had was all two years old. He had no idea what kind of woman you were, what kind of mother you would be. So he decided to protect Katie and himself by suing for permanent custody. To do that, he had to find out everything he could about your past. And while the detective was doing that, Daniel was finding out about your present from you. And falling in love."

Sarah started to protest, but Beth stopped her with an upraised hand.

"If it hadn't been for Tony, you never would have known about this background check. He would have married you, and you would have lived a long, happy life, never suspecting what he had planned. But he found out something that upset him so badly that he couldn't hide it from you. He had to discuss it with you. And that was the catalyst that destroyed everything. So you see, he's as much a victim as you are. A victim of circumstances."

Sarah stared at her for a long time, then shook her head. "You know, I always wanted to watch you argue a real trial, not a divorce, but something like that rape case you handled last year. You're good. You're very good. If I weren't feeling the pain myself, I'd probably even believe you."

After a moment, Beth jumped to her feet. "You're right. The guy is a heartless son of a bitch, and he's not worth a second thought. Come on, start packing your stuff. There are two beds in my motel room, so you might as well use one of them." She began tugging the blankets out from beneath Sarah, giving each one a thorough shake before haphazardly folding it and laying it on the arm of the couch. "We're meeting with Ryan at one o'clock tomorrow in Adams's office. We'll take Katie and tell the bastard that if he wants to see her, he can damn well pay for the privilege. Then we'll get the hell out of this dreary little town."

"I don't want him to pay," Sarah protested. "He can see her whenever he wants. He's her father, and he loves her."

Beth looked annoyed with her. "How do you know he loves her? You said yourself that he's a lying, untrustworthy bastard. Quit taking his side, Sarah. He's not your lover, he's not your fiancé—he's your enemy. He's the man who used you, who slept with you, who let you believe he loved you so he could take your daughter away from you. Quit acting like you still love him.''

Sarah's response to Beth's callous speech was anger, hurt, denial. She wanted to defend Daniel, to tell Beth that she was wrong, to cry out that she *did* still love him and always would. But she knew that was precisely what her friend wanted: to trap her into admitting that Daniel was a good man, that she was hurt and disillusioned but still very much in love with him. Then, once she'd done so, Beth would start working on her subtly, slyly, about the advantages of forgiveness. She would use Sarah's own unhappiness in Daniel's favor, and by the time she finished, Sarah would be apologizing to Daniel for ever questioning his honor. Beth could do that with witnesses and juries—that was what made her such a good lawyer—but she wasn't going to get away with it with *her*.

Sarah stood up, wrapping her hurt feelings around her like a cloak, and started across the room. ''I'll get the rest of my things.''

In the bathroom she changed into jeans and a clean sweater, then packed everything she owned in less than ten minutes. Beth helped her load the boxes into the trunk of the small car, then waited at her own car while Sarah locked the door for the last time.

She crossed the new boards that Daniel had placed in the porch nearly a month ago, then stared for a moment up the mountain. She couldn't see his house from here, not even a hint of it, but she knew it was there. Knew *he* was there.

''Do you know where the motel is, in case we get separated in the big city of Sweetwater?'' Beth asked cynically.

Sarah nodded as she walked to her car.

''Then let's get out of this place.''

Daniel walked through the woods, carrying Katie where the path was steep, letting her walk when the ground was level. It took them a long time to cover the mile that separated their house from the Peters place—too long, but not long enough. He didn't know what he was going to say when they got there. Sarah had been right about one thing Sunday; words were difficult for him. That was why he'd held her when they had argued, why he had touched her and kissed her and made love to her—to tell her the things he couldn't find the words for. But she wouldn't welcome his touch now, and he didn't communicate so well without it.

He had stayed away Monday and Tuesday, in spite of the need to see her that had eaten away at him. She didn't want him anymore, didn't love him anymore, and she had a right to be left alone. But today Katie's frequent questions, her constant trips to the window to see if her mother was coming back yet, had overridden his resolve to leave her alone. Today his need had won. She would probably throw him out, but at least he could see her. And at least Katie could spend some time with her.

When they reached the field that surrounded the farmhouse, Daniel picked up Katie and quickened his pace. When they rounded the front of the house and he saw that the car was gone, he stopped short. Maybe she had gone into town to get some groceries, call her lawyer, do her laundry. There were a dozen reasons why she might have gone out for a while.

But when he climbed the steps and looked through the window, he saw that the house was empty. The blankets were gone, along with the boxes that had lined one wall.

Sarah was gone.

Katie patted his face until he looked down at her. "Mama?" she asked.

There was such hope in her eyes that his heart ached. "No, honey, Mama's not here," he whispered in a thick voice. Sarah was gone, and he was afraid she would never come back, not to him.

November 1

At precisely one o'clock on Thursday afternoon, Sarah and Beth were shown into Zachary's office by Alicia, who was on her way out. Zachary rose from his desk and greeted them both warmly. It hurt Sarah that she wasn't able to return the greeting. She wasn't even able to meet his eyes.

Beth sat down in one of the two chairs, crossed her legs, looked the other lawyer directly in the eye and said, "In case your client hasn't already informed you, Mr. Adams, the wedding is off. We're here to accept custody of Katherine Lawson. If Daniel Ryan still wants to file a lawsuit challenging that, go right ahead, but be assured, I'll fight you—and I'm damn good at fighting."

Zachary came around the desk and crouched in front of Sarah's chair. "Sarah, what happened?" he asked, his voice colored with concern. He touched her left hand, noticing as he did so that the pearl ring was gone.

"What happened," Beth said coldly, "is that she found out how your client has deceived her. He betrayed her trust. And with his plans for a custody suit he betrayed the spirit of the agreement he signed with her."

Sarah reached across to touch her lawyer's arm. "Hey, we're not enemies here, okay?" Then she looked at Zachary. "I found out about Daniel's plans, about the private detective, about trying to prove that I'm an unfit mother." Her voice quavered on the last part, and she wiped her hand across her eyes.

Zachary stood up and leaned against his desk. "The private detective was my idea, Sarah," he admitted openly. "Daniel never would have thought of it." After a moment, he asked, "Is he okay?"

Sarah shrugged. "I already told him that he can see Katie whenever he wants. He's not losing her."

"But what about you? He's losing you, isn't he?"

This time her shrug was accompanied by a sigh. "Do you think that makes any difference to him?"

"Sarah, you know he loves you. You've got eyes—you see how he looks at you. You know how he takes care of you, how he treats you."

She shook her head. "He lied to me, Zachary. I thought he was a very special, honorable, good man. But I was wrong."

"No, you weren't," he argued. "And you *know* that. He *is* honorable and good and—"

"Let it drop, Zach."

Three heads swiveled to see the man standing in the doorway. Cuddled in his arms was Katie. When she began struggling, he let her down, and she trotted across the room to Sarah, climbing into her lap and giving her a kiss. "Go home, Mama," she said imperiously, sliding to the floor once again. "Come on, Daddy."

"No, honey," Sarah whispered as Katie tugged her hand. The girl gave up after a moment and wandered off to explore Zachary's office. Sarah felt Daniel's eyes on her, but she refused to look at him, refused to acknowledge his presence in any way.

"I wasn't going to bring her," he said, the words directed solely to Sarah. "I thought that maybe if I didn't, you would come back. But I figured your lawyer would send the sheriff out instead.

Beth acknowledged the correctness of his assumption with an arched brow. Sarah had no reaction at all.

He came a few steps closer, then asked hoarsely, "Can't you even look at me, Sarah?"

She was afraid of what he might see in her face if she did. Afraid of what *she* might see in *his* face. There was such anguish in his voice, such raw need. If she looked at him and saw it, she would forget everything, forgive anything.

When she kept her face turned away from him, he gave up. "Her things are packed. They're by Alicia's desk," he said, his voice flat and empty. He pulled an envelope from his pocket and offered it first to Sarah, who wouldn't take it, then to Beth, who did. "There's some money there, to find a place to live. I, uh . . . I'd like to see her—"

He was going to cry, Daniel thought, closing his eyes tightly. He could feel the burning all the way into his soul. It blocked any more words from clearing the lump in his throat.

Beth filled the painful silence. "You can see her whenever you'd like. We can draw up an agreement and leave it with Zachary."

Daniel nodded, then once again moved closer to Sarah. This time he stopped in front of her, crouching there, trapping her in the chair. With the gentlest touch she'd ever felt, he turned her face, forcing her to look at him. "I'm sorry," he whispered brokenly. "I'm sorry I betrayed you. I'm sorry I hurt you. But I'll never be sorry that I love you."

The tears that she'd promised herself she wouldn't cry came anyway, sliding down her cheeks. She squeezed her eyes shut to slow them, and when she opened them again, he was gone.

"What do you want, Sarah?" Beth asked, her voice sharp in spite of its softness. "He offered you money, marriage, love. Are you looking for a pound of flesh? I think you got that, too, in the heart you tossed back."

Katie came back to her mother, reaching out a chubby hand to wipe at her tears. "Go home, Mama," she pleaded, noticing for the first time that her father was gone. "Go to Daddy."

Sarah lifted Katie into her lap and hugged her close. "He lied to me, Beth," she whispered.

"So what?" Beth looked and sounded disgusted. "You said you thought he was an honorable man. He's still got honor, Sarah, in spite of what he did." Then she laughed sharply. "*What he did.* For God's sake, Sarah, what did he do besides fall in love with you?"

"He *lied*!"

"He tried to protect his daughter. Then he tried to protect you by not telling you about the detective. Telling you would only have hurt you because by then, he didn't want to sue you—he wanted to marry you."

"But how can I trust him now?"

"What's he going to do, Sarah?" Zachary asked impatiently. "Keep Katie away from you? He's already given her to you."

"He gave you his daughter," Beth said, touching the girl's hair. "After a gift like that, how can you not trust him?"

Sarah dried the last tears from her eyes. "Why does it matter to you, Beth? You don't even like him."

"But *you* love him, and he loves you, and in this world, that's a pretty rare thing. Don't lose it because he made a mistake."

In her lap, Katie made one last plea. "Let's go, Mama. To Daddy."

"No, honey," she said, brushing the girl's hair back. "You're going to stay with Beth for a while, okay? She'll take you to the park and play." She made the promise knowing that Beth hadn't played with a child since she was one herself.

Katie looked at the redhead, then clung to Sarah. "No."

Zachary lifted her from Sarah's lap and swung her around. "You stay with Beth and me, kiddo, and I'll get you some of my mom's chocolate cake, okay?"

The dark blue eyes lit up, and she giggled. "Cake, umm."

"Beth, can I use your car?" Sarah had left hers at the motel, and it would take too long to walk back and get it.

Beth handed over the keys with a dry warning. "Don't leave this child in my care for very long."

The drive to the top of the mountain had never seemed so long, but at last Sarah was there. She parked next to Daniel's pickup, then climbed the steps to the porch. She raised her hand to knock, but the door was ajar. After a moment's hesitation, she opened it fully and stepped inside.

The house was quiet. She decided to check upstairs, certain that he would be in his room or Katie's. A moment later she found him in front of the fireplace in his bedroom, staring at the pictures there. "Daniel?"

He turned quickly, surprised by her presence. A muscle in his jaw twitched as he struggled for control. He quietly asked, "Where is Katie?" He'd said good-bye to his daughter once. He wasn't sure he could do it again.

"I left her with Zachary and Beth." She came farther into the room, stopping at the opposite end of the fireplace. The picture on the mantel in front of her had been taken on Katie's first birthday. She looked sweet and adorable and loved—so well-loved. "I wanted to talk to you."

He silently watched her. He wanted to reach out to her, but he couldn't. He wanted to beg her forgiveness, but he couldn't do that, either. How could she forgive the things he'd done? All he could do was wait.

Sarah traced her finger over the picture frame. *So well loved*. Love had been the driving force behind everything Daniel had done in the past year. He had changed his life to accommodate Katie, had been both mother and father to her, and when faced with the possibility of losing her, he had taken the only steps possible to keep her.

She understood that kind of love. Hadn't she felt it for Tony? There was nothing in the world she wouldn't have done to keep her son with her—*nothing*—even give up her daughter. She had seen that all-encompassing love in herself as proof that she was a good mother. But instead of

seeing that same love as proof that Daniel was a good father, she'd chosen to look at him through the layers of pain
and heartache, and she had condemned him for it. She had
been wrong—understandably so, but still wrong.

"I'm sorry."

Daniel flinched at the quiet words. He didn't want to hear
that from her, not when he was the one who should be saying it. He grimly shook his head. "I was wrong," he said,
his voice a deep rumble. "I should have been honest with
you, but when you agreed to marry me, I—" He gave a
weary sigh. "I thought I could have it all—you, Katie, a real
family. I thought we could live the rest of our lives together, and you would never know what I'd done, would
never hate me for it."

He turned away from her then, his gaze settling on the
row of photographs. "I've been alone most of my life,
Sarah. When your lawyer brought Katie to me, it was the
best thing that had ever happened in my life. For the first
time somebody needed me. She loved me unconditionally.
I was her entire world, and she was mine." He paused to
clear the hoarseness from his voice. "In the beginning I
thought I could keep our agreement. I thought I could have
her for a year, then give her back to you . . . but I couldn't."

"So you decided to sue for custody."

He nodded. "I wanted to believe that you were unfit because that was the only way I could have her, but I knew it
wasn't true. Even before I found out about Tony...I knew."
He squeezed his eyes shut and rubbed them with the heels of
his hands. "Sarah, I'm sorry for the things I said and did.
I'm sorry for the lies, for hurting you.... I wanted you to
stay with me, to marry me, to have a family with me, to love
me." He shook his head helplessly. "I never wanted to hurt
you."

"But you did," she whispered. "You hurt me a lot. I've
spent the last couple of days telling myself that I was foolish and stupid for believing in you, for loving you." She saw
the anguish, dark and bleak, in his eyes when he looked at
her, and it wrenched at her heart, but she continued with-

out a pause. "But the only foolish or stupid thing I've done is let you go. Because in the end, when the pain is gone, I'm still going to love you Daniel. I'll always love you. And I'll always believe that you love me."

He stared at her for a long time, searching her face for confirmation of what she'd said, and he found it in the soft, tender look in her eyes and the sweet, gentle curve of her lips. For a moment he was afraid to believe; then he knew he had to, because he loved her, and with love came trust. "Can you forgive me?" he whispered, moving toward her.

She took a step, too, closing the distance between them. "For what? Loving our daughter?"

He raised his hand to her face. It was trembling when it cupped her cheek. "I do love her," he murmured in a thick voice. "And I love you." Bending his head, he kissed her sweetly, tentatively. He tasted her hunger, as quick to flare as his own, and her need, as unending as his own. "Will you marry me, Sarah? Raise our daughter with me? Have babies with me?"

Tears glistening in her eyes, she smiled. "I would be honored to marry you."

Pulling her closer, he kissed her once again, sealing her promise. This time his mouth was hard, hungry, demanding, yet incredibly gentle—like the man himself, Sarah thought in a daze. When he ended the kiss and swept her into his embrace, she gave a soft laugh and twined her arms around his neck. Her next words came out with a whoosh as he lowered her to the bed.

"I love you, Daniel Ryan."

*   *   *   *   *

COMING NEXT MONTH

#313 TIME WAS—Nora Roberts

When Caleb Hornblower comes to after the craft he was piloting crashes, he doesn't understand how very far from home he is. He has traveled not only through space, but through time, only to discover that home is what he finds in Libby Stone's arms.

#314 TENDER OFFER—
Paula Detmer Riggs

Alex Torres returned to southwestern Ohio to help his ex-wife, Casey O'Neill, fight the takeover of her company. But in the ruthless corporate world, it was not the only battle to be waged—he also had to regain the respect and trust of the woman he'd never stopped loving.

#315 LOVE IS A LONG SHOT—
Joanna Marks

Laura Reynolds's testimony had been crucial in sending Quinton Jones to prison for a crime he didn't commit. Now Quint was back, and Laura desperately wanted to set the record straight. But she knew that once he found out who she really was, he would be bound to break her heart.

#316 FLIRTING WITH DANGER—
Linda Turner

Someone was trying to drive beautiful heiress Gabriella Winters insane. So she fled her family mansion—only to run headlong into the arms of Austin LePort. There was more to this handsome hobo than met the eye, and soon Gabriella found herself truly mad...madly in love.

AVAILABLE NOW:

Available now from

◯ SILHOUETTE®

Desire™

TAGGED #534
by Lass Small

Fredricka Lambert had always believed in true love, but she couldn't figure out whom to love... until lifelong friend Colin Kilgallon pointed her in the right direction—toward himself.

Fredricka is one of five fascinating Lambert sisters. She is as enticing as each one of her four sisters, whose stories you have already enjoyed.

- Hillary in GOLDILOCKS AND THE BEHR (Desire #437)
- Tate in HIDE AND SEEK (Desire #453)
- Georgina in RED ROVER (Desire #491)
- Roberta in ODD MAN OUT (Desire #505)

Don't miss the last book of this enticing miniseries, only from Silhouette Desire.

READERS' COMMENTS ON SILHOUETTE INTIMATE MOMENTS:

"About a month ago a friend loaned me my first Silhouette. I was thoroughly surprised as well as totally addicted. Last week I read a Silhouette Intimate Moments and I was even more pleased. They are the best romance series novels I have ever read. They give much more depth to the plot, characters, and the story is fundamentally realistic. They incorporate tasteful sex scenes, which is a must, especially in the 1980's. I only hope you can publish them fast enough."

S.B.*, Lees Summit, MO

"After noticing the attractive covers on the new line of Silhouette Intimate Moments, I decided to read the inside and discovered that this new line was more in the line of books that I like to read. I do want to say I enjoyed the books because they are so realistic and a lot more truthful than so many romance books today."

J.C., Onekama, MI

"I would like to compliment you on your books. I will continue to purchase all of the Silhouette Intimate Moments. They are your best line of books that I have had the pleasure of reading."

S.M., Billings, MT

*names available on request

SILHOUETTE DESIRE™
presents
AUNT EUGENIA'S TREASURES
by CELESTE HAMILTON

Liz, Cassandra and Maggie are the honored recipients of Aunt Eugenia's heirloom jewels...but Eugenia knows the real prizes are the young women themselves. Every other month from December to April in Silhouette Desire, read about Aunt Eugenia's quest to find them worthy men and a treasure more valuable than diamonds, rubies or pearls—lasting love.

Coming in December: THE DIAMOND'S SPARKLE

Altruistic attorney Liz Patterson balks at Aunt Eugenia's attempt at matchmaking. Clearly, a shrewd PR man isn't her type. Nathan Hollister, after all, likes fast cars and fast times, but, as he tells Liz, love is something he's willing to take *very* slowly.

In February: RUBY FIRE

Passionate Cassandra Martin has always been driven by impulse. After traveling from city to city, seeking new opportunities, Cassandra returns home...ready to rekindle the flame of young love with the man she never forgot, Daniel O'Grady.

In April: THE HIDDEN PEARL

Maggie O'Grady loved and lost early in life. Since then caution has been her guide. But when brazen Jonah Pendleton moves into the apartment next door, gentle Maggie comes out of her shell and glows in the precious warmth of love.

Aunt Eugenia's Treasures
Each book shines on its own, but together they're priceless

SD-AET-1

Indulge a Little Give a Lot

An irresistible opportunity to pamper yourself with free gifts (plus proofs-of-purchase and postage and handling) and help raise up to $100,000.00 for **Big Brothers/Big Sisters Programs and Services** in Canada and the United States.

Each specially marked "Indulge A Little" Harlequin or Silhouette book purchased during October, November and December contains a proof-of-purchase that will enable you to qualify for luxurious gifts. And, for every specially marked book purchased during this limited time, Harlequin/Silhouette will donate 5¢ toward **Big Brothers/Big Sisters Programs and Services**, for a maximum contribution of $100,000.00.

For details on how you can indulge yourself, look for information at your favorite retail store or send a self-addressed stamped envelope to:

INDULGE A LITTLE
P.O. Box 618
Fort Erie, Ontario
L2A 5I3

ONE PROOF OF PURCHASE
To collect your free gift you must include the necessary number of proofs-of- purchase, plus postage and handling, along with the offer certificate available in retail stores or from the above address.

CSIM-2

Harlequin®/Silhouette®